NO GREATER HELL

No Greater Hell

Lost and Found, Inc., Volume 4

Jerrie Alexander

Published by Jerrie Alexander, 2016.

NO GREATER HELL

First edition. May 17, 2016.

Copyright © 2016 Jerrie Alexander.

ISBN: 979-8224521647

Written by Jerrie Alexander.

Table of Contents

To Jim, who always told me I could accomplish anything I made my
mind up to do.

NO GREATER HELL

ISBN: 978-1-941205-11-2 E-Book Edition
ISBN: 978-1-941205-12-9 Print Edition
ISBN: 979-8-224521-64-7 Second Print Edition
Cover illustrator: Bethany Cagle
www.brynnacurry.com[1]
Edited by: Amy Knupp, Blue Otter Editingwww.BlueOtterEditing.com[2],
and Pamela Dougherty, www.thewriteactor.com[3]

Published in the United States of America

---

1. http://www.brynnacurry.com/

2. http://www.BlueOtterEditing.com

3. http://www.thewriteactor.com

Acknowledgments

I would be remiss if I didn't acknowledge the following people. Their support, advice, and enthusiasm were invaluable.

Pamela Dougherty and Amy Knupp who helped me polish this story until it shone.

Kym Roberts listened to my ideas, helped me fill plot holes, and write the elusive back of the book blurb. I appreciate you more than I can say.

Kayla Bartley, thank you for your honesty and support.

Alexa Pressley, you are the best brainstorming partner in the world.

To Jackie Pressley, you remain my greatest contribution to mankind. I'm blessed that you're my daughter.

To my personal hero, Jim. You fought the biggest battle of all and won, thank you for your unwavering love and support.

Any mistakes are my own!

Last but not least, thanks to my readers. You are why I write. Thank you for writing and encouraging me to write Jake's story. I hope you love this story as much as I loved writing it.

Other Books by Jerrie Alexander

Single Titles:
The Green-Eyed Doll
The Last Execution
Someone to Watch Over Me
Flirting with Fate
Series: Lost and Found, Inc.
Hell or High Water
Cold Day in Hell
No Chance in Hell
Series: Killer Affections
Till Justice is Served
Till the Dead Speak (coming soon)

Prologue

Jake Donovan hated good-byes. Walking into the offices of Lost and Found, Inc. for the last time would be a bitch. He was finally square with the law and the government. Relocating would help him close the book on his life as Johnny Darling, and then everyone could move on. But he hated the feeling he was turning his back on his friends. Hated letting down the people who'd helped him get his life back.

That Kay and Nate Wolfe had finally accepted his decision brought Jake an enormous amount of relief. He hadn't arrived at this conclusion easily or without a lot of soul searching. If, in fact, he still had a soul.

Nate and Kay had stood by Jake through his surgery and rehab. They'd been his lifeline, the only thing he could cling to when he finally faced the consequences of his actions. Their numerous trips to the hospital during his surgery and recovery had been the glue that held him together. During their visits, they'd tried to hide their concern for his well-being, but their anxiety showed through their efforts at normalcy, and their unease only added to the guilt he carried. Guilt that still held him prisoner.

Nevertheless, Nate and Kay had given him back his life, and today he'd return the favor.

He crossed the parking lot, paused for a second to steel his emotions, and then opened the door. Using Nate's corny entrance line, he called out, "Honeee, I'm ho-ooome."

Kay jumped to her feet and rushed to meet him. Her long brown hair swirled around her shoulders. "Yes, you are."

Jake and Kay were both thirty, yet she stood there beaming up at him as if she were his mother. He pulled her into his arms and squeezed. He owed this tiny woman a debt, one he could never repay.

"I was afraid you wouldn't show."

"I wouldn't lie to you."

"I'm sorry I doubted you." Her hands gripped his biceps tightly. "Come on back; Nate and the guys are waiting."

His heart double-clutched. He could only hope she understood why he had to leave. "That husband of yours is one lucky bastard."

"I know. I tell him that all the time," she said with a weak laugh.

Kay was the glue that held Wolfe's Pack together. She'd taken on that role during the group's college days long before the Lost and Found, Inc. agency was founded. The business had brought her, Nate Wolfe, Marcus Ricci, and Ty Castillo back together, and she still mothered the group, except for Nate, who she'd married.

Jake kissed the top of her head, put his arm around her shoulders, and together they walked around the cubicles toward the conference room.

Jake stopped at Ty's old desk, which now belonged to Dalton Murphy. Six months ago, Dalton had taken Nate's offer to leave the FBI and join Lost and Found. It had been a lucrative business decision for the company, as government contracts had increased dramatically since Dalton's addition to the team.

"You coming?" Kay asked Dalton.

"You bet." He stood and shook Jake's hand. "I'm sorry I couldn't do more for you. I hope the state's refusal to issue you a PI license didn't factor into your decision to leave us."

"Not one bit," Jake said truthfully. "I get that my past was a factor but I appreciate you trying." Out of the corner of his eye, he saw Nate rise and move to the doorway. "We better get in there. The boss is watching."

Nate waited until they were all in the room and seated before he joined the founding partner of the company, Marcus Ricci, at the far end of the small conference table.

"I'm not going to get maudlin and go on about how much we're going to miss you, but I'm not going to lie. You are family, and we'll always be here for you. With or without a license, your job is here and our door is open."

"Thanks. I appreciate that." Jake's chest ached. He didn't deserve all this kindness and suddenly found himself choking back a swelling in his throat. There had to be a way to change the subject. Sitting in the middle of the table was a pan of barbecue and a couple containers of beans and slaw. "Wow. Is all this for me?"

"You expected a cake?" Marcus grinned. At the same time, the big man's dark eyes bored into Jake. Marcus had always been able to ferret out secrets and truths, so Jake looked away.

"No," Jake said. "Thank God."

Kay took over the job of dispensing the food, giving Jake his plate first. "Did you say good-bye to Holly?"

"Kaycie," Nate scolded. "That's none of your business."

"It certainly is," Kay fired back. She rolled her eyes and waited.

"It's okay to ask," Jake said, knowing this conversation was necessary, and wanting to get it over with. "Why would I say anything to her? We all know why Holly stopped coming by the office. She couldn't look at me without cringing." He held up his hand to stop Kay from responding. "You brought this up, so let me finish." He looked down for a second, then back at his friends. "Look, Holly has a new life. I stopped by Dallas Mercy Hospital this morning and saw her walk out with a group of people I've never seen before. They were all talking and laughing together. Why would I intrude?"

The truth was, he'd dropped by the hospital more than once. Hell, he'd been two steps away from becoming a stalker when he'd received word that his last remaining relative, his dad's brother, had died.

So Jake had spent the past few weeks helping his aunt at their small horse ranch, and found the time in the country a welcome relief. Working outside, using his hands and back, he'd felt as if he was actually contributing to something worthwhile. The hot Texas sun wrung out every ounce of strength he had and yet each morning, he'd willingly crawled out of bed and looked forward to repeating the process.

Marcus accepted his plate of food from Kay, pinched off a piece of meat, and passed it down to Diablo, his shepherd-collie-mix rescue dog. "So where is Murdock, Texas?"

"It's where nobody knows about me."

"Not funny," Kay said.

"Your location won't be a secret around here for long. Kay will have you pinned down before you get out of town." Marcus leaned down and scratched Diablo's ears.

"It's southwest of Houston, but close enough to the Gulf Coast to reach the ocean in a couple of hours. I'll text you the address after I get there." Jake ignored the fact that Nate's right eyebrow lifted in doubt.

"The ranch isn't fancy. In fact, the barns are bigger than the house. My family always believed that if you built a good barn, it would pay for the house. The place is five hundred odd acres of grass and weeds. My aunt and uncle built a reputation for quality cattle and horses, and now she needs me. I'm going to help her finish what he started."

"I remember. You have experience ranching," Dalton said.

"My dad raised Hereford cattle. We worked out of four-wheelers, but we had a couple of horses."

"You'll come back when we get the new compound open?" Kay asked. "It's going to be complete with offices for everybody, a training gym for employees, and a bunkhouse for when our agents need a place to crash." She shot a look at Nate. "I'm hoping to get my PI license."

"It's about time you got into the field." Jake knew how badly she wanted to become a field agent. She'd been training hard.

"So you'll come back for the big day?"

"I don't know." Not wanting to lie to her, Jake met her gaze with his. "No."

She opened her mouth as if to argue. Nate cut her off by asking her to pass the coleslaw.

Jake shoved a forkful of beans into his mouth and said nothing else.

The group ate in an uncomfortable silence, thankfully broken when Diablo dropped a big paw on Jake's leg to beg for food. He jumped, giving everyone a laugh.

"Hang on," he said to the dog. As he pulled off a chunk of chopped beef to share, the talk switched to Diablo, who Marcus had smuggled into Texas from Colombia. Raised by the notorious drug lord, Manuel Ortega, the dog had been trained to kill on command, and was considered unredeemable by everybody except Marcus. But Diablo had proved them wrong by accepting new training, and he'd grown to worship Marcus. Man and dog had adjusted to each other beautifully.

Jake hoped his own transition to a new life would be as easy.

Just getting through today was trying as hell. The group of people surrounding him ranked up there with the best, a team that worked well as a unit, helping people when all other resources had failed.

Reluctantly, he stood and started his good-byes. He tried to make it quick, giving a friendly hug to Nate and Marcus. Dalton reached out his hand, and Jake accepted it as an honest gesture.

He and Dalton had gotten off to a rough start. Understandable, since Jake had been living as Johnny Darling for a human trafficking ring at the time. FBI agent Dalton Murphy had worked the case, ultimately arresting Jake for kidnapping Holly. That arrest led to the removal of a brain tumor that had saved his life and restored the part of his memory that was Jake Donovan.

Kay held Jake tightly for a few minutes, then she whispered, "Take care of yourself."

"I will."

She turned and buried her face in her husband's chest. Jake kissed the back of her head and then walked out the door.

These people had saved his life. They'd taken care of him even though he didn't deserve the sweat off their brow. Nothing would ever lessen his gratitude. He committed everything they'd done for him to memory.

He didn't remember the monster he'd once been, but they did.

With each step, his breathing grew labored, as an imagined metal strap tightened around his chest. With each step away from the comfort and protection of his friends, the band tightened. And with each step, he opened the door to his new future.

A big hand landed on his shoulder. "We all have our private hell. I hope you find the way back from yours. Take care, my friend."

Jake turned around to face Nate. "You too."

"You won't find redemption by living in isolation. You'll find it here." Nate tapped a finger on Jake's temple.

Jake shook his head. "I'm not looking for redemption. I'm just hoping for a little peace of mind."

Chapter 1

Two years later

Murdock, Texas

Jake settled his ball cap on his head, shading his eyes against the morning sunlight. He blinked against the glare as he scanned the Donovan Cattle Ranch for damages. Arms over his head, he reached for the sky, stretching his stiff joints. Spending six hours underground in a storm cellar had left his long frame tied in knots. Neither he nor Aunt Alice had slept, not with the torrential rainfall and high winds pounding against the only door out of this oversized grave of a shelter.

A battery powered weather radio had kept them up to date on the deadly hurricane as it had swept across the Gulf of Mexico. According to the weatherman, numerous tornados had hit inland, dumping untold inches of rain. He and Alice had known exactly when the storm had passed over the ranch.

It was graveyard quiet now, without as much as a whisper of a breeze. Even the birds had stopped chirping. Probably too scared to announce the danger had passed.

While this area of Southeast Texas didn't flood often, being prepared was always a good idea. Alice and Jake had monitored the weather channels, took seriously the warnings that the impending storm was expected to be one of the most intense in history, and spent the past few days working nonstop to get the ranch ready. Jake had moved the cattle and horses to the back pasture away from the creek. Strong and determined, she worked harder than any two men, and her nephew's level of respect and affection for her grew every day.

Now she stood silently beside him, her blue eyes stained with red streaks from the lack of sleep. Her salt-and-pepper hair stood at odd angles, mussed from dragging her fingers through it as the wind had howled and battered the door above them. She pulled an old sailor's cap from her hip pocket and socked it on her head.

"Thank God. The old place is still standing." Alice struck out toward the house, her boots sinking in the mud. "Looks like the wind blew off a few roof shingles."

Jake was looking the other direction. "Pasture is standing in water and a few trees are down."

"I'll take a check inside. You'll check on the livestock?"

"Yes, ma'am." Jake breathed a sigh of relief. They had expected the worst, and so far nothing pointed toward disaster. Alice wouldn't say it, but she was worried about what he might find.

The four-wheeler would get stuck, so Jake went straight to the barn, where he slipped on a pair of tall rubber boots. Rapidly moving water had cut a shallow trench in the usually hard dirt road running from the house to the outbuildings. It was nothing that couldn't be fixed.

The odor of wet wood and soggy cattle pens went unnoticed as he stepped through the gate leading to the pasture, and started his search. His boots sunk into the mud, making a slurping sound with each step.

A couple of the corral fence posts had been uprooted. He found young trees dotting the pasture that would have some day provided the livestock shade from the broiling Texas sun. Today their jagged roots pointed skyward, having been yanked unnaturally from the earth.

Within a few hours, Jake located the livestock. His heart began to sink as he counted four dead, then he stared in amazement at a new-born calf and her mother. He gathered the tiny heifer in his arms, knowing the mother would follow, and carried it back to the barn. Secure in an empty horse stall with a fresh pile of hay, both animals would be fine.

He'd turned four brood mares and a gelding out into their pasture a few minutes before he and Alice had gone into the storm cellar. Duchess was close to foaling, and Jake was anxious to find her. He walked to the west fence and whistled. He waited a few minutes and tried again, hoping to hear hooves sloshing through the mud or horses nickering as they always did at meal time.

Their absence concerned him. Losing one horse would break Alice's heart, but if anything happened to Duchess, she'd be crushed. Jake slipped through the railing and went in search of the mares.

He found them in the far corner of the field. He approached calmly, speaking soft words of encouragement. Two of them backed away, skittish. All four mares were pregnant by a local stallion and were normally docile, but the storm had rattled them. But Buster, who always nuzzled Jake's pocket for a treat, came right up to him.

Jake did a quick visual and found no injuries. Duchess was the matriarch of the group, so he removed his belt and slid it around her neck. "Good girl," he whispered, running his hand up her neck. Together they led Buster and the other three mares back to the small paddock and into their stalls.

One at a time, he rinsed them off, rubbed them dry, and then loaded their stalls with fresh grain and hay. None showed signs of miscarrying. More good news to share with Alice.

Jake returned to the house, tugged off the rubber waders, and dropped them on the back porch steps. The heat and humidity had taken a toll on him, soaking his clothes clean through.

He turned on the hose and rinsed his boots, then bent over and ran water over his head, arms and hands.

Alice opened the door and handed him a towel. "If you'd let me cut off about four inches of that hair, you'd stay a lot cooler."

"You're probably right." He laughed and brushed off her comment. His "hippie hair" had been a long-running joke, starting the minute it had gotten long enough to brush the tops of his ears.

"How'd the livestock look?"

"Better than expected. Lost four cows, but the horses are fine. They are clean, dry and fed. A few trees in the upper forty were uprooted. We fared better in the small pasture on the hill. Not near as much damage up there as in the lowland." He handed the towel back.

"Duchess?" Alice's eyebrows rose.

"She's good. Helped me bring the other horses up."

"That's a load off my shoulders. "She pointed up to the roof. "Not one leak." She patted the porch rail as if to say 'good job.'

"I'll get up there and nail down those loose shingles."

"That can wait. The power is out and the ice won't last long. I made a jar of sweet tea. It's instant, but it will do for now. Come rest for a minute. I'll pour you a glass."

"I'm fine. I'll get something to drink later."

"Now Jake, don't you be arguing. I need you inside for a second."

Jake followed the fifty-five-year-old-tough-as-nails woman rancher into the house. She was an attractive woman with small laugh lines bracketing her smile. Her upbeat personality made up for Jake's occasional bad days. They'd worked hard to keep the ranch going after his uncle Charlie died. Her last vestige of fight seemed to have died when she'd walked out of the storm shelter full of fear. It was good to see her behaving normally.

"I'll pour," he insisted, taking the tea jar from her. "We got lucky. The storm sounded much worse than it was."

"Yes, we did." Alice picked up her cell. "I pulled up the weather. We're a heck of a lot better off than the cities and cattle ranchers closer to the coast. Connersville caught the worst of the tornadoes. Lots of people injured or missing, even more without homes."

Jake hated the sadness in her voice. But he had something he knew would cheer her up."I have a surprise for you."

"You do?" Her face lit up. "What is it?"

"Guess what I found nuzzled next to Bessie?"

Her eyes brightened a little. "You didn't find a calf?"

"Yep. I spread out a couple of bales of hay and put baby and mama in the back stall. They're both going to be fine."

Jake heard a vehicle drive up outside. He stood and walked to the door. "Claude is here."

"That's why I wanted you to come inside. He called. Wants to talk to you."

Sheriff Claude Welborne parked his four-wheel-drive jeep out front, got out, and walked to the porch. Jake bit back a smile, knowing that Claude had a crush on Alice as big as the main barn. She brightened up when he came around. Recently, they'd started going on an occasional date, and Jake was glad for her. She'd grieved for two years, and Uncle Charlie wouldn't have wanted that.

Jake and Alice met Claude on the front porch. A smile lit up Claude's face the minute he saw her. He almost glowed.

"I was glad to hear you two had made it to the shelter in time."

"We're fine." Alice jerked off her cap and ran her fingers through her hair. "Come have a glass of sweet tea. Might as well use the ice."

"The electric co-op will have a crew working on your transformer this afternoon. Power will be up before dark." Claude toed off his muddy boots and followed her inside. "The house looks good. You get a headcount on the livestock yet?"

"Four dead cows." Jake waved off Alice's offer of a refill. "The fences held, which helped a lot." Claude had spent a weekend helping Jake fence off the back pasture. "I guess we did a good job."

Alice motioned Claude to join her at the kitchen table. Her gaze dropped as he crossed the room, and the corners of her lips lifted slightly. No doubt, she'd noticed Claude's big toe sticking out of the hole in his sock. There was definitely a future for those two. Jake would give them some privacy as soon as he learned what Claude wanted.

"We were going to check on the new heifer." Jake placed his empty glass in the sink. "You wanted to see me?"

"That's right." Claude's tone sounded serious. "I came to ask you for a favor."

Jake leaned against the kitchen counter. "I'm listening."

"Rey Santos, the police chief in Connersville, has put out a call for help. It's not a big city, somewhere between three to four-hundred-thousand folks. Large enough to have one hospital – a regional medical center that serves the whole county. The Rio Grande feeds a small local lake that has flooded, washing out a few roads in its path. Hasn't gotten out of its banks in a hundred years, but this storm has turned it into a raging monster. Luckily, the few families impacted by the lake were evacuated. Rey's in a bad way and could use another strong back."

"The number of homeless and missing people is growing by the minute. Looting is always a problem after a disaster like this one." Claude took a drink of tea and then cleared his throat. "I'm shorthanded or I'd send one of my men. Rey is a good guy. It would mean a lot if you'd help him out."

Jake shook his head. He'd moved to the country to be left alone. "I can't leave Alice to fix the roof by herself."

"How about if I take care of anything she needs? And give you my word they'll be done right?" Claude asked.

"Go." Alice's voice was full of conviction. "If I need something done and can't do it myself, Claude can handle it."

"He can't deputize me." Jake glanced at Alice. Her expression told him nothing. How much of his past had Alice shared with Claude?

"I know. Rey's not going to deputize every member of each team. He needs honest men with strong backs. Like you. You'll wade through the debris and mud and search for survivors. It will be hot, nasty, and maybe dangerous. Rey put out a call across the state, asking for volunteers."

Jake hesitated to answer, trying to form a refusal in his head that didn't involve telling Claude to fuck off. "Do you know about my past?"

"I do." He held up his hand. "Not from Alice. I checked you out when you first moved in." Claude turned to Alice. "I just wanted to be sure you'd be safe."

She nodded. "I appreciate your concern, but also, understand how Jake might take offense."

"None taken. In fact, I respect that you wanted to be sure I wasn't some lunatic." That Claude had cared enough about Alice to check, nudged Jake toward volunteering. "Other than the few weeks before Charlie passed, Alice and I hadn't seen much of each other for years."

"You've been a godsend." Alice beamed up at him. "I hate that my Charlie and your dad never patched things up. Now it's too late."

Jake joined Alice and Claude at the table. They made a handsome couple. Maybe a serious romance would develop if he got out of the way. "This Santos, is he a friend?"

"I worked with his father years ago. Rey took the job in Connersville less than a year ago."

Jake's uncle had been full of wisdom and country slang. *Stuck between a rock and a hard spot* seemed to fit this situation. "Where do I report when I get there?"

Chapter 2

The oppressive heat inside the building drained the last dregs of Holly Hoffman's strength. She dampened a cloth and walked outside. Wiping her face, she hoped the moisture on her skin and the wind might cool her off. Unfortunately, the summer breeze she hoped for was a no-show.

A pickup approached, and Holly tried to get a look at the driver. When she'd called her friend Kay Wolfe at the Lost and Found agency to let her know she was leaving for Connersville, she'd learned that Dalton Murphy had also driven down to volunteer with a search-and-rescue team. Seeing him today would be more than welcome. But the pickup drove by without slowing. Silly of her to expect to run into him amongst all the many places he could be, but then again, this was an emergency medical station.

Had it only been a few years ago that her biggest problem in life had been selecting a vacation spot for her and her best friend, Kay? Holly sighed, remembering all hell had broken loose right after their discussion about going to the beach. Then she'd been kidnapped, held hostage, and almost murdered. That experience had changed her, made her want to make a difference in people's lives. And that desire had led her to get her nursing degree and apply for work at Dallas Mercy Hospital.

The Helpful Hands group, which consisted of doctors and nurses who volunteered to help in disaster areas, worked out of Mercy. Holly had signed up to join them right after she'd been hired as an ER nurse. This assignment was her first time working with the team.

Connersville's one hospital didn't have enough room or staff to handle the kinds of injuries a major hurricane brought, so Holly and her team had been assigned an empty elementary school, where they turned the cafeteria into a workspace. She couldn't imagine the pain and suffering this town had experienced.

An armed guard turned toward her. His face appeared to be set in stone, as not one muscle or nerve twitched. His gaze held hers for a second before he returned his attention to the entrance to their makeshift emergency room. That the medical team had been assigned protection was comforting and sad at the same time. They'd brought their own equipment and meds, which made them a target for looters and gangs.

The coat of perspiration covering her skin chilled, sending a shiver up her spine. She suddenly felt that going outside had been selfish, when so many needed her help. She nodded at the guard as she walked past him. His dark eyes gave away no emotion.

A child's cry bounced off the walls, tugging at her heart. The head nurse, Suzanne Richards, finished wrapping gauze around his arm. She picked up a syringe from the tray, and the little boy went ballistic. Maybe five years old, he wiggled and squirmed in his mother's arms. His tiny hands coiled into fists and thrashed in the air. He scrunched his face into a knot and was wailing at the top of his lungs. Holly reached her hands out for him, and without hesitation, he climbed into her arms, clinging to her.

Holly carried him to a small ice chest, opened it, and grabbed a bottle of water. She carried the boy to the far corner, shushing him in soft, soothing tones. "Want something cool to drink?"

His screams subsided, and his heaving chest slowed. He stared at the bottle she offered as if deciding whether he wanted a drink or not. His small hands wrapped around the cool plastic, pulling it to his lips, and he drank big gulps.

"Better?" she asked. His nod warmed her heart. She only had to look around at the children who needed medical attention to know that joining this team was the right decision.

Dr. Emil Abroon stepped around the corner. Deep set lines bracketed his mouth, aging him well beyond his years. His olive complexion did little to conceal the crow's feet or circles under his eyes. Holly had seen him around the hospital but hadn't actually met him until this trip. After a couple of days watching the way he treated people, she'd grown to respect his compassion and dedication.

"Such a small person to be raising such a big ruckus," he said as he approached. "Perhaps I can help." Dr. Abroon touched the boy's forehead. "No fever."

The child buried his face against her shoulder. His fingers dug into Holly's arm. "I think he's afraid of you."

"White coat syndrome. I don't see anything except the scratch on his leg, but a lot of these children haven't had any of their childhood shots. He probably needs a tetanus shot."

"I think that's what started the ruckus."

"Let's talk to his mother."

She followed Dr. Abroon to her work area and played with the little boy while the doctor spoke with the mother and Suzanne. Holly had the child calm, sitting on her table and smiling by the time the examination began again.

"Hold him just as you are now," the doctor instructed her. In less than a couple of minutes, the boy was running alongside his mother, smiling broadly, and showing off the gauze bandage on his arm and the Band-Aid above it.

"The child warmed up to you quickly." Doctor Abroon's stoic expression melted into a slight smile before he moved to the next patient.

Holly turned to the line of people waiting and motioned a young girl to come forward. She was in her early teens, with long, chestnut hair framing dark, soulful eyes. Her shorts and tank-top were battered and baggy. Her cheek presented scratches and bruises, but the condition of her shoulder concerned Holly more.

The girl moved slowly, as if wary of what might happen next. Holly patted a chair and searched for something to open a dialogue with the girl. The loss had been heavy in this area, and a deep fear shone in her eyes.

"That's a pretty bracelet. Did you make it?" Holly asked.

"My mother." The girl's physical condition wasn't good. She carried her left arm across her body, cradling her wrist in her right hand.

"Your mother is very talented." Holly knelt in front of the girl.

The girl stared at Holly for a long moment. "She was."

"She passed away?"

Her eyes darkened as if a curtain had fallen to shield them. "She's dead."

"I'm sorry." Holly blanched at the girl's tone of voice. Had death become so commonplace that she could speak those words in a cold and flat manner? "What's your name?"

"Maria."

"That's beautiful."

"There's more, but that is easier for people to say."

"Maria it is," Holly said. "I need to take a closer look at your shoulder. I believe it may be dislocated."

Maria's head moved forward slightly, giving Holly consent. She eased the tank top strap to the side and found the knot under Maria's skin.

"The doctor will have to put it back in place, but I promise you that relief will be immediate. Before you leave, you'll receive medicine to relax your muscles and help with the pain. It's important that you keep your arm close to your body, so I'll fix you up with a sling."

"Will it hurt?" Maria turned her body toward the door.

Holly wasn't going to lie or make false promises. "I'm sorry, but it's the only way to make the pain stop. When you're finished with the doctor, come see me. I'll give you a cold pack to take with you."

"It won't just go away?" the girl asked.

"No." Holly glanced behind them. "Did your father bring you?"

"No. He's dead, too." The girl's dark eyes reflected no emotion, only acceptance.

Holly's heart dropped to her shoe tops. "I'm so sorry."

"It happened a long time ago."

"Who takes care of you?"

The girl's chin lifted. "I take care of myself."

"I'll walk you over to the doctor's nurse. We have a specialist who will take a look at your shoulder." Maria followed as they crossed to where a doctor's work area had been set up.

Room dividers found in storage had been set up, offering a small measure of privacy. A row of cots was lined up in front of the closed-off area. Holly patted an empty bed and sat next to Maria, waiting with her until one of the doctor's nurses waved them inside. Holly succinctly described Maria's injury.

"Remember to come see me before you leave," Holly instructed Maria. She grabbed Holly's hand. "They'll take good care of you, I promise."

Dr. Abroon looked up from a patient and nodded.

Holly returned to her job and found her line had grown. She tried her best not to rush through, to give each individual the attention they deserved. She prayed she wouldn't miss some underlying damage and send a truly injured person away with just a bandage. After a few cuts and scrapes, she motioned to the next person in line.

A thin, dark-haired woman approached cautiously. Her eyes scanned the room, back and forth, as if looking for someone.

"Have a seat," Holly said. "Are you injured?"

The woman took her time answering. "Yeah," she said, perching on the edge of the chair.

"Are you looking for someone?"

"No. I was just checking out the place."

Holly began her examination, checking for sprains or other injuries. She asked questions, sometimes getting a yes or no answer, other times no response at all. The woman's eyes were glassy, pupils dilated, and she picked at the sores on her arms. She wasn't the first addict the medical team had seen over the past few days. Finding nothing wrong with the woman except a few scratches, she cleaned, applied ointment and Band-Aids.

"Try to keep those scratches clean and you'll be fine."

"I'm in pain." The woman's voice was whiny and pleading.

"I think a good hot meal would be just the thing to make you feel better. Stop by the volunteer food truck outside for a sandwich and a bottle of water." Holly turned to clean off her table.

The woman grabbed her wrist. "I need something. A painkiller," she pleaded. "You can get it. Help me out."

"I can't." Holly waved her hand across her medical supplies. "I have nothing stronger than aspirin."

"Fucking bitch." The woman had morphed from begging to furious. She took a step toward Holly.

The woman's loud outburst startled Holly. She did her best to maintain her composure but fear wound around her spine, stopping at her throat. The guard from the front door was walking in their direction, bolstering her courage. She swallowed her panic and stood her ground. "I will not give you narcotics of any form. You need medical help to kick your addiction."

"I don't need nothin' from you." The woman's lips thinned revealing yellowed teeth.

The guard stepped between Holly and the addict. "I'll escort you to the door. Now."

His tone was low and cold, leaving no reason to doubt how serious he was. He waved his hand, showing the way outside. When the woman was out of sight, Holly sat to catch her breath. Suzanne hurried from her work area to Holly's side.

"Holy crap," Suzanne said. "I thought for sure she was going to take a swing at you."

"So did I." Holly reached for her bottle of water, not at all surprised to find her hand shaking. "That's a scene I never want to repeat."

"You were so calm, way calmer than I would have been."

"I doubt that." The line at Holly's work area had grown, so she tried to push the incident from her mind and returned to work.

Long after the addict had gone, the woman's rancid scent lingered. She could still see the agony in her eyes; still feel the anger that had spewed from her. The hopelessness on her face as she was escorted from the building haunted Holly. What was going to happen to that poor woman?

Chapter 3

At twenty-four years old, RG Rogers had never been in a chair as comfortable as the plush leather recliner his ass was currently enjoying. He'd scored this particular hangout by following an old man home from the gas station. With three bedrooms and two toilets, the rancher's house seemed huge to him. Best of all, the place didn't smell like stale beer, cheap wine and human shit.

RG's discontent with the bowl of crap that life had handed him itched like a cheap wool shirt. Things had gotten so bad that he and Lavon Kelly were now babysitting Angel Garza. Why? Because the money was fucking unbelievable.

Angel's big brother, Ivan, was rumored to be a high-priced hitman, but nobody knew for sure. He was older, maybe thirty, and traveled a lot. After their mother had died, Ivan had moved his crazy-ass brother to the other side of town to live with him. But little brother wouldn't stay on his meds and went through caretakers faster than shit through a goose. Nobody else would take the thankless job of Angel's caretaker.

Ivan wanted somebody to make sure his mountain of a brother didn't start any new shit and wind up in jail. It didn't take RG long to understand why the previous sitters hadn't stuck. Angel was a spoiled, crazy motherfucker, and that was when he actually took his meds.

Within a week, RG was ready to pull his fucking hair out. Angel was supposed to have a psychotic disorder, whatever the hell that meant. He wanted what he wanted when he wanted it, and fuck the rest of the world. RG expected him to start chasing cars and biting at the tires any minute. Truth.

Angel's insistence they come to Connersville had come during one of his more demanding stages. They were stealing penny ante shit, but the turnover of goods would be fast. The more drugs and high-end merchandise they hauled back to Houston, the more money they'd make.

Soon as RG had enough cash, he was getting the fuck out of town. His cousin in Chicago would vouch for him and hook him up with the right people. Then he'd make some real dough. Yeah, the big money was up north.

Then Ivan could find somebody else to watch his idiot brother.

RG glanced out of the window at the open fields. There were no neighbors. He couldn't even see the nearest house. How did people live like this? Out in the middle of nowhere? It was beyond his understanding, but still, this was the perfect hideout. Nosy neighbors would have meant trouble. So did live owners, but he'd let Angel handle that problem. Angel enjoyed killing.

RG dragged the old man's hunting knife across the sharpening stone, and then held up the blade to inspect his effort. He spit on the stone, then repeated the process. The home owner's collection of guns and hunting knives had been a nice surprise.

The back door slammed open, bouncing off the wall. He didn't have to turn in his chair and look. Angel's behavior was getting more erratic every day.

"RG?"

Without looking, he knew Helena had come in the room with Angel. The putrid stench rolled off the bitch and filled the room.

"She's late."

"The line was long," Helena whined. "I stood out in the heat for hours."

Angel had picked the junkie up their first night in town. She'd been begging for a hit and offering to do anything for it. Now RG liked pussy as much as the next swinging dick, but not one as nasty as hers. Angel wasn't as picky. RG had agreed to let her hang with them because she lived in the area.

So far, she'd given them the location of one lousy drugstore to hit. The drugs were there, but so was the owner. Old fucker had camped inside thinking he could protect his business from looters. He'd been wrong.

RG turned to face her. Her skin glistened with sweat, and her hands trembled like an old woman. Her head jerked with the telltale spasm of a junkie in need.

"Cut the sob story. What did you see?"

"They're set up in the cafeteria, just like you said. I counted five nurses up front. They worked on some people up there, but if you were hurt bad, they sent you to the back. That's where the doctors were." She fidgeted, shifted her weight from one foot to the other. "I gotta have something. Please."

RG ignored her. "What else did you see?"

She clawed at a sore on her neck. "Three vans parked next to the building and two of them four-door pickups." Helena came closer, wagging a bony finger in the air. "There's a trailer backed flush to the building. I'll bet that's where the drugs are."

"Good to know." Now he could lay out a plan. They would fill the old rancher's empty horse trailer and use his pickup to haul ass out of town.

"I did good, didn't I?" She perked up. "Good enough for you to help me out?"

"We didn't make no deal." RG just wanted her out of his sight.

"But I can work for you. Check some more of those medical places."

"Angel?"

"Yeah."

"Get her out of here."

"No!" Helena cried. "You can't turn me out like this."

RG flicked his wrist for her and Angel to go. "I said to get her out of here."

Angel clamped his teeth closed and scowled. There was that weird look in his eyes. Now, what?

"There's something else. I saw a guard," she said.

"Tell me about the guard." Bitch had been holding back.

"Dude stands outside the front door. Black pants and shirt, with a pistol on his hip and a rifle slung over his shoulder."

"Did you recognize him?"

"Never seen him before. But his eyes were cold and mean."

"Some reporter said the sheriff called in outside help." RG lifted his beer and took a drink. "It won't stop us. We're going to score and then take our asses back to Houston. Get rid of her," he said to Angel.

"No." Angel shook his head.

"What the fuck?"

"She's mine." Angel had a tight grip on her arm.

"We don't need any witnesses."

"No," Helena cried. "You'll protect me, won't you."

Angel stood his ground. "You're mine, right?" He pulled her closer. "Right?"

"That's right. I'm Angel's woman." Her hand slid between his legs and massaged his cock. "We have fun together, don't we? There's more I can do for you."

"I'm keeping her."

Helena's about-face from whining to honey-sweet was pathetic. Angel looked over his shoulder and they left the room. RG shrugged. Angel could keep her as long as he wanted. The bitch would do plenty for Angel before she died.

****

Jake had seen pictures of tornado damage before, but nothing had prepared him for seeing it up close and personal. The uprooted trees, roofs blown off, and dead livestock he'd seen on his drive into Connersville had shocked the hell out of him, but that was just the beginning. The devastation in town was even worse.

Wide swaths of homes and businesses were gone, leaving behind small parts and pieces of lives. Brick walls had crumbled, some turning into rubble while others remained intact, leaning against each other as if for support. Homes where people had lived had vanished, leaving sad remnants of what once had been.

People were digging through the debris, hoping to salvage what they could. Some were stacking lumber and downed tree limbs into a pile. The sound of an occasional police siren or fire truck pierced the eerie silence.

Here and there, a house stood unscathed by the high winds, hail, and rain. But each one looked out of place in the middle of such destruction.

Jake reported to the police station as instructed, filled out his paperwork, and waited while other volunteers received assignments and left. A uniformed officer picked up a clipboard and read. He walked straight toward Jake.

"Jake Donovan?" the officer asked.

Jake stood and accepted the handshake offered. "That's right."

"Officer Tom Parker. Tom, to you." He smiled and his forehead wrinkled. "You're riding with me."

"I don't get it. Why am I with you?"

"I don't question the chief. I thought maybe you two knew each other." Tom turned and headed for the exit.

"Never met him," Jake said, catching up in a couple of strides.

"All I know is that Rey, the chief of police, had a list of people from the outside that he was expecting. I think he's got a plan, but for now, I'm to acquaint you with the area."

"Works for me." Curiosity instantly settled in. How much of his background had Claude shared?

They spent the day in one neighborhood doing wellness checks requested from people who had relatives in Connersville but couldn't reach them. Jake and Tom stopped and helped when they could. Mostly they transported people to shelters and the injured to the nearest temporary medical station for help.

And a separate team had the unenviable assignment of collecting the deceased, looking for identification, and then driving the corpse to the morgue. In war, you learned to separate your emotions from death, but this felt personal.

Jake had lived in south Texas most of his life, and he thrived on the hot, steamy weather. But it wasn't the unrelenting heat and humidity that thickened the air and made it hard to breathe that troubled him—it was the tears and despair of the families who'd lost everything. Their losses stripped away any regret he might have had about coming to help.

The day flew by without Jake once checking the time. It was dark when Tom drove them back to the station. He parked the cruiser, turned in the seat, and offered his hand for the second time today. Jake grasped it tightly.

"You were a big help today," Tom said. "I'll see you in the morning?"

"You sure will."

"Come inside. The motels filled up fast. The desk clerk will have found you a room by now."

Jake went inside, accepted the curious apology the clerk gave him as he handed over a note with the motel name and address. He programmed the address into his GPS and followed instructions. The drive gave him time to reflect on the day. His respect for the residents of Connersville had grown immensely. They supported each other in a way he'd never seen. Funny, he hadn't felt tired once today, but mile by mile he slowly unwound, realizing just how much they had accomplished.

He laughed as he parked and entered the motel, understanding the apology. The place was beyond calling run-down. The neon sign out front proudly flashed the letters OTEL. He walked into the office and was hit with the smell of stale cigarette smoke.

At this point, all he wanted was a bed. He got the key and stopped by the snack machine. Two bucks later, a candy bar fell into the tray.

Motion to his left caught his attention. He turned to find a scraggly dog at his feet. Dirty and wagging its tail furiously, the animal seemed glad to see him. Jake extended his hand and was rewarded with a friendly lick.

"Well, hello. Where'd you come from?"

Jake glanced around the parking lot. No one was outside with the animal, and it wasn't wearing a collar. Jake figured the storm and flooding had separated the mutt from its owners.

He bought the animal a package of peanut butter crackers, walked to his room, filled a paper coffee cup with water and then set them outside his door. The dog wolfed down the food, drank the water, and then trotted off.

Satisfied the animal was probably going home, Jake closed the door to his musty motel room. He toed off his boots and stretched out to relax for a minute.

Chapter 4

Daylight streaming through the curtains pulled Jake from a deep sleep. He rushed through his shower, jumped in his pickup, and sped into town. He ate the candy bar he'd bought last night on the way to Connersville. He arrived a few minutes late to the briefing, so he slipped in and sat in the back of the room.

He listened as a cop dressed in a crisp white shirt and black jeans talked. "Last night, seventeen looters were arrested, and that number grows every day. Some came from as far away as Louisiana and Oklahoma. They're stealing everything from copper to televisions. We took guns off half of the people we locked up, so stay safe out there."

The crowd broke up into their groups. Jake grabbed a paper cup, filled it with some badly needed caffeine, and then went outside to where Tom's cruiser was parked.

"Jake," Tom called from the doorway. "Chief wants you to ride with him this morning."

"Why?" Jake coughed as his sip of coffee went down the wrong way.

"He doesn't share his reasons with me." Tom chuckled as he walked to his cruiser. "I told him you were a veteran and had handled the day like a pro. Maybe he's got a special assignment for you."

"What made you think I was in the military?"

"Old-fashioned observation. You've seen death, and you saw it yesterday. It disturbed you, but you didn't allow it to derail you." Tom gripped Jake's hand. "Ask Rey why he always looks like he just put on a clean uniform. It's a mystery none of us can solve."

"Why do I feel that question might get me in trouble?"

Tom laughed. "Go. You'll like Rey."

Jake went back inside. When he'd signed up as a volunteer, he hadn't identified himself as Claude Welborne's friend, figuring the fewer people who knew about his past the better. He met the chief in the hallway.

"Jake." The chief extended his hand. "I appreciate you coming. We need all the able-bodied men we can get."

"No problem." Jake liked the way the chief interacted with his men and volunteers. His easy way of speaking and what appeared to be a calm nature were positive traits to have in a situation so volatile. His handshake was firm and strong, always a good sign where Jake was concerned.

"You wanted to see me, Chief Santos?"

"It's Rey. There's no rank or class distinction here. C'mon, ride with me. We'll talk."

Jake followed the chief to his car and slid inside. The chief got behind the wheel and drove onto the highway.

"Why do we need to talk?" Jake braced himself for a lecture concerning his past.

"Tom said you have a good head on your shoulders. He thinks you'd hold up well under pressure."

The tension building in Jake's neck eased. "What have you got in mind?"

"My men are working nonstop. I may need to add, well, I can't call it a citizen's patrol, but I'm thinking I could use some help. These looters are out of control. I've got to get my arms around the situation before somebody gets killed."

"Sorry, no badges for me."

"I can accept that. You've had a rough time. I don't plan on making it worse."

"So Claude Welborne called and told you about me?"

"No. You impressed Tom Parker and that's hard to do. So I dug out your registration. When I read you'd listed Murdock as home, I called Claude. He had nothing but praise for you."

Jake smiled, imagining the scene. "My aunt was probably standing next to him, telling him what to say."

Rey laughed. "Claude needs a good woman. His wife died around the same time as my dad, and he's been alone ever since." Rey stopped at one of the food wagons. "Hang on." He got out and returned with two coffees.

"Thanks. I needed this." Jake blew across the hot liquid.

"It comes with a price." He held up a finger at Jake's raised eyebrows. "Hear me out. I read some of your background. I saw your ties with the Lost and Found agency. We'll work together today, but tomorrow, I may pair you up with an old friend of yours."

"An old friend?"

"You two are connected through the agency. He's here and already deputized."

"Are you talking about Nate Wolfe?"

Rey shook his head. "Dalton Murphy. He arrived a few hours before you signed in yesterday."

"I wouldn't exactly call him a friend." Dalton had done a lot to square things with the Feds for Jake, but working as a team was another thing altogether. "I'd suggest you check with him first."

"He doesn't have a say. This town is my responsibility, and I know what it needs." Rey turned the cruiser onto a side road. "Dalton is working on this side of town today. We may run into him."

"Good enough." Jake and Dalton had both come to work. Spending time together might be interesting.

"Did you sustain much damage from the storm?"

"We had a few downed trees and minor flooding. The destruction I've seen here in Connersville makes what happened at home a minor inconvenience."

They worked their way through an older neighborhood, taking the time to assist families, driving them to shelters or for medical help. Late in the afternoon, they came across a house where neighbors were trying to move pieces of a collapsed roof. One of the women waved frantically. Rey parked and together they ran across the street.

"We thought Mr. and Mrs. Barnes were at their daughter's house in Tyler. She called me when she couldn't reach them."

"You folks need to move back," Jake said. If the couple was under the rubble, the pieces of the house had to be removed carefully. "Let's move the big pieces and work our way in."

"You heard the man," Rey said, moving to grab one end of a two-by-four stud.

Jake positioned three people who'd been helping and gave them instructions on what to move and when. He grabbed a section of roof. He squatted and then lifted, standing the shattered lumber on its end and tossing it to the side. The house looked like it had imploded, and moving the parts and pieces required slow, careful movements.

Rey hoisted up one end of a ceiling beam. Jake grabbed the other end, and together they heaved it to the side. The group tossed the rubble, piece by piece, out of the way.

"Look." Rey pointed at the edge of a mattress.

"I'll bet they're right here." Jake tossed several small pieces of lumber onto the growing stack of debris.

The mattress moved.

Jesus, his heart shot to the back of his throat. Someone was alive under there. He grabbed the corner and threw it aside.

Wedged in a bathtub, a silver-haired couple clung to each other. The man was ghostly gray, and the woman was small and frail, but she managed to offer a wisp of a smile.

"Anybody have water?" Jake didn't know who handed him the bottle, but he ripped off the bottom of his shirt, wet the rag, and fell down on his knees. He gently patted the couple's faces while Rey checked for injuries. His nod gave Jake the go-ahead to get them out of the tub.

"Ma'am, I'm going to slide my arms under you."

She shook her head, refusing to release her grip on her husband. "Take him. Please."

"We wouldn't dream of separating you two," Jake said. "You're both going to be fine."

"He has a bad heart." Her gaze searched his face.

"Trust me?"

She nodded and released her husband.

"The chief will bring him." Jake lifted her into his arms. She couldn't have weighed more than ninety pounds. He stood his ground, allowing her to keep an eye on her husband as Rey picked him up.

Neighbors had two makeshift stretchers waiting at the back of a pickup. Rey placed the man on one, then Jake laid the tiny woman next to her husband.

She was right to be worried. The elderly man hadn't spoken a single word. Jake jumped on the bed of the truck.

"Hand him up first." He smiled at her. "Then his wife. I'm riding back here with them."

Rey closed the tailgate and turned to the pickup owner. "Stay behind me."

Jake took a seat next to the couple's heads. He placed two fingers on the man's neck and found a faint and erratic pulse. "Let's go." He smacked the back glass with his palm, then looked back at the ghostly grey pallor of the man's skin.

"Thank you," the man barely mouthed. The gratitude on his face etched a place in Jake's memory.

"My pleasure." A calmness settled in Jake's heart. He couldn't remember the last time he'd felt this kind of usefulness. Couldn't remember the last time his life held meaning.

Rey flipped on the siren and led the procession onto the road. Jake had no idea how far they had to travel to get the couple help. It felt like forever before they parked in front of an elementary school, where people stood in line waiting for help.

Rey got out, barking orders. In minutes, both stretchers had been pulled from the pickup bed. "This is a temporary medical aid station. I'm going inside to make sure somebody sees this couple right away. You coming?"

"No. I'll wait here." Jake was content to stay out of the way. He watched as the couple disappeared into the building.

His torn shirt had long ago stuck to his body, and he'd started to think his aunt might be right about getting his hair cut. He spent most of his time alone, working the horses and tending to the cows, not worrying about his appearance.

Jake leaned against the passenger-side door and waited. People came and went in a steady stream. Some needed no more than a bandage, and some would require stitches.

His high from the rescue subsided as he waited, allowing his lack of sleep to catch up with him. That twenty-five-mile drive to his motel was starting to look good. Maybe tonight would be better. Hell, he deserved nightmares for the horrible things he'd done as Johnny Darling. He'd been told so often how Holly Hoffman had huddled on a cot, shivering in fear of him. Today he still had trouble knowing what had actually been said or what was a memory—and if it was a memory, how accurate was his recollection? He was lost, except that he had no doubt that he should've been killed during her rescue. He'd never understand why Nate hadn't killed him.

"You look tired." Rey pulled Jake out of deep thought. Tom had been right about Rey looking sharp at the end of the day. Rey handed Jake a bottle of water.

"I'm good." Jake opened the bottle and gulped down half the contents.

"So you're crashing at the Sleep Right Motel. Hey, I'm sorry you got sent to that dump, but I didn't know of anywhere else with vacancies."

"I've slept in worse."

"So banging headboards didn't keep you awake?"

"Not at all." Jake laughed, blowing off the question and getting in the car.

"Keep your head down." Rey joined him and checked his messages. "There's trouble at that motel occasionally. Just be aware."

"No worries." Jake didn't want trouble, but he could only be pushed so far. "Where are we headed?"

"A drugstore on the outskirts of town. Tornado missed it all together, but the owner had taken his shotgun and camped out inside to keep the looters out. Sons-a-bitches drove right through the front door. The poor bastard was in his sleeping bag when the vehicle ran over him."

"Shouldn't you have taken one of your detectives?"

"They're already there, along with a forensic team. You'll have to meet up with Dalton another time. He and a couple of my men are on a call. A couple of gators were spotted a mile away from Larkin's Alligator Farm. Rounding up and herding a bunch of alligators home could be a full day's work." Rey slipped his cell into his pocket and started the engine.

"Chief," a female called loudly. "Wait."

Jake jerked his head in the direction of the woman's voice. The heat had to be playing tricks on his vision. He closed his eyes, then opened them in an attempt to refocus. His lungs tightened.

Holly Hoffman, her blonde ponytail flopping wildly, was running toward the cruiser.

"Jesus, I don't fucking believe this," Jake muttered.

His stomach rolled into a ball. Sure, they'd seen each other a few times since he'd returned to Dallas. He'd always had the sense she was uncomfortable in his presence, which made perfect sense. There was no way in hell to make it up to her. He would never try to blame his behavior as Johnny Darling on a brain tumor.

Because of their mutual friends, especially Kay Wolfe, Jake and Holly had reached an uneasy peace. Still, she must've been thrilled when she'd heard he'd moved away.

"You know her?" Rey asked.

"You could say that."

She slid to a stop by the driver's side window.

"The couple you just brought inside? The woman wants the name and telephone number of the man who carried her."

"That would be Jake."

Holly leaned down to eye level. Her mouth dropped open, and she stared as if she were looking into the jaws of a shark. The air stilled as Jake scrambled to gather his thoughts, which at the moment was impossible. What were the odds of running into her in freaking Connersville?

"Holly." Speaking her name was the best he could do.

"You're the hero she's talking about?"

"I'm not a hero, and I'm not under arrest if that's what you're wondering." That he gave a shit about what she thought, and that he'd felt compelled to announce it, pissed him off royally. He gulped down a drink of water because every drop of spit in his mouth had dried up.

She didn't respond. Instead, she walked around to his side of the car. She tapped on his window and waited until he lowered it.

"I almost didn't recognize you." She reached in and grasped his bicep. His muscles bunched as a major electrical storm shot up his arm. It was a moment that he'd never forget.

"Yeah." He scrambled for a response. "It's the long hair and scruff."

"No. You've put on weight and your color is much better than when you were released from the hospital."

Jake couldn't pull his gaze away from hers. She was more beautiful than ever. Her blue eyes could pierce a man's soul and cut straight to the bone.

"Thanks," he said. He searched her eyes but found no hate, no disgust, and no fear. The grip on his lungs eased.

"Mrs. Barnes is telling everyone about the blond man who rescued her and her husband." Holly's tone hinted at surprise but not shock.

"It was a group effort. The chief and a few neighbors did most of the work."

"That's not true," Rey chimed in. "If she was referring to the man who carried her, that's Jake."

"She asked me to catch her hero before he got away. Are you okay giving her your phone number?"

"Sure." Jake looked around for something to write on.

Rey handed him a business card and a pen. Jake jotted down the number on the back and passed it to her. His fingers brushed hers. She jerked her hand back as if he'd shocked her.

"Thanks," she said, backing up a couple of steps. "I'll give this to her."

Instantly and for no reason he could understand, Jake didn't want her to walk away. "I hear Dalton Murphy's in the area. Have you seen him?"

"Once. He brought a man in this morning who needed stitches," she said. "The guy had cut his arm breaking out a window. After the doctor sewed the guy up, he was hauled to jail for looting."

Rey cleared his throat.

Jake snapped out of his daze. "We have to go."

The corner of her lips lifted. She gifted him with a smile before she stepped back from the car. "See you."

"You bet." He sounded like a tongue-tied teenager.

He watched as she hurried into the building. What the hell was she doing here? This area wasn't safe. Who was protecting her? Was Dalton keeping an eye on her?

Rey checked his messages, then drove away. Taking the first exit, he drove south. "I'm going to have barricades set up in a few neighborhoods. Damned looters are tearing up what's left of the town. They're even stripping the grocery store shelves."

"Bastards." Jake almost regretted that he couldn't be deputized.

"You got that right," Rey said, muttering something under his breath. "Hey, you got pretty uptight just talking with that nurse. She's the woman from your past, isn't she? The one who went to bat for you and testified that you saved her life."

"You probably already know the answer to that."

"I don't know all the facts, but I'm not stupid. I read far enough to know you're right with the law. That makes you right with me. As far as I'm concerned, your past is just that."

Chapter 5

Holly's thoughts drifted to Jake again. She'd unsuccessfully tried to shake him from her mind, to push his piercing blue eyes out of her memory. The sun had streaked his hair, leaving it the color of wheat. His skin reflected long hours working in the sun and gave him a healthy glow, and he'd put on weight. From what she could tell, his body was all muscle.

Had his mind healed too?

Jake's bicep had tensed when she touched him, sending tremors up her arm straight to her heart. Yet he'd left the impression that he hadn't been pleased to see her.

"Excuse me. Are we done?" An angry voice snapped Holly out of her daydreams.

"I'm sorry." Heat flooded her face. How long had she stared at the thermometer? The boy and his mother were both scowling. Holly wished for a hole to crawl into. "Your son's temperature is normal. Try to keep his scratches clean. If you'll take him to that table"— she turned and pointed—"the nurse will give him a tetanus shot. After that, he'll be ready to go."

Holly understood why the woman was short on patience. Without electricity, the heat inside the building was stale and stifling. She glanced at Suzanne. The head nurse was sending the last patient in her line out the door.

"Time to shut it down for the night."

"Okay." Holly checked her watch. The afternoon had passed quickly.

Suzanne, her dark hair pulled back in a severe knot, put both hands on her lower back and stretched. Exhaustion had etched a few new lines around her eyes, making her look older than her thirty-five years. Holly watched the woman, thinking she'd use the word tireless to describe Suzanne. She'd lost her husband to suicide after he'd returned from Afghanistan, and now her job filled her life.

She joined Holly, helping pack supplies. "My feet hurt."

"I hear you. I may soak in the tub tonight until my fingers and toes wrinkle." Holly rubbed the back of her neck.

"We'll take turns. Just don't use all the hot water." Suzanne's chuckle was warm and friendly. "The influx of injured should slow down over the next day or two. But who knows how many people are still missing. That older couple who came in a few hours ago, they were lucky."

"What happened to them?" She'd given Jake's number to the woman, but had been too busy to check on her and her husband.

"Dr. Abroon ordered an ambulance. They're to be transported to the hospital in Vale City. I haven't seen the ambulance yet. Have you?"

"No. Are they still waiting? I'll go to check on them."

"Okay, but come right back," Suzanne cautioned. "The van will be loading shortly. We'll need to be ready to go to the motel. You could get stuck here for hours."

Holly shrugged her shoulders. Maybe she wasn't so tired after all. "The van will come back, right?"

"Sure, but you've done enough today."

Holly placed her last box of supplies on the pull cart. "I'm okay with staying. The poor woman was terrified, but she was still so brave. I want to be sure she's okay."

Holly walked to the back of the room and into the surgery area. She saw nurses and doctors preparing to leave. A few passed her on their way out, but she made her way to the couple, who were lying side by side. Both had IV drips that were slowly rehydrating them.

"Mrs. Barnes?" Holly spoke softly, hoping not to startle her.

The woman smiled, just a slight lift of her mouth.

Holly lifted the woman's thin and fragile wrist. Mrs. Barnes's heart rate was slow and steady. "How are you feeling?"

"Stronger. Safe." The scratches on Mrs. Barnes had been taken care of, but her face was flushed. She turned her head toward her husband. "I wish the ambulance would come."

Holly's heart tugged. "I'll go ask for an update. First, I'm going to check on your husband."

Mr. Barnes smiled. "She fusses over me too much," he grumbled. "I'm fine."

Holly checked his blood pressure. "You are better. And you'll be fine." She joked with him, wondering how many years the couple had been together. How many emergencies had they been through together?

"I'll be back."

Holly located Dr. Abroon helping with a stack of supplies. She joined him and finished putting the last of the supplies on a cart.

"Thanks," he said. "Shouldn't you be loading yourself into one of the vans? They're leaving in a few minutes."

"I can't leave Mr. and Mrs. Barnes. They've been here a long time," she said, walking with him to where the Barnes couple waited. Holly took Mrs. Barnes by the hand.

Dr. Abroon slipped his stethoscope from around his neck, listened to Mr. Barnes's heart, and then moved around to repeat the process on his wife. "It's not necessary you stay. I'll be here."

Mrs. Barnes's grip tightened and Holly couldn't turn away from the woman's troubled gaze. "I don't mind. I'll sit with them."

"Suit yourself." He smiled. "I'll check on the ambulance."

"He's been very attentive," Mrs. Barnes said. "I hope he's right about my husband."

"Dr. Abroon is one of the best." Holly pulled over a stool and sat next to Mrs. Barnes. "Can I get either of you anything?"

"No, thanks," they answered at the same time.

"I heard the doctor say your ride was leaving," Mr. Barnes said. "You should go."

"I couldn't rest, knowing you two were still here."

"Well, we appreciate you staying," Mrs. Barnes said. "Are you from around here?"

"I live in Dallas. I hate to admit it, but I've never been this close to the coast."

"A homebody, right?"

Holly laughed. "I had a beach vacation planned with a friend, but that was a long time ago."

"We have a small house within walking distance of the beach. Now that our children are grown and scattered across the state, we don't use it much. When this is over, you'll stay there."

"I couldn't."

"You can. You must. I want you to write down our number."

"Mrs. Barnes, you're too kind."

"It's Irene. I think we can skip the formalities." The corners of her mouth lifted. "Don't you?"

Holly located a piece of paper, pulled out her pen, and said, "You're right. Give me your number." While she did not intend to impose on Irene, Holly went along with the idea.

Two pops silenced the conversation.

"Was that...?" Irene's eyes flashed wide.

"Gunshots." Holly knew exactly what the sound was. She'd spent more than one afternoon at the gun range.

Crashes that had to be furniture being upended sent her pulse racing. She worried that Mr. Barnes's blood pressure would do the same. Holly held her finger to her lips asking for quiet.

Gathering all her nerve, she flattened herself against the wall and inched her way toward the front where Dr. Abroon had gone. Holly's mind jumped from thought to thought. If looters had gained access to the building, they would soon make their way to the back and find them.

She reached a doorway and stopped. She clamped her hand over her mouth. Outside in the parking lot, two men stood looking down at Dr. Abroon. Blood puddled and oozed from under his body, and the friendly spark in his eyes had gone dark. Holly's legs trembled and threatened to crumble.

One of the men shouted in Spanish to an unseen accomplice. Damn that she'd never gotten fluent in that language. A pickup backed up to the side door. Those men would be coming inside soon. Moving fast, she returned to Mr. and Mrs. Barnes.

Holly concentrated on staying in the present. She couldn't allow old memories to take over her actions. *Hold it together. You can do this.*

"What is it?" Irene asked.

"Looters." Holly decided against telling them about Dr. Abroon. "We have to hide."

She looked around for a safe place for all three of them to take cover. The cubicle dividers set up for patient privacy offered no real protection. The only choice they had was to take the one hallway leading the opposite direction from the men. She had no idea what she would find at the end of the hall, but she had to take a chance.

"I'm going to push you both down the hall and into one of the classrooms." Holly took the IV bag off Mr. Barnes's stand and placed it at his side. Then she walked to the foot of his bed.

"Nobody is pushing me. I'm getting up." He looked at Irene. "I'm fine."

"We'll both walk." Irene pushed the thin sheet to the side and swung her feet to the floor. She picked up her drip bag and her husband's. "You lead. We'll follow."

Holly would never forget the sight of the Barnes couple holding hands, displaying bravery under horrible circumstances. They gave her strength and courage.

The little troop moved slowly down the hall past classroom after classroom. The tables and chairs had all been removed, leaving the rooms empty. She had to find cover. An outside door gave her hope until she saw the heavy chain and padlock.

After they'd gone far enough that she felt she couldn't be overheard, she pulled out her cell and dialed 911. After explaining the situation, the woman instructed her to stay on the line.

Holly closed her eyes and made a decision. She ended the call.

"May I have the telephone number of the man who carried you inside?"

Irene pulled the wrinkled card from her pocket and handed it over. Holly's hand shook as she called the last person she'd ever expected to ask for help.

"Donovan." The voice was strong and steady.

"This is Holly," she said, talking fast so he wouldn't interrupt. "I'm stranded at the school with the Barnes couple. We need help."

"I'm on my way." There was the sound of movement on the line. "You called 911?"

"Yes." Holly saw an exit that wasn't locked. The chain hung loose. "We're going out a back door."

"I'm going to hang up and call the chief of police. I don't want your phone making a sound, so put it on silent and call me in five minutes."

"Okay." She disconnected.

"Stay back." Irene pressed down on the bar and pushed the door open just far enough to see down one side of the building. She turned and pointed to a classroom. "Take a peek outside."

Holly ran to the wall of windows, looked both directions, and then rejoined the couple. "The football field is directly behind us. There's no cover between here and the stands or the field house."

Irene reopened the door. "Let's get out of this building."

"Okay. But we're going to move slowly. Once we make it to the field house, we'll find cover." Holly stepped in front of the couple. "Stay close."

Holly took a big breath and moved into the open. It had been a few years since she'd felt this vulnerable. They had no time to spare, so she grabbed Irene's hand. Holly flattened her back against the wall just as she'd done earlier. If they could make it to the end of the main building, then cross the two-lane driveway separating the school from the athletic building, maybe they'd be safe.

She stopped after a few feet to check on Mr. Barnes. Stepping around Irene, Holly pressed her fingers on his carotid artery. His heart rate was weak and irregular.

"I'm fine. Keep moving." His jaw was set and his lips were drawn into a thin line.

"He's right," Irene whispered. "We don't have options."

Holly knew they were right. She nodded and resumed their slow walk. She continued their trek while pulling out her phone and tapping redial.

"Damn it, Holly," Jake snapped out rapid-fire. "Five minutes was ten minutes ago. What's happening?"

"We took the south exit out of the main building and are moving toward the football field house."

"I talked to Chief Santos. You'll hear sirens soon. That will be him or one of the other units dispatched."

"You're not coming?" Right in the pit of her stomach, a large ball formed. He'd saved her life once. Would he do it again?

"Of course I am. But I'm still on the highway. Don't hang up. Put your phone in your pocket. When you're safely hidden, tell me where you are, and then I want you to stay put until I tell you it's okay to come out. Okay?"

"Okay. I don't understand why the ambulance never showed."

"Don't worry about them. You keep your head down."

She paused and listened for any sounds. "No sirens yet."

Holly slid her phone into her pocket. Fear washed over her, turning the sheen of tension sweat to rivers of icy chills. They would be out in the open with nothing to protect them. "Ready?"

"Yes," Irene said.

"Wait." Holly concentrated on the faint sounds in the distance. She breathed deeply. "I hear sirens."

"Sounds like angels singing to me," said Irene.

"Then let's wait here." Holly walked the few feet to a set of concrete steps. "This must be the exit that was chained closed." She reached for Mr. Barnes's arm. "Let's get you both off your feet."

Irene eased herself down next to her husband. "That's better."

A woman screamed. The sound was pure terror. Had another one of the nurses stayed behind too? Holly whirled in the direction of the cry.

She saw a woman turning the corner, staggering and running blindly. She stumbled, flailed her arms in the air, and rebalanced, doing her best to stay on her feet. Right behind her was a hulk of a man doing his best to catch her.

The woman's feet went out from under and she landed face-down. The sound of her face hitting the hot pavement echoed down the alley, sending a gut-wrenching reaction through Holly. She ran to help as fast as she could.

The hulk reached the unmoving woman. He grabbed her shoulders, jerking her to her feet, and tried to make her stand. Blood ran from her forehead, nose, and mouth. He stopped and stared at Holly as if trying to decide what to do. He started dragging the limp woman toward the front of the building.

"Stop," Holly screamed. "Leave her alone."

His face contorted in anger. "She's mine."

"Hear the sirens? The police are coming."

The man stopped. An odd expression crossed his face. "She's mine," he repeated.

"No." Holly paused just out of his reach. "She is not yours."

The man dropped the unconscious woman, and her head hit the hard concrete a second time. He took a step toward Holly. She hoped she hadn't made a huge mistake by getting too close. She'd never be able to fight him off. Afraid to take her eyes off him, she stepped back.

"You can take her place," he spit at her. His dark eyes were full of hate.

The sirens grew closer.

"Angel," a male voice yelled. "Get your ass over here."

Without hesitation, the hulk turned and jogged around the corner.

In seconds, the sound of tires squealing mingled with the sirens. Holly batted back tears of relief as she dropped down to her knees. Blood had already soaked through the woman's hair. Holly took her pulse and found a faint heartbeat. The pavement was hot as hell, but she dared not move the woman to the shade of the building.

"He's gone. You're safe now." She offered soothing words but knew they didn't help ease the poor woman's pain. "We'll get you to the hospital."

The woman gasped, trying to pull air into her lungs. She coughed and blood bubbled from the corners of her mouth. "He's crazy. Nobody is safe."

"Stay with me. The police must be close." Holly pushed the matted hair away from the victim's face, and suddenly recognized the addict from her previous visit to the clinic.

"He promised me," she sputtered.

"Who promised you?"

"Angel. He said I belonged to him." She gasped. Her breathing was becoming more and more labored. "I tried to get away."

A police car slid around the corner and came to a stop right in front of them. A uniformed police officer exited the cruiser.

Relief washed over Holly. "Thank God," she said. "This woman needs help."

"Are you injured?"

"No. This is her blood."

"Step back and let me take a look," the officer said. "I was a medic a few years back," he answered Holly's unasked question.

She backed away, knowing steadier hands needed to take over.

A second car stopped behind the first. Another officer and Dalton Murphy got out.

Holly started to speak, but the only sound she made was teeth chattering. Suddenly, she was freezing in ninety-degree weather. Energy leached from her system faster than water down the drain. Something blocked the sunlight. She looked up.

Without saying a word, Jake Donovan lifted her to her feet and guided her to some steps, holding her elbow as she sat. He rested his hand on her back, his fingers spread as he rubbed a spot between her shoulder blades. Unexplained peace enfolded her, comforting her. She turned and looked into his sea-blue eyes.

Chapter 6

The relief Jake saw in Holly's eyes punched him in the gut. "I'm here. Nothing is going to happen to you."

"Thank you," she said. "You got here faster than I expected."

"The chief sent an escort." His gaze dropped to the injured woman's face. She was either unconscious or dead.

Dalton and a police officer approached. "That couple has to be transported to a hospital." She pointed toward Mr. Barnes and Irene, who were leaning against each other. "The man has a weak heart. He needs a doctor. Now."

Jake looked in the direction Holly indicated. "That's the Barnes couple. Why are they still here?"

"Good question."

"We've got this." Dalton and the officer helped the couple into the back of a police cruiser.

The cop who had taken over for Holly stood up and shook his head. "She's dead."

"She fell, and then a man chasing her grabbed her. I yelled, and he just dropped her." Holly pulled away from Jake.

"I'm sorry." Jake wanted to say something to offer comfort, but not one soothing word came to mind. At least none that didn't sound cheesy as hell.

"I've seen her before. She came into the clinic wanting pain meds. But she wasn't hurt, so I refused."

The chief walked around from the front of the building and joined them. Jake made introductions.

"I'm pleased to officially meet you." Rey shook her hand. "Sorry that it's not under better circumstances." He squatted and rocked back on his boots.

"Me too."

"I understand the Barnes couple is on the way to the hospital. You can stop worrying about them," Rey said.

Two men came over, placed the dead woman on a stretcher, covered her with a blanket, and took her away.

"Dr. Abroon is dead too." Holly's body trembled.

"There was nothing you could've done for him." Rey paused as the dead woman's body was loaded into a van. "I understand you led Mr. and Mrs. Barnes to safety. That was brave."

"Not brave. Scared." Holly glanced around at all the activity. Once again, Jake felt her pain in the deepest part of his gut.

Chief Santos nodded. He leaned over and placed his hand on her shoulder. "Two of my men are with the doctor's body. The medical examiner and his men will take good care of him."

Dalton walked back to them. "How can I help?"

"You didn't go to the hospital with the Barnes couple?" she asked.

"No. I figured Kay and Nate would want me to make sure you're okay." His gaze drifted to Jake. "Jake, I'd heard you were in town."

Jake stood and extended his hand. "Good to see you."

"You too." Dalton clasped Jake's hand.

So, détente was still in force. Jake wondered if this uneasy peace would last if they had to work together. He could understand that Dalton was distant. After Jake's brain surgery, Dalton had been instrumental in Jake Donovan's probation. But that didn't mean they had become best friends.

"I'm sorry you went through this," Dalton said, moving closer to Holly.

"I'm glad you're here," she said. Jake immediately stepped away, giving Dalton room.

Another patrol car and an unmarked vehicle came into view seconds later.

"My CSI crew is here," the chief said. "Ms. Hoffman, how about I drive you to the hospital. On the way, you can fill me in on all the details."

"I'm fine." She held up her hand. "Protocol. I get it. I don't need to see a doctor."

Rey blew out a slow breath. "If I put you with a forensic artist, do you think you can describe the man who was chasing the victim?"

"Yes." Holly closed her eyes. "I'll never forget his face."

"Great. I'll make arrangements to have our best artist meet us at the station. We'll take your statement and get started on a drawing while things are fresh in your mind." Rey started to walk off.

"What happened to the ambulance?" Holly reached for him, catching him by the back of his shirt. "We waited and waited, but it never came."

Words had spilled from her mouth and tears trickled down her cheeks. The pain in her voice sliced through Jake. He had never felt so helpless.

"We found an ambulance a mile or so from here on the side of the road. The EMTs are dead." Rey muttered something under his breath. "Neither of them carried a weapon. Whoever stopped them ransacked the ambulance and murdered two innocent people."

Jake understood enough Spanish to understand the chief's mumble. He'd referred to the killers as sons-of-bitches. The weight of the city seemed to be riding on Rey's shoulders. It showed in his eyes, hardened now, and determined.

"If you're sure you don't need medical attention, let's get started." Rey took a step back, allowing Holly to stand. "You can get cleaned up at the station, and then I'll take your statement." He turned to Jake. "Can you give Dalton a ride to his motel?"

"Sure thing. Or we can follow you and wait. She'll need a ride."

"I'll provide transportation to her motel."

Jake opened his mouth to protest but clamped it shut. He had no right to disagree. "Good enough."

"I would like the both of you to stop by my office around seven in the morning. We'll talk assignments." Rey escorted her to his cruiser.

Holly glanced back. Her gaze skimmed Dalton and then landed on Jake. She held him in limbo, telegraphing a message. He hadn't seen her in a long time, but he'd never forgotten how she used to look at him when she stopped by the Lost and Found office to see Kay. He read the fear in her eyes. It felt good to know he wasn't the cause of her discomfort.

He sincerely hoped she'd return to Dallas and get out of harm's way.

In just the short time he'd been here, he'd witnessed total strangers breaking a sweat to help each other clear debris and rebuild. Yet at the same time, there were the sorry bastards who came to Connersville to loot and steal from residents who had already lost so much.

Jake and Dalton walked to the pickup. Neither spoke as they got inside and buckled their seat belts. Jake started the engine and drove around front to the stop sign.

"Are we just going to sit here?" Dalton turned off the radio. "Why don't you dig that burr out of your ass and tell me what's on your mind?"

"Look. I don't have an ax to grind with you," Jake said. "Especially if you and Holly are together."

"All you saw was me trying to calm her down."

"All I'm saying is more power to you." Why had his eye twitched? "She deserves somebody who'll make her happy."

"What are you talking about? There's nothing but friendship between us."

He paused for a second, then "Where's your car?" A load slipped off Jake's shoulders. He didn't want to feel relieved, but there it was. He pulled away from the stop sign and drove to the main road.

"At the Broad Street Precinct."

"And that would be where?"

Dalton laughed. "We got a case of the blind leading the blind unless that GPS works. I have no idea where we are."

"It works." Jake entered the information and waited until the map appeared on his screen. Then he realized that the mood inside the pickup had gotten lighter. "When's the last time you ate?"

"Around six this morning." Dalton looked at his watch and chuckled. "Fourteen hours ago."

Jake blended in with the traffic. "Keep an eye out for a place that might be open."

"Take the Main Street exit. The tornadoes bypassed the downtown area. The rain washed out a number of the town's businesses, but some of them are up and running. It's fucking amazing how one entire section of town is destroyed, yet other parts of it survive."

Dalton was right. The farther Jake drove into the heart of Connersville the more shops he saw open. Water pooled in a few places, but this area had been lucky.

"Have you talked to the crew back at Lost and Found?" Jake had been putting off mentioning them, expecting an ass chewing for dropping off the radar altogether.

"Not since I left. Probably should give Kay a call. I'll catch hell if I don't."

"Now you know why Ty started calling her Little Mama back when we were in college. She's a natural-born worrier." Jake laughed at the memory. He thought about his friends often. His finger had hovered over the call button many times, but he'd always pulled back. They needed to move on, without Jake's baggage haunting them.

"So you remember that?"

"I remember a few pieces of things that happened before I was shot down." Jake decided to clear the air. "The doctors said the tumor had probably been growing for years. The helo crash caused trauma to that part of my brain, waking it up, so to speak, and wiping out my memory bank. But it's possible everything will come back—or not."

"So removing the tumor saved your life but at a great cost."

"I'm hoping it will all come back eventually," Jake said, hoping that he was right.

"I get why you needed a fresh start, but Nate and Marcus worry about you. Occasionally, they talk about hunting you down. Of course, they use Kay as an excuse. How long since you were in Dallas?"

"Two years this month. I wasn't the only one who needed a fresh start. Holly had almost stopped coming around after I got square with the law for my crimes as Johnny and government for being AWOL." He spotted a couple of restaurants and a bar ahead, and slowed the pickup down. "Pick a spot."

"How about O'Neill's Bar and Grille? I could use a beer and a burger."

"Works for me." He hoped Dalton had dropped the subject. Jake turned on the blinker and then stopped in the turn lane at the red light.

He remembered pieces of his college days and Wolfe's Pack. How they'd stuck together like a band of thieves through four years of school. Or maybe he'd heard the story so many times that he just believed he'd pulled them from his subconscious mind. It didn't matter how he knew they had a history. The fact was he owed them his life. Wolfe's Pack had stood by him even after they'd learned the horrible things he'd done. They'd blamed his illegal actions on the tumor in his brain. And Jake's doctors had testified that he shouldn't be held accountable.

Ah, but there was the rub. He *should* have been held accountable. The government had given him a medical discharge. The Feds, thanks mostly to Dalton, had bowed to the medical findings, and everything was settled with two years probation. Nate Wolfe stepped up and took responsibility for Jake, promising to keep an eye on Jake during that period.

A horn honked, pulling Jake out of his thoughts. He'd sat through the light, and Dalton hadn't said a word. "Sorry. My mind wandered."

"How are you, really?"

"I'm good. Don't know that I've remembered anything else. Sometimes it's hard to distinguish between what I really remember and what I've been told."

"Well, that may be for the best. Don't you think?"

The light changed, and Jake made sure he took his turn, freeing the cars waiting in line behind him. He drove into the parking lot and turned off the engine. "I wish I knew."

****

"You stupid fuck." RG swallowed the urge to hit Angel. "You can't even follow simple instructions. Helena wouldn't have gotten away if you'd killed her when I said!"

A flurry of emotions raced across Angel's face. His whole body trembled. "She was mine, and I wasn't done with her."

RG closed his eyes for a second and pulled himself together. He'd gone too close to the edge, too close to forgetting he'd promised Ivan Garza that Angel would be safe. The dummy had no idea how badly he'd fucked up.

"Angel, tell me exactly what happened."

"She belonged to me." Angel just stood there staring, clenching and unclenching his fists. "She heard what you said, so she ran. What'd you think she was gonna do?"

Angel could be violent when pissed, but RG hadn't seen this level of fury. He tried to remain calm. "Think back. You chased Helena around the building and then what?"

Angel scowled. "I caught up with her when she fell."

"And then you killed her?" RG needed the right answer. "Yes?"

The big dummy shrugged his shoulders. "She'd hit her head and was bleeding, but she was alive. That lady yelled—"

"What lady?" RG's blood pressure shot through the roof.

"I don't know. A nurse!" Angel's voice had shot up an octave. "You called and I came running."

"Awww, fuck me. There was a witness?"

The rigid lines on Angel's face drooped. At last, he understood. "I want that nurse."

RG jumped to his feet. "No, you stay away from that clinic." He wasn't doing time because of this bastard. "Oh man, that's just great, now I have to clean up your mess." A jackhammer had taken residence inside his brain.

"I don't think so."

RG's fingers coiled around a large bottle of benzos sitting on a table. *No.* He wouldn't give in to temptation. He'd come to Connersville with a purpose. When the trailer in the barn was full, they'd go home to Houston. The take he'd raked in from just two drugstores would bring a nice chunk of change, and that money would help him get established in Chicago.

"Now I have to find that junkie bitch and the nurse. Shit, I'll have to kill them both."

"No." Angel's head swung from side to side. "That nurse is mine." Angel's lips curved down at the sides. "I'll kill her when I'm ready."

RG blew out a breath. "You can't have a new one right now. Look, you need to go make sure Lavon is packing last night's haul into the trailer nice and tight." Lavon had come along for the ride. He took orders okay. If he kept it up, he might get to be RG's wingman.

Angel troubled RG. Ivan would go nuts if his brother fucked up and got arrested. They'd have to keep Angel on the ranch and out of town. RG picked up the remote and turned on the TV. He'd watch the local news and see what he could learn. Dead or alive, Helena had probably made the headlines.

A few punches on the remote and he found local news. The abandoned school filled the screen. A hot redhead held the microphone in front of her mouth while pointing to a trailer. Angel had helped Lavon and RG rip the side door off its hinges.

His fucking head hurt just thinking about how close they'd been to getting busted. The "lady" must have called the cops. How else would they have shown up so fast?

Then there was Angel, who hadn't killed Helena when he was told. He'd nearly blown the entire setup.

RG leaned forward. The chick on TV was telling everyone about the heroic nurse who'd tried to save the life of the unidentified woman.

The nurse and the old couple posed a problem. Had all three seen Angel? At least, Helena was dead.

Finally, some good news.

Chapter 7

Like most sports bars, O'Neill's Bar and Grille had TVs on every wall and above the bar. Thanks to the local news station, anyone with a set knew about the doctor's murder and the nurse who'd tried to save the dead woman. No names were given, but Jake wasn't taking chances with Holly's safety. She'd been through enough.

He shifted in his seat, stretching his long legs across to the passenger side. After they had eaten, he dropped Dalton off at his car. Then Jake drove to the police station and parked across the street.

Minutes turned into hours, and still he waited. Finally, fear that she'd somehow left and he'd missed her was too much. He had to know, so he got out and walked across the parking lot.

Just as he stepped onto the sidewalk, pain slammed into his right temple. White light filled his vision, blinding him as wave after wave of nausea washed over him. He staggered forward, slamming his shoulder into an object that didn't move. He wrapped his arms around it, clung tightly, taking deep breaths, willing the headache to ease. It didn't help. Sweat ran in rivulets down his face, but Jake didn't release his grip to wipe his cheeks.

He must have looked like a fool hanging on to the immobile object like it was a long-lost lover. Slowly, the pain subsided and his vision started to clear.

A hand clamped down on his shoulder.

"What's wrong, buster? You have too much to drink?" an officer in uniform asked.

"No. A blinding headache."

"Right. Then you won't object to a breathalyzer test."

"I know this must look bad." Jake pushed away from the telephone pole. "But I'm not drunk." He frowned as he tried to size up the cop standing in front of him. Jesus, he couldn't have been over twenty-two.

"Jake?" Holly's voice had him turning on his heel.

She stood next to a female officer, who was looking back and forth between him and Holly as if she were watching a tennis match.

"I..." Words caught in his throat. He hadn't planned on coming face-to-face with her.

"I hope you haven't been waiting long." She turned to the officer escorting her. "He's my ride to the motel."

"You didn't mention that someone was picking you up," the woman said. Her eyes narrowed as her gaze slid up and then down his frame.

"I wasn't sure he'd be able to make it."

"I'm not sure he's capable of driving anybody anywhere," the young cop said.

Holly came forward and looked Jake right in his eyes. "He's not drunk if that's what you're thinking," she said to the cop with his hand on Jake's shoulder. "If it will help the situation, I'll drive."

Jake was stone-cold speechless.

Holly glanced at the female officer. "This will save you a trip."

"It's all right, Phil," the woman said. "Ms. Hoffman is vouching for him."

Holly thanked the officers and took Jake's arm. "Can you walk?" she whispered.

He nodded. His headache had been replaced by total confusion.

"Where are we parked?"

"Across the street."

They turned away from the cops and walked to his pickup as if they were old friends. Why? Why would she stand up for him? Why hadn't she let them haul him inside? He stopped at the hood of the truck.

She held out her hand, palm up. "Keys."

"I can drive."

"They're watching. Give them to me."

Jake scrubbed his hands over his eyes. His headache was almost gone, but much more of this weirdness and he was afraid it might come back. He handed her his keys, held the door for her, and then went around and got in on the passenger side.

"I'm sorry that I put you in an uncomfortable spot." His brain scrambled for a sane explanation as to why he was even at the police station. Finding none, he tried the truth. "I just wanted to be sure you got back to your motel safely."

"How long have you been out here waiting?"

"Not long."

"That sounds kind of stalker-ish, doesn't it?" She started his pickup, dropped it in gear, and then drove away like it was something she did every day.

"It does when you say it out loud."

"You didn't think I was safe with the police?"

What did she want from him? Why was she digging? "You were on the news."

"I was?"

"Not by name but the story is out there. How did the drawing come out?"

"The forensic artist was amazing. The chief said his officers will get a copy as will the media."

"Did this guy get as good of a look at you?"

"He must have." She glanced at Jake. "I'm sure he did." Her breath caught. "Wait, you think he'll come after me?"

"I think you should take precautions."

"Like what?"

"Well, for one, you shouldn't be alone." This time, when she glanced at him, he saw a spot of fear in her eyes. "Maybe Dalton can drive you back and forth to work until these thugs are caught."

Holly took the exit to the freeway and headed north. "That's not necessary. I ride in the van with the other nurses. I share a room with one of the nurses, so I'm never alone."

"You were alone today."

"I stayed behind today because of Mr. and Mrs. Barnes. It was a fluke that I was at the school when those looters showed up."

Jake mulled that over for a few miles. He wasn't convinced a van full of nurses constituted a safe place, but at least she'd be in a group.

"I appreciate you worrying about my safety." She parked in front of one of the nicer hotels in the section of town that had escaped damage. "But I think you're suffering from some kind of guilt. You need to get over the past."

"Nothing I've done negates the fact that I kidnapped you." Jake dragged his hands through his hair. Getting over his past wasn't an option.

"Not even the fact you saved my life twice?"

"Not even." What was she looking for? Of course, as a nurse, she'd want to help him heal. Whatever she had in mind, he wanted no part of becoming her patient.

"Then maybe we could talk about why you were holding on to the telephone pole at the police station."

"Nothing happened." Jesus, why was this woman so curious? She should hate his guts.

"It wasn't alcohol. You're not drunk."

"I had a headache." He held up his hands in the time-out sign. "It's no big deal. I haven't had one in a long time. They usually produce a flash of memory, but this one brought nothing."

The motel marquee lights cast off a glow and played with the angles of her face, highlighting her creamy soft skin, high cheek bones, and cupid's lips. Her blue eyes always seemed to sparkle as if she was on the verge of laughter. The past couple of years had been more than kind—Holly was even more beautiful.

"Do you mind me asking how much you remember?"

"Enough. Let's leave it at that." Jake got out, walked around his pickup, and opened the door for her. "Holly, look. Just....in case this gang decides a dead witness is a good witness, please stay with the group. Don't venture off alone."

"I won't." She slid off the seat and looked up at him. A faint hint of citrus drifted from her hair and slammed into his senses. "I appreciate you coming to the school and the station."

God, he was so attracted to her, but knew he couldn't allow himself to enjoy her standing this close. She'd dealt with fear before, and he'd been responsible for the lion's share. He stepped back and waited for her to go inside.

"No problem."

She didn't walk to her room. In fact, she seemed to be waiting for something.

Jake scanned the parking lot. "Want me to walk you to your room?"

"That's not necessary." She gripped his arms, lifted onto her toes, and kissed him on the cheek. "Let go of the past, Jake. I have."

Color him speechless, dumbfounded and confused. Every emotion in the book raced through his mind. He stared down at her and could not manage to force a single syllable out of his mouth. While he struggled to connect his brain with his tongue, she walked across the parking lot, unlocked the door to her room, and closed it without looking back.

Jake got in his pickup and started the long drive back to the motel. He touched his cheek, and realized that he could still feel the warmth of her lips on his skin. He quickly shook off the tenderness rising in his heart. He couldn't handle her forgiveness.

His motel sat off a long, dark stretch of road outside of a tiny spot in the road named Tipton. There was no red light to slow down travelers, no post office, and no police station. A hometown breakfast joint attached to the only gas station were the only things open late at night.

Jake drove past them and into the motel parking lot. The stray was lying in front of his door. He should have known better than to give the mutt something to eat and drink. He went inside, filled a paper cup with water from the bathroom faucet, and gave it to the dog. A trip to the snack machine and two bucks bought another package of peanut butter crackers. Jake ripped open the package and placed it next to the cup. The food was gone before he'd inserted the key into the lock.

He closed the door behind him, ready for some peace and quiet. His eyelids were heavy and energy was seeping from his body fast. He shucked his boots and stretched out on the bed.

****

Jake's eyes popped open. Had he dreamed the sound? He glanced at the clock. It had barely been an hour since he'd dozed off. A high-pitched cry had him out of bed. He stuffed his feet into his boots, crossed the room, and threw open the door.

A stranger was approaching the cowering dog. He drew his leg back, ready to kick the animal. Jake stepped out into the parking lot.

"Hey," he yelled. "Cut that shit out." He snapped his fingers and the dog ran to him. The poor thing leaned against his leg.

"The son of a bitch growled at me." The man walked toward Jake. "Ain't no mongrel going to get away with that."

"You feel like kicking somebody, try me." Jake walked closer. "It takes a sorry bastard to kick a helpless animal."

"Just keep your fucking mutt away from me." The asshole staggered off to one of the rooms.

Jake squatted down, stroking the frightened animal's back. Its coat was a mottled mixture of dirt and short brown hair. It stared up at him, and the trust in those sad eyes sealed the deal. "It's hotter than hell out here. You can come inside, but you're getting a bath. Got it?"

He opened the door, and the mutt followed him inside. They went straight to the bathroom, where Jake stripped down to his underwear and drew a bath. He lifted the dog into the warm water, realizing it was female. "So were you separated from your owners because of the storms, huh?"

She stood patiently and allowed Jake to scrub her with the tiny bar of soap the motel had provided. He found only a couple of fleas, which he caught and killed. Then he tenderly rinsed and dried her before setting her on the floor.

"Wonder if anybody is looking for you." He'd find a veterinarian's office in the morning. If she had a chip, maybe she could be reunited with her owner. "It's one in the morning, and I'm talking to a dog."

By two o'clock, Jake had showered and mopped the water off the floor with the already wet towels. He stretched out on the bed, rolled over, and then patted a spot on the rug next to the bed. "Come on."

The dog made three circles and then flopped down. Jake set the alarm, turned off the table lamp, and concentrated on catching a few hours of shut-eye. He was barely aware when the mattress dipped on the opposite side of the bed, and the dog curled up in the bend of his knees.

Chapter 8

A shower running pulled Holly from a deep sleep. After leaving the military, Suzanne had kept her morning routine. In a few minutes, the hair dryer would come on, which meant Holly was running out of time to rest. She pulled the cover over her head and tried to block out the new day.

But it didn't work.

Yesterday had been a nightmare. She'd spent two years trying to put her kidnapping behind her, burying the experience deep in the recesses of her mind. Dalton's number was programmed into her cell, yet she'd reached out to Jake for help.

The sound of the blow dryer meant she had a few minutes before the bathroom became open for her use. She sat up, turned on her cell, and thought about calling Kay. She'd want to know that Jake was in Connersville, but she probably wouldn't appreciate the phone ringing at six in the morning.

Suzanne stepped out of the bathroom, dressed and ready to go. Her hair had been pulled back into one long braid. A natural beauty, she was one of those lucky women who could put on mascara and lipstick and be stunning.

"Good morning." Holly went to the small dresser they shared, gathered her clean underwear, stopped by the closet, and grabbed her clothes.

"Morning. I'm going to the donut shop while you get ready. You deserve a treat." Suzanne grabbed her purse and the van keys.

"Hey," Holly said, stopping Suzanne at the door. "Thank you for not demanding I relive everything last night. I was exhausted."

"No worries. I'm just glad you're okay."

The door closed and Holly hurried to get ready. She showered quickly, applied fresh makeup, and then dressed. When she stepped out, Suzanne was sitting at the small table in the corner.

"Breakfast is served." She waved her hands over a napkin holding two chocolate-covered donuts. In front of the empty chair sat a giant cup of coffee.

"Careful, you'll spoil me." Holly wasted no time sitting down and taking a welcome sip of coffee. She allowed the caffeine a minute to wake up a few brain cells before launching into the events at the school and police station. Suzanne didn't ask questions. She listened quietly, letting Holly tell the story. "I hope the police catch this gang or whatever they are."

"One of their pictures is on the front page." Suzanne unfolded the newspaper lying on the table. "If they catch him maybe he'll lead them to his buddies."

Holly studied the drawing, then read the story in silence. The chief had given a brief account of what had happened. He hadn't divulged the doctor's name pending notification of relatives, and he hadn't identified her by name. She appreciated his discretion.

"Tell me more about this mystery man who drove you home."

Holly felt her cheeks heat. "Jake?"

Suzanne's eyes widened. "The same Jake you told me about?"

"Yeah. He's one of the volunteers. He gave me a ride, that's all."

"Right. That's all."

A knock on the door ended the conversation. Holly finished her coffee, ignoring the silly grin on Suzanne's face. "We'd better go. The rest of the team will have questions. Did anyone speak to Dr. Abroon's family?"

"Dr. Paul was going to call last night." Suzanne stood and walked to the door. "The team met and talked about canceling our mission and going home early, but Dr. Abroon wouldn't have wanted that. We voted unanimously to stay."

Holly and Suzanne hurried to get into the van. Holly answered their questions on the way, battling the sadness that filled her with each retelling. The closer they got to their destination, the more they all wondered if the police would let them inside.

The back parking lot and one section of the school was cordoned off by yellow and black crime scene tape, but the clinic was allowed to open. People were already lined up to go inside. A group of onlookers recorded the activity with their cell phones, but the police kept them on the other side of the street next to the three news vans parked at the corner.

Chief Santos met the medical team in the parking lot.

"Good morning." His tone was formal but pleasant. "We'll get out of your way as soon as possible. I've given instructions to disrupt your work as little as possible."

Dr. Paul stepped up, identified himself, and shook the sheriff's hand. "We're glad you're here."

"We've managed to keep Holly's name from leaking to the media, but they're on the hunt, and they are relentless. I'd appreciate you asking the rest of your team not to speak with the press. In fact, it would help if they refused to speak to anyone about what happened here yesterday."

"We'll simply say that we're not at liberty to talk about it," Dr. Paul said.

"Perfect." The chief turned to Holly.

"The media is dying to know who worked with the forensic artist. We'll do our best to keep you anonymous."

"Thank you." Holly fell in step with the group and said nothing during the walk indoors.

The guard was in place at the entrance. Today, he'd been joined by a uniformed officer. Neither man made eye contact with the doctors and nurses as they entered the building.

Suzanne, Holly, and the other nurses quickly set up their stations. Dr. Paul spoke to one of the guards, and the front doors were opened, allowing the sick and injured inside.

A few patients were curious and asked questions, but most were dealing with their own losses and just wanted a little help. The morning sped past.

A little girl Suzanne had just treated for splinters in her arm paused at the door on her way out and asked her mother if they could stop at the food truck.

"Suzanne, want to divide up in groups and grab a bite? We should eat something."

"Good idea," Suzanne said.

Holly turned back to the next person in line until one of the nurses returned from lunch to take her place. She and Suzanne then crossed the parking lot and were greeted by a silver-haired man, his smile wide and genuine.

"We brought enough food to go around and lots of cold water," he said.

Holly and Suzanne both shook his hand. "We can't thank you enough," Holly said as Suzanne got in line.

"It's our pleasure. We try to give back when we can."

"Where are you from?"

"Ballinger, Texas." He nodded at the second line forming. "I'd better get inside the truck before the missus gets too far behind."

Both lines were backed up so Holly joined the closest group and struck up a conversation with the man in front of her. When she looked around for Suzanne, she saw her friend waving a sandwich and bottle of water as she turned to go back inside. Her voice grew loud and angry.

"No. I have no information to share with you or anyone else." The crowd of media had managed to get around the cops' protective barrier?. "Get away from me."

Before Holly could come to Suzanne's defense, the guard from the front door appeared.

"You were told to keep your distance. Go back across the street," the guard barked out.

"This parking lot belongs to the city. We're on public property," a reporter yelled so the crowd could hear. "We have a right to be here."

The officer left his post at the door and joined them. "You're disturbing the peace. Leave now, or you can write your story from a jail cell."

Holly got her food, thanked the woman, and turned to join her friend. A gunshot rang out. Suzanne's mouth dropped open, her lunch fell from her hands and she sank to the ground. The crowd scattered, screams came from all sides, and a hand locked around Holly's arm. She dropped her food and tried to run to her friend.

The guard pulled Holly behind him. "Let's get you inside."

"I have to help."

"You could be next." He shoved her inside, released her, and hurried to cover the policeman who had lifted Suzanne into his arms.

Holly held the door open and yelled for Dr. Paul.

Dr. Paul ran forward. His gaze stopped at the blood on Suzanne's top. "Bring her back here."

The officer disappeared behind the dividers with Suzanne. Holly waited, knowing the doctor and his surgical nurses wouldn't want her to interfere. Fear built up, making it hard to concentrate. She returned to the front lobby, where the guard who'd ushered her inside was calmly herding the people inside the school out of the building.

He paused when he saw Holly. "How is she?"

"I don't know." She refused to entertain any thought except that Suzanne was going to be okay. "There was a lot of blood."

He closed and locked the door bringing the flurry of activity to a halt. "One of the cops called it in. Help will be here soon."

"What is your name?" she asked.

"We don't share personal information with clients." Cold, dark eyes warmed just a smidge as he shrugged. "Don."

"Liar."

He lifted an eyebrow. "If you say so."

"Who do you work for?"

"The chief of police." Don walked away. He paced the front of the building, pausing at each window to scan the outside.

Holly returned to the doctor's corner.

The officer who'd carried Suzanne to the back walked around the partition, drying his hands. Blood had soaked the front of his shirt. He tossed the paper towels into the biohazard bin.

"She's alive. The doctor didn't give me any more information than that. I can tell you an ambulance will be here soon."

Holly's stomach was in turmoil. Why was this happening? And to her friend? Was this random or related to yesterday?

Multiple sirens filled the air. Don moved to the entrance door and waited until the first officer stood on the other side before he flipped the lock.

Holly scanned the faces as the chief and his men poured through the door. She'd never felt so useless. She wanted to be at her friend's side but knew they wouldn't allow it, so she joined the group of nurses who'd gathered and were saying a prayer for Suzanne.

She thought about calling Jake but didn't. He believed she had Stockholm syndrome, a psychological phenomenon that started after he'd kidnapped her.

He was wrong. She saw beyond the tough, confused man. She saw his heart. Jake Donovan wasn't a criminal. Johnny Darling was the cold-blooded killer.

Chapter 9

The media had saved RG the trouble of figuring out who to silence. They had rushed to her like a pack of hungry wolves. The cop had backed them up just enough for a clean shot. He calmly drove back to the ranch, taking the time to let his nerves settle. He totally understood Ivan's choice of professions. The thrill of killing was better than sex.

RG parked in back of the house, noting that the rancher's car was gone. He went inside and walked through the kitchen into the living room. Lavon was sprawled on the couch watching television and eating from a package of cookies.

"Where's Angel?"

"Gone." Lavon stood and brushed crumbs off his shirt onto the carpet.

"Gone where? Goddamn it. I told you not to let him out of your sight. You fucking better know where he went." RG's hand slid behind his back. If Lavon fucked with him, he'd kill him where he stood.

"He was pissed at you," Lavon said. "Pussy spent the morning ranting about getting another woman. I was glad when he shut the fuck up."

"Why did you let him leave?"

"How was I supposed to know he was gonna split?"

RG's cell rang. A glance at the caller ID sent panic straight to his gut. Few people scared him, but Ivan Garza was a cold motherfucker with ice in his veins. Telling him his brother was missing meant trouble.

He tried to keep his voice casual. "I was going to call you. It's all good. The nurse is dead."

"Good. I'm picking up Angel. Put him on the phone."

Fuck. "He ain't in the house right now." RG's brain scrambled for answers. If he could stall Ivan long enough for Lavon and RG to bring that stupid fuck home, things would be okay.

"Give me directions to where you're staying."

RG's bowels growled. "You're in town?"

"I am. Directions?"

He did as told, giving the address and word-of-mouth directions. "I can come to you. This place is hard to find."

"Have Angel call me." The line went dead.

"Fuck." RG turned on Lavon. "This is your fault. Ivan will be here soon."

"Nothing we can do about it. You think Ivan is gonna be pissed that Angel ain't here? You ain't seen nothing. Wait until Angel finds out you put a cap in that nurse."

****

Ivan's head was going to explode. After driving down two wrong roads, eating the dust that seeped in through the car's piss-poor ventilation system, he spotted RG leaning against the trunk of a car. Ivan parked, killed the engine, and studied his surroundings. He knew better than to assume anything. Being aware had kept him alive.

RG walked to the front of Ivan's rental and waited. The motherfucker's eyes were glazed with fear. Ivan pushed open the door and got out.

"Come inside, boss. We gotta talk."

"Where's Angel?"

RG scurried in the house, reminding Ivan of a scared rat. Ivan followed. Something stunk. His own fear nagged him. If something had happened to Angel...

"Ask him," RG said. "None of this is my fault."

Lavon jumped off the couch. "Fuck you."

"Don't make me ask again." Ivan could almost smell the stench of fear rolling off RG. Lavon was too stupid to know he was close to death.

RG regurgitated information on the past few days in a flurry of stutters, starts, and stops. Ivan could barely keep his hand in his pocket.

"Where do you think my brother went?"

Lavon stuck out his chest. "He's looking for that dead nurse, but he doesn't know she's dead." Lavon shifted his weight from foot to foot.

"Why didn't one of you go with him?"

"I was at the school, killing the witness like you said."

"The school?" Ivan hated having to pull information from people.

"The city turned it into a hospital."

"It's probably where Angel went," Lavon said.

Ivan turned his attention to Lavon. If he was scared, he didn't show it. That meant he was either good or stupid. "So you were here with Angel?"

"Yeah." Lavon's shoulders straightened.

"And you let him leave when he barely knows how to drive a fucking car?"

"I didn't know he was leaving until I heard the engine. The idiot walked around raving about 'replacing the woman' all morning."

RG stopped shuffling his feet. He stared slack-jawed at Lavon.

"What did you call my brother?" Ivan pulled the pistol from his pocket.

"Hey, I didn't mean no disrespect."

Ivan spotted a gun cabinet full of weapons. He opened it, removed a rifle, and ran his hand over the smooth stock. "So how do I find my brother?"

"Like I said, he probably went to that school. That nurse works there."

"The nurse you killed?"

"The witness I killed." RG was shaking so bad his voice trembled. "But Angel doesn't know that."

Ivan was wasting time. "How long ago did he leave?"

"A couple of hours," Lavon said. "He's probably still looking for the school building."

A news bulletin on the television drew Ivan's attention. The reporter was standing in front of a school. "Shut up and sit where I can see you. I want to watch this."

News vans, cop cars, and people milled all over the parking lot. The woman holding the microphone described the earlier shooting of a nurse. No witnesses had come forward.

"That's because nobody saw me," RG boasted.

Lavon opened his mouth but was silenced with a wave of Ivan's hand.

"The victim was transported to the hospital for surgery." The newswoman held up a finger as if to tell the viewers to wait. "While Chief Santos has declined my request for an on-camera interview, it's believed this was an effort to silence the nurse who identified this man as Angel"—a drawing of Angel filled the screen—"in connection with the murder of Doctor Elhag Abroon."

She held her finger to her ear. "My sources also tell me the nurse shot earlier is not the witness who provided this description."

Ivan's blood ran cold. They knew what his brother looked like and knew his name. The bitch had given the artist a good description. There was no doubt the man was Angel. He slid his hand through the rifle strap and shifted it over his shoulder. Removed his pistol and checked to ensure the clip was full before turning to leave.

RG and Lavon were standing by the back door. "Let's go find Angel," Ivan said.

When both men hustled outside onto the porch, Ivan pulled his pistol out and put a bullet in their backs. The sound of gunfire ripped through the otherwise quiet countryside. He walked to RG and kicked him in the side. Dead like he deserved. Lavon rolled over on his side and opened his mouth as if he had something to say. Ivan shut him up with a bullet between his eyes.

He pushed the tendrils of madness and fury crawling through his mind. Why hadn't he turned down the job until he'd found reliable caretakers for Angel? Now he was out there all alone with nobody to control his actions. Ivan's hands shook as he placed the rifle on the floor of the car. He got in, focused his mind on the task, and asked the car GPS for directions.

The skies, heavy with storm clouds, grew darker with each mile he drove. Without so much as a sprinkle, rain began falling in sheets. The windshield wipers fell short of keeping his vision clear, but he kept going.

Anger churned in his gut, mingling with fear that Angel might be caught wandering around this school/hospital and be arrested. If his brother was there, Ivan would find him. In a fucked up way, this was his own fault. If he hadn't taken the New Mexico job, none of this would be happening.

The tires lost traction on the slick highway, and the rear end of the car fishtailed. He steered into the slide, easily regaining control. No way was he ending up in a ditch. He had to get to the makeshift medical station.

A half mile from his destination, Ivan parked. The rain had tapered off, so he walked the rest of the way. He saw news vans parked across the street, telling him he was at the right place. A small crowd stood under trees with their cell phones out. Why? Were their lives so dull they hung around crime scenes hoping to catch their fifteen minutes with something that goes viral? Just in case a cop was nearby, he skirted the area and walked farther around to the side of the building, climbing up a grassy rise. He lost his footing, his body lurched forward, and he landed on his knees.

He hated getting dirty. Once he got Angel away from this place, he had some hard decisions to make. He had promised his brother that he'd always take care of him. Angel would never survive in jail; a private hospital was looking better all the time.

Angel's voice pushed the rain and mud from Ivan's mind. He crawled on all fours to an opening in the brush. A group of cops had surrounded Angel and a woman. He was hanging on to her while facing drawn pistols. Fuck. He was trying to kidnap a woman in broad daylight right in front of the law and the media.

Ivan wiped away the wetness from his eyes. What was Angel screaming? Ivan made out two words: *she's mine.* He started to run to Angel but stopped, standing there helpless as the scene unfolded, and he tried to figure out what to do.

The woman broke free. One cop grabbed her and together they ran inside. Angel slammed a cop to the ground, fell on top of the man, and clamped his hands around the bastard's throat.

Three cops were yelling at the same time. All three fired their pistols. Life moved in slow motion as the sounds of multiple gunshots mixed with the pouring rain. His baby brother's body flinched and jerked and then crumbled like a brick wall under the pressure of a wrecking ball.

A cop walked over, grabbed Angel's lifeless body, and dragged him off the man. Then he helped the fallen guy to his feet. They looked down at the body at their feet.

A man wearing a white shirt and western hat joined the group that now stood over Angel. Rain poured off the brim when he bent down and touched his fingers to Angel's artery. He shook his head, turned his back, and strolled away.

Ivan held his head in his hands to keep his skull from exploding. His vision blurred as tears mingled with rain and slid down his cheeks. He'd promised his brother that he'd always be safe. Yet Angel lay on the ground like a piece of trash.

Every single person involved in Angel's death would pay the ultimate price. Ivan vowed not to stop until he'd killed the cops and the bitch who had started it all. If RG was to be believed, that nurse, the one who just escaped, had set Angel on the road to his death.

Ivan joined the crowd huddled under a clump of trees, wiped his eyes, and got his bearings. He kept his ears trained on the media. Sooner or later they'd learn something, and they wouldn't care who heard as long as they got to broadcast the news.

A camera woman noticed his arrival. She cut him a smile. One of those, *I'm interested and available* smiles. Normally his dick would have jumped to attention, but not today. His mind was too full of anger. Still, she could come in handy, so he smiled back, and moved close enough to start a conversation. He needed information and this was a good place to start.

Twenty minutes later, he still hadn't been able to get her alone. He leaned down, whispered in her ear, and made a date for dinner. He'd try to get the information somewhere else. He was far too busy to mess with some bitch in heat. Only as a last resort would he keep the date.

Ivan walked away in a daze. The sense of loss weighed down on him. It wasn't Angel's fault their mother had been a junkie. No one had ever been able to explain why Angel and Ivan had been born with no sense of right and wrong. Perhaps it was an inherited trait bestowed on them by their father, who had left without compunction.

Anger boiled through his veins with the heat of molten lava. He drove away from the makeshift clinic, got on the freeway, and tried to decide his next step.

The rifle currently resting on the back floor of his rental just might be the answer.

Chapter 10

Jake and Dalton finished setting up sawhorses on one of the hardest hit cul-de-sacs. The sprinkle they were working in was rapidly turning into a lot more.

"We're about to get really wet." Jake laughed as he looked at the sky. He was already wet with sweat and figured a little rain might cool him off. But before he finished his thought, all hell broke loose.

"Just what this area doesn't need." Dalton made a dash for Jake's pickup.

Jake barely managed to hit the button and unlock the door before Dalton grabbed the handle. Dalton got in, and Jake followed.

"It's a bad break." Jake started the engine, turned the air conditioner to high, and relished cool air hitting his wet body. "The river hasn't crested yet, so there's more flooding on the way."

Setting out the sawhorses to block the road completed their assignment for the day, so Jake waved as he drove past a patrol car with the two officers inside. They would enforce the barricades, and Jake didn't envy them the job. The homeowners hadn't been allowed to go home yet, and today's downpour would, no doubt, extend that order.

"You surprised me today," he said to Dalton.

"How so?"

"I figured I'd have to carry you, but you held up to the heat and work. You pulled your weight and then some."

Dalton chuckled. "I'm not sure if I should say thank you or fuck off."

"Neither is required." Jake realized he actually liked the man.

"I was doing my job," Dalton said.

"Read minds much?" This time, they both laughed.

The police radio issued to them this morning sat in the seat between them. Dalton had carried it around with him at first, but after listening to hours of chatter that had nothing to do with them, he'd left it behind.

"We probably need to check in. I'm betting the city will need help handing out sand bags." Dalton turned on the radio.

The talk was rapid-fire and sent the hair on the back of Jake's neck standing on end. He listened closely as someone called, "Three-eleven. Shots fired. Suspect dead. Dispatch CSU to Stanton Junior High."

"Dispatch crowd control and supervisor?" the voice on the radio asked.

"Negative."

"Fuck," Dalton muttered as Jake pressed harder on the gas pedal.

"Buckle up." Jake swallowed the bile rushing to the back of his throat.

He turned the wipers to high and pushed his pickup's speed as he raced up the entry ramp to the freeway and wove through the traffic. He hadn't completely familiarized himself with all the streets, and Dalton turned out to be a decent navigator, never once mentioning Jake's speed.

Something about Holly pulled him to her. He was kidding himself. It was guilt. Guilt for kidnapping her. Guilt for using her as barter to secure evidence to keep his boss's son out of prison. Guilt for not releasing her before he had to kill that same slime-bag to save her life.

A car changed lanes, pulling directly in front of Jake. He slammed on the brakes, sending his pickup into a swerve. An excellent driver, he turned his wheel into the slide and corrected his vehicle's path.

"Sorry. The bastard could've given a signal." He glanced at Dalton, whose face was as unreadable as it had always been. "If Holly's been shot..."

"She's fine. The suspect is dead."

Dalton's words gave Jake no peace. "I need to see for myself."

"Then take the next exit. We can avoid the end-of-day traffic and go the back way."

Jake did as told, anything to shave a few minutes off their driving time. They arrived to find police officers and their patrol cars blocking each entrance to the school grounds. Jake parked on the outskirts of the parking lot.

"See if you can reach Rey on the radio," he said to Dalton. "He'll clear the way for us to go inside."

They got out and waited in the drizzle while Dalton tried to reach the chief. Seconds ticked by, giving Jake's imagination time to create dozens of possible scenarios. None of them good.

"You're clear through the front entrance," Rey said through the crackling radio.

"About fucking time." Jake crossed the street in long strides. He moved through the crowd, ignored the grumbles, moving forward until he stood facing a guard who looked enough like the Hulk to be his kin.

"Names?" The guard shifted his assault rifle, keeping his attention on Jake and Dalton.

"Dalton Murphy and Jake Donovan," Dalton answered.

The big man nodded once, and then wordlessly stepped sideways.

Jake stepped into the doorway and scanned the area. Small groups of people were huddled together, but there were no honey-colored blondes to be seen.

"Where are the nurses?" he asked the guard.

"Don't know. I'm not working inside." His tone suggested Jake's question might have been a stupid one.

"No shit. But you have ears. Were any of them taken to a major hospital?"

"Not to my knowledge."

Jake entered the building and walked to the closest group of people. Some were obviously patients who'd been receiving treatment when all hell had broken out. A few were wearing white coats, but Holly was nowhere to be seen. He ignored the stares as he pushed past them and walked behind the row of office dividers.

His breath caught in his throat. His heart jumped around inside his chest. All he could see was the back of Holly's head, but she was perched on an examination table while a doctor inspected her arm. Her feet were bare, and her hair looked like a tumbleweed.

"She's fine," Dalton said from behind.

"Doesn't look fine."

"I'm going to find Rey. See what I can do to help."

Jake was so focused on Holly that he didn't realize Dalton had walked away. Then, the people in the room, staring at him, drew his attention. A few scanned him and went back to their conversation. Others scrutinized him. He felt them gawk, wondering why this man with stringy wet hair was staring at one of the nurses.

Hell, he was as confused as they were. Why had he rushed across town to check on Holly? She was nothing to him, so why did he give a shit that someone had roughed her up? His relief that she was okay bordered on freakish.

The doctor stopped and stared at Jake like he was something to scrape off his boot heel. Fuck it. He had to know if she was hurt. "How is she?"

"Jake, I'm okay." Holly turned to face him. Unless he was blind, the tension in her eyes eased when she saw who was asking.

"Good to know." He walked closer, dragging a hand through his wet hair and knowing he probably looked like a shaggy dog. "What happened?"

"I was at my workstation when that man, Angel, grabbed me by the arm. He said I was his now. He dragged me out the back door."

"Was he alone?"

"I didn't see anyone else." The fear returned in her eyes tenfold. He rolled his fingers into fists to keep from pulling her into his arms. "Nobody in their right mind would try to kidnap me in front of all these people."

"I'm sorry about all this."

"If the police hadn't been here, he might have taken me." She blew out a sigh. "I'm so glad it's over.

"How'd he get in?"

"Someone said he killed the guard on the back door. I don't know how long he'd been inside when he grabbed me."

The red marks on her arms were already on their way to being bruises. He clamped his jaw shut to keep from uttering words unfit for her ears.

"Maybe he was going to kill me for interfering? I'm not sure."

"But you're okay?" Jake tried to sound reassuring while his mind was churning.

She gifted him with the slightest of smiles. "Yeah. I am."

Shit. Her expression sent electric impulses shooting through his body. She shouldn't be looking at him like he was a superhero. He'd explained Stockholm syndrome to her more than once. Hadn't she listened? Hadn't she learned anything in nursing school?

He needed to be far away from her, because being around her fucked with his mind. She was like kryptonite to Superman...shutting down his system. "I'll get out of the way. Dalton's around here somewhere. I'm sure he needs my help."

A hint of disappointment clouded her eyes. At least that's how Jake read it. "Well." She slid off the table and looked around for her shoes. "Thanks for checking on me."

He wound through the group of people crowding the area and went out the back door in search of Dalton. The rain had stopped and the heat was already rising.

Dalton nodded as Jake approached. "I'm guessing Holly is pretty shaken up."

"She seems to be holding it together," Jake said, doing his best impersonation of someone who didn't care. He shook hands with the chief.

The brim of Rey's western hat had protected his face from the rain, but his shirt and slacks were soaked. Still, there was no doubt that he was in charge of the crime scene. Rey pushed the Stetson back, removed his sunglasses, and then looked around the parking lot.

"To say it was stupid of this guy to come here would be the understatement of the decade. But he did. Witnesses reported he was rambling but not making sense."

"Surely he wasn't alone?" Dalton asked.

"We've questioned everybody. No one saw an accomplice," Rey said. "If he wanted her dead, an old-fashioned drive-by would have been easier."

A big, icy hand slipped in between Jake's ribs and squeezed his heart. "Maybe he wasn't planning on killing her right away. Maybe he was taking her to his buddies."

Rey nodded. "I'm putting Holly under protective custody for a few days."

"I'm not sure that's enough. You won't be able to keep her name away from the media." Jake wanted her as far away from Connersville as possible.

Dalton moved closer. "He's right. Every weirdo around will be trying to reach her."

The sound of rifle fire ended their conversation. Spectators and policemen rushed for cover amid a barrage of bullets. "Get down," Rey yelled.

Jake, Dalton, and Rey dove behind a cruiser.

Two of Rey's deputies were hit. One was dead, the other — Tom — desperately tried to drag himself to safety. Jake ran into the open, hooked his hands under Tom's arms and pulled him behind the car with them. A bullet bounced off the pavement where they had been standing.

Rey was propped against the cruiser's front tire. A red stain covered the front of his normally snow-white shirt. Jake had never wanted a gun so badly.

The gunfire stopped as abruptly as it had started. The voices of women crying and people yelling filled the air.

"Son of a bitch," Rey said with a cough. "Stay here. Give my men time to sweep the area. We'll carry the wounded inside."

"There's no time. You're going first," Jake said.

"No." Rey's voice was weak.

"Jake's right," Dalton said.

The officer Jake had pulled to safety pushed himself up on his elbows. "I'm okay. Go."

Dalton reached down and caught Rey's ankles. Jake slid his hands under the chief's arms and they hurried inside.

Pandemonium was the only way to describe what was happening inside the building. The front doors had been closed and locked, no doubt to keep people safe, but apparently everyone wanted outside.

As badly as he wanted to make sure Holly was safe, he tamped down the fire in his belly and went back to help Tom. He'd lied when he'd told the chief he was okay, and Jake knew it.

Tom's face was pale, but he tried to stand.

"Put your arm around my shoulder." Jake grabbed him. "Now lean into me. Let me carry the load."

One step at a time, they made their way into the building. Jake handed him over to another white coat. "Hang in there," he said as they whisked him away.

Jake and Dalton walked to the front door and stood with the guard. The rain had stopped, the sky had cleared, and the sun was trying to break through the clouds. It was oddly quiet.

"Until Rey can talk, we'll have a hard time finding out anything," Dalton said.

Jake dug his fingers into his scalp. "Too many pieces of this puzzle are missing. If these men are hell-bent on getting to Holly, you need to take her and disappear." Dalton would protect her with his life if it came to that. "Without talking to anyone, just take her to Dallas."

Dalton rubbed his chin as if considering Jake's idea. "That's not a bad idea, but Dallas isn't the answer."

"Why not? The new facility sounds like a fortress."

"It's close, but if Holly's name gets out, connecting her relationship with Lost and Found will be easy." Dalton's eyebrows pulled together. "Kay is pregnant again. They don't talk about it, but she miscarried last year. I don't know anything about babies, but no way can stress be good for mother or baby."

Jake smiled at the news. Nate and Kay would make great parents. "How far along is she?"

"I don't know, but she's big." Dalton glanced back at the area where the doctors had taken Rey. "Have you seen Holly?"

"Not since we came back inside."

Dalton moved closer. "Nobody here knows you or where you're from. You have to be the one to insist that she go with you."

"You're suggesting I kidnap her? I've been there. It didn't end well."

"I'm not suggesting that. Let's see what she says."

Chapter 11

Holly and the nurses moved to their workstations and started packing up. It gave her something to do and took her mind off her scrapes and bruises.

Why was this happening to her? She had run to stop that woman from being attacked on instinct. How did that make her important enough to kidnap? Chilly fingers wrapped around her spine. Would Angel's friends try again?

She sensed Jake before he spoke. Her skin heated whenever his eyes were on her. She turned to find him and Dalton.

"I appreciate both of you for coming."

"No worries," Jake said.

"We need to talk with you." Dalton's frown dug furrows in his forehead.

Jake, on the other hand, was stoic and unreadable.

"Okay. Give me five minutes." Holly closed the plastic tote she was packing into and set it on a cart next to her table. She joined them at the front door. "If you're wondering about Chief Santos, he's still in surgery."

"Nothing yet," Dalton said.

"Walk with us," Jake said.

The hair on her arms quivered. Something was up. A few steps away from the crowd, she stopped. "What's this about?"

Jake's eyes darkened as he looked down at her. Was that a flash of concern? If it was, it vanished quickly. "Rey wants to place you in protective custody. As far as we know, the shooter was looking for you."

"Let's face it, your presence here puts others in jeopardy," Dalton added. "This group of thugs is either lucky or damned good. After the kidnapping attempt, security swept the area and found nothing. Hours later, one of them came back and unleashed that barrage of bullets."

His words stung but sometimes the truth hurt. "I know."

Both Jake and Dalton weren't saying anything she didn't already know, but hearing somebody say it out loud sent her stomach rolling. "Look, I'll be fine. If the airports in Houston are open, I'll get a ride to town and fly home."

"You won't be safe there." Dalton cut a quick glance at Jake. "If your name gets out, and we have to assume it will, you won't be safe in Dallas.

Nobody fully understands what happened today. Until we do, you should stay out of sight, maybe at Jake's ranch."

She scrambled to come up with a safe place to go. "The Lost and Found compound is isolated—" Holly stopped midsentence. "No, I can't put them in danger, not with Kay pregnant."

"I agree," Dalton said. "If these men want to find you, they won't hesitate to kill Nate or Kay. This shooter has proven that he doesn't care about human lives."

Holly tried to wrap her head around everything Dalton was saying. Now she understood why Jake had turned into Mr. Stone Face. Dalton was trying to shove her off on him.

"You'll be safe with me at the ranch," Jake said. His tone, cold and stiff, pushed Holly's nerves to the edge.

"I can disappear without your help." She shifted her gaze to Dalton. "Wait here. I'll see what I can learn from the deputy chief of police. If there's a plan in place, I'll go with it."

Before they could speak, she turned her back to them and walked to the area where the chief had been taken. But checking on Chief Santos wasn't her major reason for a quick exit. She needed to think. Jake obviously found the idea of her staying at the ranch ridiculous. Why was he acting as if she were a contagious, incurable disease?

Dr. Paul was the first person with any authority she ran into. Holly waited until he'd finished his conversation and then touched his arm.

"Holly," he said. His face bore the look of a man who'd shouldered a lot of responsibility that he didn't necessarily want. "How are you holding up?"

"A little jumpy. Chief Santos thinks I should be in protective custody, but I don't know what he had planned. I'm looking for his second-in-command."

"I think he's still outside." Dr. Paul cleared his throat. "Look Holly, I think protective custody sounds like a good thing after all that's happened today."

His words sealed the deal. She couldn't stay here and didn't want to turn her safety over to complete strangers.

"How was Chief Santos?"

"The bullet broke a rib. Luckily, it missed his vital organs. It could have been a lot worse." Dr. Paul lowered his voice. "You'll be leaving soon?"

"Yes. I would appreciate it if you didn't mention our conversation with anyone. I'll contact the sheriff with details."

"Of course. If anyone else inquires, I'll tell the truth. You left without a forwarding address."

"Thank you. Please ask the team to keep my identity confidential."

"I will speak with them privately. Stay safe. I hope to see you at work when all this is over."

"Me too." Holly couldn't help but wonder if or when "all this" would be over. She turned to see Jake was standing a few feet away. In long strides, he closed the gap between them.

"Dalton is right. My aunt's ranch is the safest place for you."

"Exactly how did you reach that conclusion? A few minutes ago you almost choked on the idea. You think because of our history that I should...what? Hate you? Be scared of you?" Jake opened his mouth as if to argue, but she wasn't finished. "If I can understand you weren't yourself, why can't you?"

The dark cloud behind his eyes returned. The nerves in his iron jaw twitched. "You remember every detail of everything that happened. I don't. What else is out there that I don't know?"

"It doesn't matter. Johnny Darling wasn't and isn't Jake Donovan."

"It matters to me." Jake glared at her. His broad chest expanded and then relaxed as he breathed out a long breath. "The only people in this town who know how to reach me are the police department. It makes perfect sense for you to stay at the ranch."

"I really don't know what else to do. Why would these men go to all the trouble of hunting me down? The only one I could have testified against is dead."

"The cops will identify the dead guy and go from there. They will run his DNA, fingerprints, and picture. Maybe that information will lead them to the rest of them. Dalton is sticking around to lend Chief Santos a hand."

"This is crazy. Those men came here to steal narcotics. Now look what it's turned into." Holly's mind was racing. She'd spent a lot of time in therapy getting her life back together after the kidnapping. And now this? "So this bastard got away?"

"The cops are still looking." Jake's gaze swept the room. "I'll get you to my pickup safely." He glanced around the room. "Hang on a second."

She opened her mouth to speak, but Jake had already walked away. He spent a few minutes on his cell phone before speaking with one of the other nurses. A few minutes later, he motioned for her to come there.

"My aunt's expecting us."

"You couldn't have told her everything."

"She knows enough and understands." He handed Holly a light-weight hoodie. "I borrowed this with the understanding she'd never see it again."

Holly waved at the nurse, who looked thoroughly confused. "I'm surprised you found anything."

"It's raining again, so covering your head won't draw attention. We need to go before it stops." Jake motioned for Dalton to join them. "Dalton and the chief will be the only people who know where you're staying."

Dalton's lips were drawn into a grim line as he approached. "You two reach an agreement?"

"We did." Holly tried to read his thoughts but couldn't. "I'm going to the ranch."

"Think you can get a ride to your vehicle?" Jake asked Dalton.

"Sure thing."

Jake held out his truck keys. "If you'll bring my pickup close to the front door, we'll be ready. I'll call you when we get to my aunt's ranch but not until I have clean phones."

"Clean phones?" Holly asked. "Isn't that overkill?"

"Nothing is overkill until we're sure nobody is looking for you," Jake almost growled.

"He's right." Dalton twirled the keys around his finger. He held Jake's gaze for a minute before shifting to Holly. "He'll take good care of you. If either of you need anything, call me."

Dalton walked away, leaving behind a sadness that settled in her heart right next to her fear. Right now all Holly wanted to do was crawl into a hole and hide. People were dead. Her dear friend shot along with the chief of police.

Holly's presence put everyone she was near in danger. And the word *why* kept circling through her mind.

"It's raining harder. We need to go." Jake held the hoodie while she slipped it on.

"I'm ready." She led the way, pausing at the door to cover her head and face as best she could.

Dalton had parked so the passenger door was closest. Jake ushered her inside, hurried around the front, and quickly changed places with Dalton.

"Go," Dalton said, stepping back and closing the door.

Jake's foot came down on the gas pedal and the pickup lurched forward. Holly turned in the seat to wave good-bye, but Dalton was already gone.

Jake kept his gaze on the highway, avoiding the main roads for a while before taking a ramp onto the freeway.

Holly was full of unanswered questions. She didn't even know where this ranch was located. What exactly had he told his aunt and what if she wasn't okay harboring a hunted woman?

Jake was silent as he drove north. That he kept coming to her rescue said a lot about the real Jake Donovan, the one who would always have a place in her heart. The young man she remembered had matured. The long hair and scruff on his face couldn't hide the fact he was masculine and handsome. Working at the ranch had strengthened his body, hardened him, and transformed his muscles into works of art. Something as simple as turning down the radio or shifting on the seat caused his sleeves or jeans to stretch, almost groaning against the strain.

An overhead sign drew her attention. "You missed the exit to my motel."

"Is there anything there you can't live without?" He slowed down.

"Not really, just a few clothes, some makeup, and a good book." She thought a minute. "You're right. Let's keep going."

"There's one stop I have to make."

He didn't offer any additional information, so they slipped back into their silent worlds for another twenty minutes. Jake took an exit and drove past a sign indicating ten miles to the next town.

"That's my motel." He nodded as they drove past a rundown motel. The rooms looked as if they were tied together by one long awning.

"I'm sorry." What else could she say? No need in telling him it was a dump. "You're not stopping?"

"No. Who knows if your picture will surface, but people are quick to snap away with their cell phones." He parked in front of a veterinarian's office. "This won't take more than a few minutes, but I don't want you out here alone."

"I'll go in. No problem." The rain had stopped, but Holly slipped the hoodie over her head, tucking her hair out of sight. She followed Jake inside the small office, immediately turning away from the woman behind the counter.

"I've been expecting you," the middle-aged woman behind the counter said.

"Yes, ma'am. What did you find out?"

"She's a little thin but in overall decent condition. Judging from the condition of her paws, she's been walking a while. I fed her, and then gave her the required shots."

"No chip?"

"No, but I implanted one."

"Then I guess she belongs to me."

"I'm glad you're taking her, because I really don't have room for another animal. I'll bring her right out."

The woman turned and disappeared through a door while he selected a collar from a sale rack.

The door opened and Jake knelt on one knee. He opened his arms and a large brindle dog jumped into his arms as if they were old friends. He slid the collar around her neck while she licked his cheek. The animal followed him to the counter, leaning against him while he paid the bill. As soon as he pocketed his change, they were out the door.

Holly watched in amazement, biting back questions, knowing that she'd have time on the drive. She got in the pickup and waited. Jake opened the drivers side door and patted the seat.

"Come on. You can do it."

The animal jumped inside, hopped on the seat, waiting for Jake. "Good girl."

Holly removed the hoodie and then extended her hand. The dog rested her muzzle on Holly's fingers. Soulful brown eyes stared up at her, instantly connecting.

He started the engine and turned to Holly. "I hope you don't mind sharing your ride with a dog." His blue eyes flooded her with warmth.

Holly laughed for the first time in days. "Not at all. What's her name?"

"I don't know. I figure she'll let us know." Jake buckled his seat belt and the unnamed dog rested her head on his thigh.

Holly waited until they were back on the freeway to ask her question. "Where did you find her?"

"She found me in the motel parking lot. She needed a friend." His right hand dropped to scratch behind her ears. "She was pretty rank last night. I gave her a bath."

"We'll need a leash and some food for her."

"I have a nylon rope in the tool box that will work until we get home."

"How far is it to Murdock?"

Jake glanced at her. "It's another three hours plus a good twenty minutes the other side of town. How did you know where we're going?"

"Kay often talks about you, wondering if you're happy, that sort of thing. She and Nate miss you terribly."

"Hmm," he hummed with a slight nod of his head.

So, it seemed they were back to not talking. Holly leaned back and turned her face to the scenery. The rain hadn't been as devastating inland as it had been closer to the coast. Still, water stood in all the ditches and in areas of low ground.

The signs of city living slowed faded. Soon the houses were few and far between, replaced by ranch-style homes with porches that ran the length of the house. The older homesteads, built years ago and faithfully maintained by people who truly loved their homes— those were her favorites. Flower beds planted across green yards, tire swings hung from aged trees, and the occasional plastic swimming pool to help ward off the heat—all of it reminded her of the family she'd lost years ago.

Holly shifted her head and studied Jake's profile. A man of many internal scars, his hair covered the one over his ear where a life-saving surgery had been performed. She didn't have to see the scar to know it was there. The operation had freed his personality from the monster he'd become, giving him back his identity but robbing him of his memory. She wondered if his self-loathing would ever go away.

"You're staring at me. If you have questions, just ask them." His tone was chilly and didn't sound as if he'd welcome any conversation.

"I don't have any ball busters. My questions are common ones, like how are you, really? Are you happy living on a ranch? Obviously, I don't have to ask if you're married, but maybe there's a woman in your life. Ordinary questions one might ask a friend."

His broad chest rose and then fell in an audible sigh. "You want answers? Here's what you can tell Kay. I'm fine. Yes, I'm happy living on the ranch. No wedding and no woman."

"That wasn't so hard, was it?"

"And we are not friends."

"We could be. We've both changed."

"How have you changed? You were not a timid person then and you're not one now."

"That's true, but I used to be a little quicker with my mouth. I've learned there's a time and place where that's acceptable. And I've learned how to defend myself with and without a gun."

"How so?"

He'd managed to turn the subject to her, but he was talking, even if in short sentences. She'd take it. "I took self-defense classes, and I perfected my aim."

"You have a license to carry?"

"I had that a long time before I met you. The only time I thought I might have to use it was on Nate."

She wasn't sure but she thought she heard him choke. "I'd love to have witnessed that day. What happened?"

"It was the first time he and Kay had seen each other in ten years. Suffice it to say, it didn't go well."

"Nate's always been head-over-heels in love with her. There's no way he would hurt her."

"It wasn't him who was riled up. She smacked him in the jaw. He remained a gentleman, so I didn't have to get involved."

"Then if something happens, you can save me."

Jake's answers were eating away at her patience. "You can handle yourself without my interference," she snapped.

"You don't know who I am or what I'm capable of." He cast a harsh look at her, probably meant to shut her up.

It wasn't going to work.

"I 'know' you look great, but that's not surprising. I 'know' you're still packing enough guilt to sink a ship. I 'know' you're capable of giving of yourself to save lives. I 'know' people benefited from your help over the past few days. I 'know' Mr. and Mrs. Barnes wouldn't be alive if it weren't for you."

"Maybe you should be a fortune-teller."

"You're right about one thing. We're not friends. But how I feel or don't feel is none of your business." She was rambling and close to making a fool out of herself, so she hushed.

"That's true."

"Thank you for the concession. If we're going to stay safe, we need to at least communicate civilly."

Holly turned her head and stared out the window. If she ignored him, maybe the wide-open pastures would relax her. The visibility went on for miles and miles, interrupted occasionally by a herd of cattle or rows of horse barns. She understood how someone could find peace here.

She had to stop caring how Jake felt or was doing. He pulled at her heart, generated a deep, sensual desire she couldn't explain. Protecting her emotions was going to be important during her stay.

Jake could try to convince her that they weren't friends, but it wouldn't work. He'd protected her. Defended her. Fought for her. In the end, he'd killed to save her life. As sick as he had been, down deep, he had hung on to a shred of decency.

Hell, maybe he was right. Maybe she was suffering from Stockholm syndrome.

Chapter 12

Ivan's stomach roiled with the need for revenge. The thought of his brother lying on a slab in the morgue burned through his system. Before he left to meet the reporter, he would have a plan in place.

He sat on the bed and dialed a contact in Detroit.

"Ivan, what can I do for you, Bro?" Big Mike always came through. Ivan paid without haggling and Big Mike liked that.

"I have a unique problem and know you can get it done. My brother was murdered."

"Who did this?"

"I'll take care of that situation. For obvious reasons, I can't claim his body, but I want him out of that fucking morgue. Do a good job, leave no trail or witnesses, and there will be a little extra for you. Luis Soto at Soto Funeral Home in Laredo will expect you to deliver Angel." Ivan gave Big Mike a telephone number. "You let Luis know when you're an hour or so away. He'll be ready."

"This morgue, how big of a problem will I have to get inside?"

"I don't know. You figure out how to get in and out. Steal a fucking ambulance and fake some sort of paperwork. I'm not going to lay out your plan for you."

"You know stealing bodies isn't my line of work, right?"

"You decide if you want to work for me or not." Ivan didn't appreciate it when people pushed back, especially not the hired help. "Force me to find somebody else, and I will rethink who gets my business." Ivan knew exactly what was coming next.

"It won't be cheap."

Ivan had learned long ago that love didn't conquer all—money did. "Have your best men do this job. Tell them to treat my brother's body with respect."

"It will take a day or two to pull this off."

"Get it done before they dispose of his body like he was garbage."

"Consider it done."

Ivan quickly shared the pertinent information. He finished his call with a second warning that Angel should be treated respectfully.

Ivan called Luis, explained the situation, and requested Angel's body be cremated. He trusted Luis to place the ashes in an urn and keep it until Ivan could spread the ashes somewhere.

Ivan took a quick shower and then shaved nice and close. He studied himself in the mirror while he combed his hair. He proudly flashed a white smile.

His good looks had always irritated his mother. More than once, she'd lashed out at him because he was a mirror image of his father. Ivan had no point of reference since the sorry bastard had hit the road soon after Angel was born. Dear old Dad couldn't face the fact that he'd fathered a child whose brain would never fully develop.

Nobody ever heard from him again, which was a good thing because Ivan would have killed him if he ever showed his face. Mama had mostly stayed drunk until the day she decided to commit Angel to a state home. It was a fatal mistake. That night she died in her sleep from an accidental overdose.

Ivan added a touch of his best cologne before being satisfied with his appearance. He was keeping his date with the reporter. If she knew the name of the nurse responsible for Angel's death, he'd have it before morning.

Ivan left for town early. He parked in the parking lot of the bar to wait for...shit, what was her name? He shrugged. It didn't matter. She'd never make it inside for drinks.

She'd never make it home, either.

****

Jake risked a glance in Holly's direction. Hallelujah, she'd gone to sleep. One more question or observation from her and he would've popped a vein.

Some of her hair had slipped out of the smooth ponytail she'd worn at work. A long blonde strand rested on her cheek, tempting him to brush it aside for her. Touching her wasn't a good idea, so he tightened his grip on the steering wheel and kept his eyes on the road.

There was only one way to get through this without making a fool out of himself, and that was to keep his mind on her safety.

He spotted a roadside gas station, pulled in, and then killed the engine. Holly didn't stir. The day's excitement had wiped out her energy. She was probably down for the count. He let the dog out, waited until she did her business, and then put her back in the pickup with Holly.

Once the gas tank was full, he ran inside and grabbed a couple of snacks and drinks. He was back on the highway for another hour before Holly shifted in her seat. He turned his head to find her looking at him. "You stare at everybody or just me?"

"Just you."

Her answer surprised him, but he wouldn't dare ask for an explanation.

"There are a couple of bottles of water and some cheese crackers in the sack by your feet. I bought the dog a snack too. She's probably ready for a bite to eat."

Holly pulled the sack onto her lap. She passed Jake a bottle of water and then opened one for herself. She fed the dog, and then she cupped her palm and poured the dog a drink, spilling water on her jeans. If that troubled her, she didn't show it.

"Want me to watch for a rest stop? I think there's one up ahead."

"Depends on how much farther we have to go."

Jake glanced at the clock. "Another forty-five minutes."

"Then I'm good." Holly fed the dog another cracker.

She was quiet until he drove over the cattle guard and under the sign that read Donovan Cattle Ranch. Jake slowed the pickup, giving Holly a chance to look over the property as they approached the house.

"Are you sure your aunt is okay with me staying here? It's bad enough she had little warning, but I'm a stranger."

"She is. You'll find Alice is friendly but plain spoken. She wouldn't have said yes unless she meant it. You will like her. She's the best thing to happen to the Donovan family with the exception of my mother."

"Where are your parents?"

"Dead. Mom to cancer and Dad drank himself into the path of an eighteen-wheeler."

"I'm sorry."

"Me too."

"How old were you?"

"Twenty-three. I was already in the military when Dad died."

"Tell me about your aunt."

"Alice is a well-educated city girl who fell in love with a country boy named Charles Donovan. He was always a bit of a recluse. He preferred horses, cattle, and the solitude of living in the country. A friend introduced him to Alice and she stole his heart."

"Any children?"

"A couple, but both babies died just a few months after birth. I think they stopped trying after that."

"That's heartbreaking." Holly's voice, soft and low, gave his heart a tug.

"They were disappointed but they had each other. I spent quite a few summers with them as a kid, and they seemed happy."

A feeling of peace washed over him when the house came into view. It meant he was half a mile away from home. Two huge oak trees shaded the front yard, making sitting on the porch swing in May bearable. This was where Jake belonged.

Alice had initially jumped to the wrong conclusion when he called her about bringing a woman to the ranch. He'd been quick to interrupt her and explain. This situation was serious business and she had to understand the risk of allowing a woman whose life was in danger stay at the ranch. Always one to jump in and help, Alice had readily accepted that having Holly at the ranch might pose a threat.

Truth be told, he wasn't sure where he'd have taken Holly if Alice had said no. His only other option would have been to call Nate and ask if the lake house outside of Dallas was available.

"It's lovely." Holly interrupted his train of thought.

"My uncle did a good job with the place, considering it was two hundred acres of mesquite trees and scrub oak when he bought it. Judging from the pictures I've seen, it took a lot of work. Alice came along and added the woman's touch."

"The wrought iron sign over the gate is beautiful."

A painful ice-pick stab blasted into his temple. He remembered another gate. Kay jumping out and opening that gate while begging him to hurry. The road was rough, full of potholes, but still she'd urged him on. Overcome with the memories, he stopped the pickup, dropping his head in his hands as the scene played out in his mind. He was supposed to kill her and Holly after he had possession of a ring. That ring was evidence that would've put his boss's son, Hank, away for murder.

The anger Jake had felt when he'd caught Hank about to rape Holly gripped him even now. He saw the fear in her eyes, could almost feel the weight of the knife as it left his hand, flew across the room, and then slid deep into Hank's chest.

Soft hands slid around the nape of Jake's neck. Holly's warm breath brushed across his cheek. "What can I do?"

"Just give me a second."

Her fingers massaged the tendons in his neck. The dog whined as if sensing the fear and anger in the air. Jake took a couple deep breaths, counting the seconds while he pulled air into his lungs and forced it out. The pain in his head finally subsided, a dull ache replacing the sharp, penetrating stab.

Jake straightened his spine. Holly should not be subjected to his problems. Mad at himself for showing weakness, he shook his head. "I'm okay. These headaches come and go fairly quickly."

"What happens when you have one?"

"Sometimes nothing. On rare occasions, memories surface." He pointed to the barn where Alice was waving both arms. "Luckily, it's never happened while I was driving."

Holly smiled and waved. "Your aunt is excited to see you."

"She's dying of curiosity." Jake laughed and waved his arm out the window. "She's almost as nosey as you."

"What does that mean?" Holly sat back, jerking her hand away as if he'd scalded her.

He let that question drift out the window. He wouldn't allow her to start psychoanalyzing him.

"You just don't want people to care about you."

He hit her with a hard glare. "So you do understand."

She snapped her mouth shut and returned his glare.

He'd hurt her feelings, but he'd stopped her probing. When would she realize that being his friend, lover, or nurse was out of the question? He parked and let the dog out with him. Holly hesitated before exiting the pickup and when she did, she stood off to the side.

"I thought you'd never get here." Alice gave him a quick hug, then turned her attention to Holly. "I'm Alice Donovan. Welcome to our home."

Holly came forward and grasped Alice's extended hand. "I can't thank you enough. If at any time I become a burden, please tell me, and I will leave."

"Nonsense," Alice huffed out. "I don't often get to hang out with another female. If I want a reasonable conversation, I usually talk to the cows or horses." She grinned and winked at Jake. "I see you brought a friend."

Holly put up both hands. "She's not my friend. She and Jake are inseparable."

"Then we'll leave them to entertain each other." Alice slipped her hand around Holly's waist. "Come on inside. I made up the spare bedroom for you."

Jake and the dog walked down the path to the barn. Once Alice and Holly were indoors, he pulled out his phone and called Dalton.

He answered on the second ring. "Everything okay?"

"Yeah. I won't call again until we get a burner phone, but I wanted to ask about Rey."

"The doctor says Rey should stay in the hospital for a few days, but he's already threatening to check himself out. He's awake and barking orders. I temporarily accepted a badge strictly because it makes my nosing around legal."

"That's a good idea. Keep me in the loop."

"Will do."

Jake stuffed his cell in his hip pocket and walked into the horse barn. He stopped, closed his eyes, and let the sounds and smells of the ranch surround him. Some people didn't appreciate the fragrance of fresh cut hay, horse manure, and saddle leather, but to Jake, it was pure ambrosia. He loved watching the foals run and play with their tails in the air and nostrils flared, ready to challenge the world. He never tired of the sight.

This ranch was the closest he'd gotten to finding peace. It invigorated and renewed his spirit every time.

Alice had made him feel welcome. She gave him time to work through everything that had happened without prying. There was no reason to hide his shame here. Neither she nor the animals passed judgment on him.

He honestly didn't believe he'd brought trouble to all that was left of his family, but he stood ready to protect her and the ranch. He would allow no one to disturb or threaten the tranquility of this place.

"Come," he said to the dog. He picked up a small bucket, filled it with water, and then placed it on the ground in front of her. She didn't hesitate to drink.

Jake opened the wide wooden doors at the back of the barn. He whistled, and within seconds, four horses appeared from a nearby rise, trotted past him to the barn and directly into their respective stalls. Marbella nickered as she waited for him to close the stall door and scratch behind her ears. Duchess stomped her feet, reminding him of the pecking order in the herd.

"Don't be jealous. Everyone knows you're the boss." The tension of the drive home fell away when he stepped inside her stall, then closed the gate behind him. He ran his hands down her sides, flanks, and stomach. A small bump that pushed against his palm made him smile. "I think you're close to foaling." He patted her rump on the way out. "And soon."

He fed the horses, gave them fresh water, and then looked around for the dog. Curled up in front of the small tack room and office, she hadn't shown any aggression or fear around the horses at all. He patted his leg, and she caught up with him at the door.

The sun was setting as Jake walked the path to the back porch. The dog ran ahead of him and into the small flower garden that Alice labored over with love. She sniffed a few times before dropping and rolling.

"Come," Jake commanded but got no response. The dog's front paws tossed dirt everywhere. Jake caught up with her just as she shook hard. Damned if she didn't look pleased with herself as she trotted next to him to the back porch. Jake cleaned her paws and then dusted his boots off before going inside.

The wonderful smells coming from the kitchen said Alice had been cooking ever since he'd called to ask about bringing Holly home with him. He pushed opened the screen but paused. "May I bring in the dog?"

"Is she housebroken?"

"Don't know. She made it through the night in my motel room without an accident."

"Guess there's only one way to find out. Bring her with you."

Jake washed his hands, accepted the glass of iced tea from Alice, and then sat at the table. "Where's Holly?"

"I expect she's still asleep. I gave her some of my clothes, so she could take a shower. I took a peek about ten minutes later and found her face-down stretched out on the bed."

"That's probably a good thing. She's been through a lot."

"Supper's a good thirty minutes away. You think we should let her rest a bit longer?"

"Yeah. Let her sleep."

Alice poured herself a glass of tea and joined him at the table. "So, can you tell me about it?"

"Yeah." He would tell her everything he knew. Truth with Alice was the only way to go. "You need to know."

Chapter 13

Ivan had sat in the parking lot patiently waiting for...fuck, what was her name? He'd just about decided the bitch had stood him up when she pulled in and parked. He got out and cut her off.

"I'm sorry," she purred. "This has been a huge week for news bulletins. We couldn't wrap up until we heard from the hospital." She smoothed her hand over her perfectly styled hair. "I broke the story that Chief Santos survived and will be fine."

Not news Ivan wanted to hear, but he ignored the flash of hate and slid his arm around her waist. "You don't really want to go inside, do you? I know a place where we'll have a lot more privacy."

"But I could use a drink and a bite of food. I haven't eaten since morning."

"In there, we'll have no privacy. People will be all over you asking questions. My Spanish omelet is delicious, and my house is private."

She leaned into him. "It does sound tempting."

"I'll give you my famous foot rub afterward." Man, she was eating this shit up. She'd come voluntarily, or he'd yank her ass into the car by the hair on her head.

"Sounds too good to be true. Let's go."

Ivan walked her to the passenger side, opened the door, and waited for her to slide in. "Buckle up." He smiled on his way to the driver's side. Did this cow really believe any man would touch those fat feet of hers?

He drove to the farmer's house, barely hearing her babble on about her boss and how not one soul at work appreciated her hard work. Ivan was about to scream by the time he turned onto the long driveway. He parked and turned to face her.

"This can't be your place," she said. "The Wellingtons live here."

"Shut up," he said, unable to listen to any more of her constant chatter.

"What did you say?"

"Shut. The. Fuck. Up. Did you get that? You stupid *coño*."

Her eyes filled with fury. "Nobody calls me a cunt. Take me back to my car."

Ivan backhanded her, relishing the sound as her head smacked into the window. "Speak one more word that's not an answer to a direct question and I will kill you."

Her hand cupped her cheek as blood trickled from her lip. Tears rushed down her face.

"Get out and go in the house." She opened her mouth but remained silent as she followed instructions. "Good girl." He pushed her toward the door.

She'd get to scream again soon enough.

****

Holly jerked upright and wide awake. Her heart raced as if the fiery-eyed monster in her nightmare had been real. She stretched her arms over her head and took a minute to adjust to her surroundings. A peek at the clock on the nightstand indicated that she'd slept for hours.

The door was slightly ajar and light flooded in from the rest of the house. The aroma of food drifted into her room and sent her mouth watering. Her stomach growled, prompting her to get up and follow her nose. She slipped on her shoes and walked toward the sound of Jake's voice, stopping in the doorway, hating to interrupt.

Jake turned his head as if sensing she was there. His smile changed his face from handsome to stunning. He stood and pulled out a chair.

"Join us. Alice kept your supper warm."

"I'll get your plate." Alice hurried to the stove and started spooning food onto a huge plate. "I hope you like chicken and dumplings."

Holly laughed, shaking her head. "It looks delicious but I can't eat that much."

"Eat until you're full. The rest will go in the fridge for the dog's breakfast." Alice put her hands on her hips and looked down at the animal next to Jake's feet. "What the heck is her name?"

"Daisy." Jake's eyes sparkled with mischief. The name must have just popped into his head. He leaned down to stroke the dog's side and was rewarded with a wet kiss.

For a fleeting second, Holly imagined Jake's fingers trailing against her skin. Would his touch be gentle or demanding? Her cheeks heated. Before anyone noticed, she shook off that thought and popped a dumpling in her mouth.

"Daisy, I like it." Alice nodded her head in approval. "What made you pick that name?"

"I was getting around to that." Jake gave his aunt a wide smile. "She sort of dug around in your flower—"

"My daisies?" Alice sat, pinning Jake with a glare. She leaned forward and rested her elbows on the table. "You waited until it was too dark to see before telling me, so it must be bad."

"I'll fix it in the morning." Jake hit her with a hundred-watt smile.

Alice stood, picked up a flashlight from the counter. "Holly, will you excuse us for a minute?"

"Yes, ma'am."

"Thanks. Jake and I are going to take a look at the damage Miss Daisy caused."

"Don't mind me." She already loved the relationship between Jake and Alice. So much so that she almost left her supper and followed them to the garden. Instead, Holly restrained her laugh and reached for one of the homemade biscuits and the butter. "I'll be fine."

The kitchen-dining room was huge. The large, white oak table and china cabinet sat under a wagon-wheel chandelier, giving the room a comfortable feel. She envisioned what it must have been like years ago, when all the Donovan clan converged on the ranch. Mealtime had probably been a help-yourself, boarding-house-reach, everybody-talking-at-the-same-time, event.

Pictures of horses wearing silver and leather show rigs were scattered around the room. Most included a man, sitting straight and tall in the saddle, proudly holding up a trophy or ribbon for the camera. The resemblance between Jake and his uncle Charlie was striking. Both men had broad shoulders, strong jaws, high cheekbones, and an impish look in their eyes that made you wonder what they were up to.

A paw came to rest on her thigh. "You may be in big trouble, girl." Holly pinched off a piece of chicken and shared it with Daisy. Soulful brown eyes stared up at Holly. "You just watch, Jake's going to fix things for you."

By the time he and Alice returned, Holly had finished eating and was washing and drying her dishes. "That was the best meal I've had in—well, I can't remember when. I had one too many biscuits."

"I'm glad you enjoyed it." Alice caught Holly's hands. "You have some peach cobbler before you turn in for the night. It makes you have sweet dreams."

"Yes, ma'am."

"I'm an early-to-bed, early-to-rise woman, so I'll leave the rest of the dishes to you two and see you both in the morning." Alice cast Daisy a look. "You and I will have some boundary lessons tomorrow."

Holly waited until she heard the door close behind Alice. "She's wonderful."

"That she is." Jake spooned cobbler into two bowls and set them aside. "Wash or dry?"

"You know where everything goes. I'll wash, you dry."

"I figured you and Alice would get along."

"I love her already. I'm sure she appreciated you coming to lend a hand."

"It's been a good situation for us both."

They finished the dishes making small talk. Holly caught herself doing most of the talking. Jake put the last dish away. He picked up the two bowls of cobbler.

"Can you eat in the dark?"

Unsure where this conversation was headed, she quipped, "Yeah. I have a pretty good idea where my mouth is located."

He lifted one eyebrow. "There's that smart mouth I remember. Follow me."

This was the first time he'd ever referred to the past without his eyes turning dark and hard. She and Daisy followed Jake through the house, out the front door, and onto the porch.

"It's warm out here, but there's a breeze. This is my favorite spot no matter what time of the year." Jake motioned to the chairs. "Have a seat."

He turned off the light in the living room, closed the front door, throwing them into total darkness. She felt his presence as he joined her.

"Thank goodness for the partial moon. I can barely see."

"Give your eyes a minute to adjust."

Her eyes slowly grew accustomed to the darkness. A beautiful new world opened up. The clear Texas sky had burst to life with millions of twinkling stars that spread as far as her eyes could see. She'd seen starry nights before, but out here, without city lights, skyscrapers and billboards to interfere, the sheer size and magnificence were overwhelming.

A horse nickered in the distance. Crickets called back and forth. Fireflies, something she hadn't seen in years, flickered in the dark. Daisy jumped off the porch and vanished.

"The fireflies are beautiful."

"It's mating season. I've been told that the females choose based on the most elaborate display."

"Survival of the brightest." The tension between her shoulder blades relaxed as she searched for the right word. "This view is exquisite."

"When I can't sleep, I sit out here and listen to the universe."

Holly's heart pinched at his words. She hated that the guilt of his past actions had followed him to this peaceful place, and understood why Jake had come here searching for tranquility.

Her situation threatened his quiet world. Her presence posed a threat to everything he and his aunt loved. "I shouldn't have come here. I'm asking too much from you and Alice."

"You're not. I get that you're scared, but you're safe here. Even Chief Santos doesn't know exactly where you are." Jake set his bowl on the porch, and Daisy came out of the dark to clean up any leftovers.

"People have been killed and wounded. If I hadn't taken this job, maybe none of this would've happened."

"Alice would remind you that hindsight is always twenty-twenty. Besides, you don't know what would've been."

The dog jumped to the ground, disappearing into the darkness again. "Will Daisy be okay?"

"As long as she stays out of Alice's flowers."

"I'd like to know how Chief Santos and Suzanne are doing."

"I'm sorry. I talked to Dalton after we arrived, but when I came to tell you, Alice said you were asleep. The chief is in the hospital in Connersville. I didn't think to ask about her."

"That's where she was taken."

"I'll ask next time I speak with Dalton."

"Thanks. I think I'll follow Alice's idea and go to bed." Holly stood and straightened her blouse. "Your aunt loaned me some clothes."

""So she said. You've given new life to Alice's jeans and shirts."

Holly stood and mentally debated his comment. "I'll take that compliment and turn in for the night." Her cheeks had warmed in spite of her efforts not to react.

"Leave your bowl and spoon. I'll rinse them."

"Okay." She put them on the seat of her chair. "Well, goodnight."

"Goodnight."

She made her way back to her room and turned on the light. Jake was so darn hard to read. He was distant most of the time, making her feel like a major inconvenience. Other times, he dropped his guard and she felt a connection. Holly hand-washed her underwear, then slipped on a faded T-shirt. She couldn't wait to crawl between crisp, cool sheets.

****

Holly woke to sunlight streaming through the open curtains. She rolled over and checked the time. Why did she have the feeling that seven o'clock was a late start on a ranch?

In a quick bathroom trip, she washed her face, brushed her teeth with a brand new toothbrush, and tucked her hair into a low ponytail. She removed the sleep shirt, slid on a pair of jeans, pulled on a red cotton shirt, and stuffed her feet into her work shoes.

The scent of cinnamon filled the house, pulling her down the hall to the kitchen. The closer she got to the smell, the louder her empty stomach growled.

A note on the counter instructed her that the coffee had to be reheated and cinnamon rolls were waiting for her under the cake cover. Holly picked one up, breathed in the aroma, and then sank her teeth into it.

"Sit down, child. I'll get you a glass of milk."

Holly jumped and whirled.

Alice's hand covered her heart. "I'm sorry. I didn't mean to scare you."

"It's okay. I'm just a little jumpy these days."

"I understand. I came back to change my shopping list." She pulled a pad and pen from a drawer then handed them to Holly. "I'm making a grocery run to town later. Might as well get you fixed up at the same time. If you'll jot down your sizes, I'll pick you up some clothes. A girl needs makeup and toiletries, so add them to the list."

"I'll be right back." Holly fished out all the cash she had and carried it to Alice. "It sounds very cloak and dagger, but I'm betting Jake would tell me not to use a credit card. I'm sorry to be such a problem."

Alice reached over and folded Holly's fingers over the money. "You're not a problem. I know what happened before Jake moved out here. That you've forgiven him and trust him with your life tells me you're a good person. I'm proud to help you."

Holly blinked back the tears, but one escaped, and she quickly wiped it away.

"Now see here, none of that." Alice's tone was warm. "I'm going to warm up the coffee. Jake and I are ready for a second cup."

"I slept really late to be living on a ranch, didn't I?"

"We're up earlier than usual. Jake just happened to wake up and go check on his favorite pregnant mare."

"Is everything okay?"

"She and the colt are fine." Alice poured three mugs of coffee and put them in the microwave. "We have time for you to eat your roll before we carry Jake this badly needed caffeine."

Holly finished her breakfast quickly. "I'm ready. And I want to help out around here. I know very little about raising livestock, but I'm a fast learner."

"We never turn down free labor."

Licking the remnants of sugar from her fingers, Holly walked with Alice down the path to the barn. "Tell me about your ranch."

"The barn exteriors are sheet metal and iron. During the hot summer months, you can hear them groan and pop as if in pain. The horse barn on the right is where we're headed. The one next to it is full of grain and hay with an area for an occasional sick cow. The big one to the left houses equipment and behind that is the corral. The land is sectioned into pastures; some are used for grazing and others for growing hay."

"It's a beautiful place."

"Get Jake to take you up on that rise." Alice pointed to the left. "You can get a real good look at the property from there. My Charlie cleared trees and hauled rock for years before he had the place exactly like he wanted."

"I'm sorry for your loss. Jake speaks fondly of your husband."

"Thank you. He was a good man."

They entered the barn to a much warmer environment. The morning sun had heated the metal roof, making the ceiling fans appreciated. Jake was carrying an armful of hay into a stall.

"Come see the new colt." Alice's pride shined in her eyes.

"Good morning." He flashed a smile at the two of them as he filled a large rubber barrel with the hay.

"We brought leftover coffee," Alice said, handing him a mug.

Jake stroked a pretty red horse on the nose and came toward them. Holly's mind whirled at the sight before her. His shirt, damp with sweat, clung to him, outlining his muscular stomach and shoulders.

A ball of heat settled in her lower stomach. "Good morning," she said over dry lips.

Alice handed him a mug. "I'm taking the four-wheeler up to the back forty to check on the cows. With your appetite, we're going to need food. Soon as I get back, I'm making a grocery run."

Jake stepped out of the stall and closed the gate behind him. "Better get enough for Claude." Jake turned to Holly and winked. "He has a habit of showing up around suppertime."

"Stop that," Alice chuckled. "You'll give Holly the two-dollar tour?"

"I'll put her to work."

"She's already volunteered."

"We need dog food," Jake called out as Alice walked away.

"She's right about my volunteering," Holly said. "I need something to do, anything to get my mind off why I'm here and not at home in Dallas. And I want to earn my keep."

"Holly," Alice called out from the door. "I'm placing you in charge of the coffee mugs. Jake can't be depended on to return them to the house." Alice waved and was gone.

Holly found herself alone with Jake. Her nerves were pinging around in her system. He was standing really close. "What can I do?"

"You can dump out this coffee." He handed his untouched cup to Holly. "I recommend you do the same with yours."

"Why?" She pulled her mug to her lips, and Jake caught her wrist.

"I try to fix the coffeepot the night before. Alice can cook better than most, but I recommend you never drink her coffee. That stuff will grow hair on your chest, and I'm guessing you don't want that to happen."

"And you don't want to hurt her feelings." That statement drew a scowl but no response.

Chapter 14

Ivan caught the reporter's feet, dragged her bloody body out of the house and around the backside of the barn with the others. Lavon had explained that the dead rancher and his wife were buried there, so he'd dumped Lavon and RG on top of the grave. He'd been too fucking mad to think what the heat and rain would do to their bodies. Jesus. The stench had started quickly, and it was sickening.

It was time to move to a new place anyway. The inside of the house was a mess. He wasn't cleaning up the blood and wasn't sticking around for the flies.

His anger over his brother's death had bled into his time with the reporter last night. The bitch had actually believed that he was going to drive her ass back to town. The second he'd slid on a pair of gloves, she'd known just how wrong she'd been. Funny how she'd asked for her mama seconds before she died.

The best and last piece of information he'd obtained from her was the sweetest. His target's name was Holly. He'd also learned the name of the hospital where the nurse RG had mistakenly shot was recovering. Suzanne Richards worked for the Helpful Hands Organization based in Dallas, which meant she was a valuable resource.

He thoroughly wiped down the furniture, removing all fingerprints and remnants that he might otherwise leave behind for a crime scene unit. He had one stop to make before going to Dallas.

The more information he gathered before he made the drive, the sooner Holly would die.

****

Jake opened the stall, put a halter on Duchess, and then led her out into the walkway. The chestnut colt followed, staying close to his mom.

"He's beautiful."

"He has a good bloodline." Jake stopped to show off mom and son. "We're hoping he brings a good price at auction."

"You're going to sell him?" Holly's smile disappeared.

"Alice has a good reputation for raising and selling quality livestock, especially horses."

"May I pet him?"

"Let me get him behind a gate first. Walk with us down to a larger stall." Jake moved the horse and foal down the aisle to their new home, where he'd spread a clean bed of straw.

The colt nuzzled his mother, ready to nurse again. Jake closed the gate and turned to Holly. "When he finishes eating, hold out your hand and talk softly to him. His curiosity will get the best of him."

The mare ended snack time by moving away from the colt. Holly did her best to attract the colt, but failed.

"Hang on." Jake pulled a brush out of the tack room and carried it to Holly. "Duchess loves to be groomed. If you brush her, he'll get curious and come to you. She's used to people being around her foals. If you need me, I'll be finishing up morning chores."

Daisy followed his every step as he worked. Even though his hands were busy, Jake's mind was never far from Holly. The image of her stroking Duchess and the sound of her soft murmurs put thoughts in his head that sent blood careening through his veins.

He worked harder, scrubbing the birthing stall until it was more than clean. He had to be careful with her. Keep his distance. But when he tossed the cleaning water down the drain, she was still in his head.

The sound of the four-wheeler's return was a welcome distraction but short-lived. A few minutes later, the engine on Alice's pickup broke the silence. She must not have found any problems with the herd, because she left for town without letting him know.

He washed Daisy's water bucket and refilled it. Grabbing a clean towel, he washed his face and arms before taking Holly on a tour.

Holly was kneeling down with her hand scratching the colt's forehead. Jake stood silently for a long time, not wanting to disturb them. Her words were too soft for him to hear, but she spoke as if the colt understood.

She ran her fingers down the white star on his forehead. She glanced at Jake but quickly turned away.

"You okay?" He unlatched the gate and stepped inside.

She stood, kept her back turned, and brushed the backs of her hands across her cheeks. His belly jumped up and wedged itself in the back of his throat. Holly had been crying.

Standing behind her, Jake was unsure how to react. He placed his hands on her shoulders and gently turned her. "It's okay if you're worried about your safety."

"I'm not." She kept her gaze cast downward. "Forget it. I'm just being silly."

Her eyes were shaded with sadness. "If you're not frightened, what then?"

"I just hate that you're going to sell him." She put her hand up. "Don't say it. He's an animal. It's a business. I get it. It's just sad."

"Alice all but checks the buyer's pedigree. She makes sure her horses are sold to someone who will take good care of them."

"You're sure?" A new batch of tears welled in her eyes.

Something tightened inside his chest. A need to make her happy swirled around his heart. At this moment, he'd do whatever it took to ensure she never cried again. He pulled her against his chest and patted her back.

God, she smelled good. What man in his right mind thought a woman who'd been brushing a horse smelled good? Her scent was warm and healthy with a touch of citrus, which had to be from her hair.

Her nearness, the heat from her body, the small hands wrapped around his waist generated an uncomfortable reaction in body parts that he seemed to have zero control over. It was time to put some space between them.

He took a step back, and she looked up. He could drown in those crystal-clear blue eyes. Her lips looked soft and inviting. What if he leaned down and tasted them?

Her mouth opened slightly; she lifted up, and kissed him. All reasonable thought vacated his brain. She tilted her head and slipped her tongue across his upper lip. Her hands cupped his cheek, pulling him closer and increasing the intensity.

Jake gladly returned the pressure. His only thought was he needed more. He swept his tongue inside her mouth, exploring, probing the sweetness and heat inside. She melted into him. Her soft moan rattled his very foundation.

Jake gripped the back of her shirt, pulled her tighter against his chest, imagining how her breasts would feel without the thin layers of cotton that separated his flesh from hers.

In the back of his mind, he prayed she wouldn't push him away. She slipped her hands under his shirt, burning this moment into his brain. Her grip tightened and his entire blood supply rushed south.

Jake intensified his attack on her mouth and senses. His desire for her was clearly evident as their bodies pressed together. He'd completely lost his mind.

Daisy barked, snapping Jake back to reality. What was he thinking? He was seconds away from taking advantage of a vulnerable, frightened woman. He dropped his hands and stepped back. "This is crazy."

"What does that mean?" Her lips were moist and so tempting.

Jake faltered but forced his hands to stay put. "I'm sorry. It won't happen again."

Holly recoiled as if he'd slapped her. His gut clenched as pain clouded her eyes. Turning away and walking out of the barn took a supreme effort, but for her sake, he had to do the right thing. He stopped and leaned against the railing. There could never be anything between them. Neither would ever completely forget their history. When this was over, Holly would return to Dallas and resume her career. She deserved the chance to find happiness, get married and have a houseful of kids.

Relief washed over him as Claude Welborne drove up and parked next to the house. Alice hadn't mentioned the sheriff, and Jake felt like an ass for not asking. He waved to Claude and waited while he walked to the barn.

"I ran into Alice in town. For a stable, level-headed woman, she was acting weird."

Jake laughed. "How so?" His aunt had never been good at keeping secrets.

"I asked if she'd heard from you. She leaned in and whispered that you were home. Then she said nobody else could know. I decided to come out and talk with you."

"Come with me. I need to introduce you to someone." He turned to find Holly standing behind him.

Claude gallantly jerked his hat off his head. Wearing a grin spread from ear to ear, he walked to her, holding out his hand. "I don't blame you for keeping this beautiful lady a secret. Except from me, 'cause I'm harmless." He glanced at Jake.

"No." Jake held up his hands. "No. It's not like that. Not at all."

Holly's smile was strained, but she shook Claude's hand. "Holly Hoffman."

"Sheriff Claude Welborne. Most folks call me Claude."

Jake's cell vibrated. Alice was calling. He excused himself, and walked a short distance away. He went straight to the point. "It's too late to warn me." Jake chuckled. "Claude is already here."

"Damnation. I should have figured he'd head to the ranch. He tried to wrangle an invitation to supper, and I blew him off."

"It's not a problem. He should know just in case trouble finds us."

"I'm about ten minutes out. You might as well tell him to stay." Her tone had shifted slightly, warming up as she spoke of the sheriff.

"How are things between you and Claude?"

"I don't know what you mean."

"Yes, you do."Jake could imagine her cheeks getting red. "He's crazy about you."

"And how do you feel about that?"

"Me? If you're holding back because of me, don't. Uncle Charlie would want you to be happy. Besides, I'll move on someday, and if Claude is here, I won't worry about you."

"This ranch is your home now. If not because we're family, sweat equity has earned you that claim."

Jake wasn't gaining ground. "We can argue about this later."

"Later being never. You can help me unload groceries when I get home."

Jake ended the call and returned to the barn. Claude and Holly were leaning against Duchess's stall chatting away like old friends. She had that personality that made people feel like they'd known her for years. Her male patients probably fell in love with her. And why did that thought taste bitter?

"I'm staying here with Alice and Jake until Chief Santos tells me it's safe to go home."

"We're hoping that's soon." Jake recoiled at the hurt expression that flashed across Holly's face. "You know what I meant."

"I think you were pretty clear." Her injured look segued to anger.

Claude shifted his feet. "I best be going."

"Alice will be here in a few minutes. Stick around and help her unload the groceries."

Claude's smile spread quickly. "I'll go open the gate."

"I can help." Holly turned to follow Claude.

Jake touched her arm, waiting until Claude was out of hearing range before speaking. "He's grateful for any excuse to get close to Alice. He's nuts about her."

"Smart man." Holly smiled as Claude hustled to the front gate. "I hope he makes her happy."

"I take it you explained the trouble in Connersville to Claude's satisfaction?" Jake walked back to the pasture gate, opened and latched it back. His low whistle let the horses know it was time to come inside. Holly stood next to him as the horses trotted past them into their respective stalls.

"Yes. He had a right to know."

"I agree."

"I'm impressed that the horses knew exactly where to go."

"Yeah. Horses are creatures of habit." He slapped his leg and Daisy came running.

"Aren't we all?"

****

Ivan dumped the doctor's body into the hazardous waste trash bin behind the hospital. He slipped on the dead man's white coat and name tag and entered the building. It took maybe twenty minutes before he stood outside Suzanne Richards's door. She was his best chance of finding Holly.

His blood raced through his veins but not from fear. He'd never experienced that emotion. The only things that stirred him, that truly gave him pleasure, were the hunt and the actual kill. He pushed open the door and stepped inside.

"Good evening, Ms. Richards." He smiled as he paused in the doorway.

"You're new to late rounds."

"Oh, I'm not making rounds. I came to see you." Ivan stepped inside, closed the door, and turned the lock. In one motion, he pulled his knife from his pocket and flipped it open. "Scream and I'll gut you like a pig."

The instant terror on her face gave him an incredible rush. He'd enjoyed convincing the reporter to spill her guts, and now the anticipation was just as exciting. In his line of work, he had very little interaction with his targets. Most of his clients paid for a quick kill, but the up close and personal was much more rewarding.

"What do you want?" Her voice quivered as she pushed herself up in bed. "Who are you?"

Ivan used his foot to push a chair next to her bed. He ran the smooth blade down her arm to the IV. "It's Suzanne, right?"

Her entire body trembled under the white sheet. Her gaze tracked the path of his knife.

"Pull yourself together. I have questions and you will answer them. Understand?"

She lifted her gaze and met his. Her lips moved but no sound came. He pressed the tip of the knife under the tape holding her IV in place and sliced through with ease. She winced but didn't make a sound.

"Answer me."

"Suzanne Richards." Her voice was a soft whisper.

"Now wasn't that easy? Let's go for another one. How do I find the nurse responsible for getting my brother killed?"

"Holly?" She immediately clamped her mouth shut and closed her eyes.

"What is Holly's full name?" Ivan had to get her talking. It was only a matter of time before somebody tried the door and found it locked. The hospital really wasn't a good place to gather information, but he'd work with what he had. He'd gag her if necessary. "And where can I find Holly?"

"I don't know." Her face gave no indication that she had lied.

Ivan stood and jerked the sheet from her grasp. He pulled the hospital gown up to reveal the bandage on her stomach. Perfect. With a quick movement, he ripped off the tape, removing the bandage. She cried out, he assumed more from surprise than pain.

"Shh. Now try again." He pushed two fingers against the discolored flesh hard. She closed her eyes and moaned. "It's going to get a lot worse before it's over."

"Please don't." She placed her hand over his. "I'm telling the truth. If she's not at the school, I don't know where she went."

"She's been by to check on you, hasn't she?"

"No."

"That's not much of a friend."

"She's probably afraid that she might get shot too."

"Smart girl. But shooting her isn't what I have in mind."

Ivan walked to the small cabinet and looked inside. There on the shelf was exactly what he wanted. A woman's purse sometimes provided valuable items. A quick inspection revealed what could be answers to all his questions. He glanced back at Suzanne. "Aren't you too old to keep a diary?"

"It's a private journal. Someday I want to write about my experiences with the Helpful Hands medical team."

He thumbed through the pages. "So you think you're an author?"

"I'm going to try. The organization does good work. The world should know."

He didn't try to suppress a smile. She was trying to connect with him. Trying to save her life. "If I read this, will I learn that you've been lying to me?"

Her eyes filled with tears. "I don't know where Holly is."

He stuffed her billfold and journal into his coat pocket as he walked back to her. "It's a shame we don't have more time together."

She opened her mouth to scream. He was faster. The sharp blade sunk into her soft neck with ease and slid deep. Blood gushed and spurted, but no sound escaped. He lifted the bedsheet and wiped the knife.

The door rattled as someone tried to enter and failed.

A woman called out, "Ms. Richards" Ivan sighed. Any distraction or inconvenience would be handled quickly. He moved behind the door and then flipped the lock open.

A short female bustled inside. Ivan caught her from behind and slid the knife across her neck. Blood spurted and he pushed her out of his way.

The sleeves of the white coat were wet and crimson. He slipped it off his shoulders, wiped his hands and knife, and folded it into a small square. He tucked it, Suzanne's wallet, and her journal under his arm and then quietly walked to the stairs.

Less than five minutes later, he was driving away in his rental. His time with that twit reporter hadn't been wasted. She'd directed him to Suzanne, and hopefully, her journal would give him the information to find Holly.

A new place to stay was next on the agenda. Somewhere quiet so he could read without distraction.

Chapter 15

Holly stared in amazement at the cell phones and stack of pay-as-you-go minute cards on Alice's kitchen table. Alice retrieved a pair of scissors from a drawer and opened one of the packages.

"So as not to inspire too many questions, I bought two each at the grocery store, drugstore, and the truck stop outside of town."

Alice's positive attitude just added to Holly's guilt. Was she destined to bring trouble to all the people who cared for her? Alice couldn't possibly understand the danger.

"I shouldn't be here. I think one of Nate's safe houses would have been a better option."

"This ranch is the safest place for you." Jake ripped open the second package and removed the cell phone.

"We agreed not to put them in danger, but isn't my being here the same thing?"

Alice caught Holly's hand. "Jake's right. Besides, the Donovan family doesn't scare easily."

Claude pulled a chair out, sat, and reached for one of the throwaways. "Jake, are these folks the group who helped you get your life back?"

"Yes," Jake said. "I owe them my life and sanity. Kay and Nate will do anything we ask, but she's pregnant. It's not the right time to ask them for help. "

Holly knew Jake was right. "I'm sorry. Still, may I use one of these cells to check on her?"

"Absolutely." Jake went to work, and before long, he handed a pocket-size phone to her. His eyes softened, filling with an unspoken compassion. "I loaded one hundred minutes on this one."

Alice spoke up. "That swing on the front porch is a great place to relax. You take your time and visit with your friend. When you're finished, you and Jake can ride out to check fences if you like. Get some fresh air in you."

"Ride out?" Holly hadn't been on a horse in years.

"We can take the four-wheeler if you don't know how to ride."

She knew a challenge when she heard one. "It's been a long time, and I'm sure it will come back to me, but I was taught not to ride in tennis shoes."

"We're about the same size," Alice said. "With a pair of thick socks, I'll bet you can wear a pair of my boots. There are a couple of sacks of clothes on your bed. I got everything on your list plus an extra pair of jeans."

Holly wrapped her arms around the woman and hugged her. "I'd forgotten you'd gone shopping for me. I'll put them away and then call."

Holly unpacked her new things, carefully folding the price tags and tucking them into her wallet. When she opened her bedroom door, a pair of boots had been placed on the side where she'd see them.

She carried them and the cell to the front porch.

"Lost and Found agency. How may we help you?" Kay's tone was so cheerful Holly's eyes filled with tears.

"How's the mother-to-be?" She struggled to keep a tremble out of her voice.

"Holly? Oh, my God, we've been so worried. Nate," Kay yelled. "It's Holly."

Holly laughed at her friend's excitement. "You probably scared him to death."

"He's picking up so we can both talk with you."

Holly spent the next fifteen minutes assuring them of her safety and well-being. The conversation flowed easily and turned to Kay's pregnancy. That she was in good health and hadn't been confined to bed rest was welcome news.

"I've been so worried about you." Kay's tone softened.

"Don't do that. I'm doing fine. Jake and his aunt are taking good care of me. Not knowing what's happening is hard. Was the shooter there because of me? Is he hunting me? Why?"

"Lots of people are working hard to answer those questions. You have to hold it together."

"I seem to be stuck somewhere between frightened and furious."

"Stop that." Nate's deep voice boomed through the cell. "You are not responsible for any of this."

"People keep telling me that, but that doesn't change the way I feel." She shook off the self-pity creeping to the surface. "I take it Dalton brought you up to speed?"

"Yeah," Nate spoke up. "He's staying in Connersville as long as Chief Santos needs him."

"I'm sorry you're not here with us," Kay said. "But I'm okay as long as you're in a safe place."

"To say we're isolated is an understatement. Jake's aunt is one of the most amazing women I've ever met."

Kay was silent for a second. "How is Jake?"

That was the question Holly had been expecting." Very different than you remember. Living in the country has been good for him. He's muscled, matured, yet he's not sure about having me underfoot. He's friendly one minute and hates me the next." Holly's fingers touched her lips as the memory of his kiss rushed over her.

"He doesn't hate you," Nate said. "He still hates himself."

"I'm sure of it. Sometimes he relaxes but then he pushes me away."

"The tone of your voice makes me think that you still care for him," Kay said. "Am I right?"

"Please don't tell me I have Stockholm syndrome."

"Did he tell you that?" Nate's question reminded her that he was on the other line. Heat rushed up her cheeks.

"Not for a few years."

"Then don't let it worry you." Nate was like a big brother to Holly. She welcomed his advice. "Get through this situation and then you can figure out who or what you want."

"I'd better get off the phone." She gave Kay the number, confident no one else would have it.

"Remember, we're here if you need us," Kay said.

"She means that. In the meantime, we'll do what we can through Dalton."

"I promised to help out when the baby is born. If the police catch this crazy jerk, maybe I can keep my word."

"Then we'll have to get this business done. Tell Jake to call if he needs me," Nate said.

"I will. Thank you." Holly disconnected, went back to the kitchen, and handed Jake the phone.

"How's Kay?"

"Great. She asked about you."

He nodded. "I'm glad you talked to her."

"They were both on the phone. Nate said to call him if you need anything."

"Good to know." Jake carried the stack of phones to a kitchen drawer and put them away. He glanced down at her feet. "Are you riding with me?"

She followed his gaze. "Oh, give me a minute. I left my boots on the porch."

"I'll be in the barn."

****

Jake saddled Jazzy, a chestnut mare, for himself, secured his work belt to the back of her saddle using the leather ties, and led her to the hitching post just outside the barn.

He saddled the gelding for Holly. Buster was shorter than most quarter horses, built more like a bulldog, but with a ton of patience. His only flaw was that he had to be warmed up before the rider gigged him in the flanks. He tied Buster next to Jazzy.

"Which one is mine?" Holly said from behind him.

He turned and froze in place as she walked toward him. Wearing boots and jeans with a light blue T-shirt, her hair back into a high ponytail, the old Holly smiled at him. She took his breath away.

"Hello?" The laughing lilt to her tone snapped him out of his daze.

"You look..." He decided against telling her she looked beautiful.

"Look what?"

"Like a cowgirl," he said, attempting to laugh off his awkward moment of stupidity. "Alice's saddle should be perfect for you, and Buster will give you a good ride."

"Buster," she repeated, running her fingers through the horse's mane.

"Climb aboard and I'll adjust your stirrups."

Holly put her left foot in the stirrup, swung her right leg over Buster's back, and smiled down at Jake. She'd mounted with ease and grace with a smile intended to remind him she knew how to ride. He moved from the left side to the right, making the necessary adjustments. His skin prickled under her scrutiny, but he refused to meet her gaze. He slid on the headstall and handed her the reins.

"He has to be warmed up. Walk him around for a few minutes."

"Thank you." She backed Buster up a few steps.

"For what?"

"Saddling my horse." She pushed Buster forward into a walk. "And for staring at me like you think I'm hot."

No way was he taking that bait, so he slid the bridle on Jazzy, climbed on board, and then walked her to the gate. He leaned to the side, flipped open the latch, and swung the gate wide. Then he watched and waited as while Holly rode past him.

A lone diamond-shaped patch of white hair grew right in the middle of Buster's forehead. That damn horse seemed to know why people stopped and admired him. With Holly on his back, he seemed to be walking extra proud.

"You look good on him. He's a little touchy. Don't kick..."

Her heels connected with Buster's flanks. The horse lunged forward. His back bowed, and he ducked his head straight at the ground. Every time he jammed his hoofs into the ground, Holly's ponytail flew straight out and flopped up and down. She grabbed the saddle horn and scrambled to regain her seat in the saddle, which was no easy feat since she'd lost a stirrup on Buster's first jump.

Jake couldn't hold back the laughter. She was doing a great job of sticking to the saddle. Four solid bucks later, and Buster settled down, ready to work. He shook his mane as if to say, "See how cool I am?" Then calmly waited for Jake and Jazzy to join them.

"Nice riding. I was trying to warn you when all hell broke loose." Jake turned in his saddle and waited for her response.

"You told me to warm him up." Her face was flushed and a smile ran ear to ear. "I can't believe I stayed on."

"He's done stretching his legs. You can drop the reins on his neck, and he'll wait for your command."

Holly did exactly that while she used both hands to put her ponytail back together. She patted herself on the shoulders, chest, and hips. "Just checking to make sure all my parts still work."

Her parts looked great to Jake, but he kept his thoughts to himself. "Let's get this done before dark."

They fell into an easy pace as they made their way to the back of the pasture. Today was one of those rare south Texas days when the temperature and humidity honored some kind of peace treaty. A slight breeze made for an unusually pleasant morning.

Jake stopped and tightened barbwire at a couple of places. Holly had been silent for the longest time, so he detoured to a small creek that ran through the property. The water had receded a few inches, but it still rushed over the normally exposed rock.

"Let's give the horses a drink." He walked Jazzy to the water's edge and stopped.

"Buster's won't want to go swimming, will he?"

"Not unless you walk him out belly deep. Then you'd better keep his head up." Jake dismounted and dropped his reins. She'd been unusually quiet after her conversation with Kay.

Holly did the same. She walked to a boulder and sat. "Join me."

"You've been working on something for a while. What's up?"

"Don't think you can read my mind." Her blue eyes flashed in the sunlight.

"Your face is very expressive. Professional poker playing isn't a career you should pursue." Jake braced himself. "Spit it out."

She placed her hand on his arm. Heat seared his skin. He wanted nothing more than to feel that burn on every inch of his body. To make her melt into his arms. He stiffened his back and resolve.

"Jake."

He swallowed, dug deep into his reserve, and turned to meet her gaze.

"I kissed you. Don't you think we should talk about that?"

"No." He wasn't discussing the kiss, period. "I do not."

"Well, I do." Her fingers dug into his skin.

"You're grateful. I get it. The kiss was a mistake." He pulled his gaze toward the water, anything to prevent her from seeing the lie in his eyes. "It won't happen again."

"Look at me." She stood and stepped between his knees. "Damn it. We have to put the past where it belongs. You didn't find my kiss repulsive, did you? You kissed me back, and it wasn't a we're-just-friends peck. You care for me."

Jake longed to pull her against his chest. To admit to her that not seeing her for the past two years had done nothing to erase his feelings for her. But none of that mattered. She'd moved on with her life and was happy. Period, end of story.

She pinched his arm. "Stop folding up into your own head."

"Hey." He caught her wrist in his hand as laughter burst from him. "You actually pinched me."

"It seemed the only way to get your attention." The corners of her mouth turned down. "This isn't funny, so stop laughing."

Shit. He'd pissed her off. "That you pinched me is funny as hell. Our conversation is not."

"Our conversation? When did you decide to join?" She cupped his cheeks, leaned her forehead against his. "You think you get to decide what I want or need? Well, I have news. I've been able to make my own choices for a long time. If this is going to work—"

"This?"

"Yes, this." She pointed at her chest and then his. "You have to step up."

"Step up?"

"Stop with the questions. Why do you refuse to talk to me?"

"I do talk. You don't listen." She opened her mouth as if to speak. "Hold up. You want this out in the open? Here it is. I live with the things I did every day. How can I not remind you of it every time you see my face? I don't expect you to forget or forgive the monster I was."

"There you go again. Deciding what I will or won't do. When I look at you, I don't see a monster; I see the man who saved my life."

Jake stared at her face. Her eyes had always given away her true feelings. The look in them now melted his heart. Her fingers slid up his cheek to the scar behind his ear, where surgery had saved his life. He surrendered to her warm touch and leaned his head into her hand.

"I remember a very sick young man in a lot of pain. He was confused and alone. In the end, the good in him won out. He touched my heart. Still does."

"Holly," he whispered as she was slowly untying the twisted knots inside his head and heart.

"I'm right here." Her eyes turned the color of the deep blue sea, sensuous and beckoning. Lightning bolts shot in every direction, mostly in the direction of his groin. Her head lowered until her lips covered his.

Emotions he'd kept buried deep in his soul roared to the surface. Jake dragged her onto his lap, returning the kiss, drinking from her as if his life depended on her.

He was demanding, hungry, his muscles tightening like coils. She responded with a fervor that shook him to the soles of his feet, and her soft moan drove his need even higher. He had to show her what he couldn't say in words. He pulled her to straddle his legs, cupped her head, and swept his tongue inside the sweetness of her mouth. Jake almost exploded when she slid back and forth over his erection.

The throwaway phone in his pocket buzzed. Holly moaned a sound of frustration as Jake reluctantly released her. Her lips were wet and swollen, cheeks pink with desire, and her chest rose and fell rapidly.

"You've never looked more beautiful." He tucked a stray lock of hair behind her ear, stood her up, and then fished the cell out. "It's Alice."

"Maybe she has good news," Holly said between breaths.

"What's up?"

"Nate Wolfe said you should call Chief Santos." Jake picked up on her fear rolling through the airway.

"We're on our way."

Holly had already gone to gather both horses. Trained to ground tie, neither had wandered off. She rode back, leading Jazzy. "What's happened?"

"We won't know until I call Nate. Rey Santos contacted him."

Jake mounted and together they turned their horses toward home. He pulled his horse to a stop just as the ranch came into view. He scanned the yard, barn, and north pasture. Alice stood alone on the back porch, her hand shielding the sun from her eyes as she searched the horizon for them. From a distance, everything looked peaceful.

"Jake?" Holly's hand reached for his. The fear in her eyes stabbed his heart.

"Don't buy trouble. Maybe this is good news. But whatever has happened, we can handle it." He kept his gaze trained on the road in front of them for fear she'd know he'd lied.

They rode the rest of the way in silence. The closer they got to the ranch, the more he hoped for Holly's sake it wasn't more bad news. As they approached the ranch, they slowed the horses. Alice waved and went inside.

Jake tied up both horses outside the barn, then walked with Holly to the house. Alice had three glasses of iced tea waiting on the table.

"Have a seat."

"Where's Claude?"

"He had business in town to take care of." Alice's eyes were full of sorrow. "Have a seat," she repeated, waiting until they were down. "Holly, your first name was leaked to the press."

"Damn it," Holly muttered.

"We kind of expected it. Jake agreed with Holly but played down his concern. "There were so many witnesses at that school."

"I promised Nate you'd call him as soon as possible." Tears welled in Alice's eyes. She lifted her iced tea to her lips but didn't drink.

Jake walked to her and wrapped his arm around her shoulders. The hair on the back of Jake's neck crawled. "What else did Nate tell you?"

"No." Alice's hand came up to grip Holly's. "I'm so sorry. Suzanne Richards is dead."

"She can't be." Holly stood, shaking her head. "There must be a mistake. The last I heard, Suzanne was recuperating nicely. It can't be her."

"It's true. She, a doctor, and a duty nurse were killed last night."

The color in Holly's face rushed south, leaving her ghostly pale. "Killed? You mean murdered?"

Alice nodded. "Yes."

Holly's fingers drifted across her mouth. Tears fell silently and she stared at the floor. "This is my fault. All my fault."

He quickly went to her, slipping his hands around her and pulling her into his arms. She leaned into him, buried her face in his chest, and sobbed. Her shoulders and chest heaved with her cries.

"Let it out. I've got you." He doubted she heard him speak. She was lost in pain, fear, and frustration. Her fingers dug into his shoulders and he felt utterly, completely, helpless.

Chapter 16

Holly clung to Jake, her soul crying for Suzanne. Not only had she lost an incredible friend, the world had lost a wonderful person. She'd survived a war only to have her life taken by a madman. The last few minutes of her life had to have been nothing but terror and pain. Holly cried harder, thinking of what Suzanne must have gone through at the hands of a madman.

"I'm sorry. You shouldn't have to go through this," Jake whispered. He continued to hold her, support her, and allow her to grieve. The family's loss sliced through Holly. Depression wrapped around her, heavy, like fog on the lowland.

"Take this damp washcloth, Jake," Alice said. "Holly needs to rest. I'll turn down her bed."

"Thank you." Holly closed her eyes while Jake pressed the cool cloth to her face. "I'm fine." She backed out of Jake's arms and walked to the front door. As she studied the pasture dotted with grazing horses and cattle, her sorrow was slowly replaced by anger. She dug her fingernails into her palms. "There has to be something we can do."

"There is." Jake opened a drawer and pulled out one of the throwaway cell phones. "We'll call Santos first and then Nate." Jake dialed the number and put the phone on speaker.

Worry lines were trenched around his mouth, topped by a frown burrowed between his eyes. By the fourth ring, he was pacing.

"Rey Santos."

"Donovan here. Holly and I got your message about Suzanne's murder. Two other people were killed? What can you tell us?"

"I understand a doctor and nurse are dead too. The scene must have been gory. This motherfucker cut their throats." Rey paused. "Sorry, about my language."

"Not necessary." Holly put her hand against the wall to steady herself. Jake quickly led her to a chair. "Tell us everything."

"I've seen some bad shit in my day. I've been through a war, have worked car wrecks with mangled bodies, and had a killer who painted his victims to look like dolls, but this was the worst. Goddamn, blood was everywhere."

"I don't know how you do it." Jake picked up the phone.

"Leave him on speaker." As horrible as this was, her friend was dead and she wouldn't look away from it. Jake was not going to filter information. He shook his head. She stepped closer, crowding his space. "I have a right to hear."

She understood that he was trying to protect her, that he thought the information was too horrible for her to hear. But she stood her ground, and he returned the phone to the table where she pointed.

"Go ahead, Rey." The nerves in Jake's jaws twitched as he spoke.

"Holly, none of this is pretty. You may be a nurse, but—"

"Suzanne was my friend." Holly wasn't backing down. "This involves me."

The chief cleared his throat. "She bled out pretty quick."

Holly caught Jake's hand. "Go on." Tears rushed to the surface and she battled them back.

"The night nurse must have interrupted because her body was found just inside the door to Suzanne's room."

"Has anyone contacted the Richards family?"

"I spoke to her sister. Dalton gave me Nate Wolfe's number, said he could reach you."

Holly closed her eyes, trying to imagine Suzanne laughing and happy. She'd never married. Instead, she'd spent her life taking care of other people. "Why kill her? What did that accomplish?"

"I think the shooter wanted information on Holly," Rey replied.

Jake leaned forward. "Yeah. I agree. The shooter must have thought he was silencing the witness when he shot Suzanne."

"But later he discovered he was wrong and hadn't killed me?" Holly's knees grew weak so she sunk down to a chair.

Holly closed her eyes. "She had no idea where I'd gone."

"I can only speculate as to what happened," Rey said. "Maybe she woke up and caught the bastard going through her purse. It was upside down on the floor."

Jake tightened his grip on her hand.

"Holly, what could Suzanne have told him?" Rey asked.

Old conversations with Suzanne flashed through Holly's mind. "We shared a lot of details about our pasts. She knows...knew...." Holly paused at the realization her friend was past tense. "She could have told him where I live. She knew Kay Wolfe." Holly stopped to consider everything they had shared. "The three of us had lunch and went shopping a few times."

"Family?"

"None in Texas. My mother fell in love while on a cruise and never came back. She's remarried and living on a small winery in Italy."

Jake dragged his fingers through his hair. "Why has this crazy bastard turned finding Holly into his mission? Angel is dead. There's no reason to kill the witness. You can't identify any of the others, right?" Jake turned to her. "Walk us through that day behind the school."

"I already told you everything I could remember. It happened so fast."

"That's actually a good idea," Rey said. "Sometimes, a few days later, things do come back."

Jake touched her hand. "Close your eyes and think back to that day."

Holly nodded and did as he asked.

"Try to see the alley and the woman."

After a few seconds, she opened her eyes. "He said, 'she's mine.' It was almost as if he was frantic. The woman said that he lied. That he was supposed to take care of her. "

"None of this makes sense," Rey grumbled. "There's a reason the shooter didn't come one floor up and try to kill me. He knew I was unconscious when you left and had no personal knowledge." The frustration in Rey's voice was heavy.

"I can't believe Suzanne told him anything." Holly fought to keep her tone level even though her stomach churned.

"You'd be surprised what a person will blurt out when they are terrified."

"I don't believe she told him anything."

"Rey," Jake said. "This Angel, what have you learned about him? The autopsy proved my theory that he was stoned out of his mind?"

"His toxicology screen came back with traces of your run-of-the-mill narcotics, but the surprise was the traces of loxapine in his system."

Jake's head turned her direction. His eyebrows rose in question.

"That medicine is for one of many psychotic disorders, but if there was only a trace, maybe he hadn't been taking his meds," Holly said.

"That explains why he'd grab you with all those people around. In his mind, he was ten foot tall, bulletproof, and invisible," Jake said.

"In the meantime, Dalton contacted a friend with the Feds. We sent the video from the school's entrance and the parking lot to their crime lab. FBI is going to run Angel through their facial recognition program. If he's there, we'll dig into his background and get some answers. If he's not in the system, we're still chasing our own tails."

"How about you? Are you healing okay?" Holly asked.

"Yeah. I've been through worse." Rey coughed. Holly doubted the chief was telling the truth. "The longer you stay out of sight, the more frustrated this bastard will become. When that happens, he'll make a mistake."

"Angel's fingerprints weren't in the system?" Jake asked.

"No. That makes me worry that the FBI's facial recognition program won't come up with a match. Our state lab is too backed up to rush DNA results, so the Feds are helping with that too."

"I knew he'd come in handy." Jake looked at her and grinned.

"Look." Rey's voice took on an official tone. "I've asked the FBI to take this case. Dalton will act as a go-between. Five people were found murdered on a ranch outside of town. And my hands are full."

"Damn. That sounds like an entire family," Jake said.

"It's not. It's the older couple who lived there, two unidentified men, and a reporter who's been missing a couple of days."

"Reporter?" Holly started piecing things together. "Do you think the two cases are connected?"

"It's too early to say for sure, but if I were a betting man, I'd cover the yes card."

"I may be overreacting, but if Holly is tracked to this ranch, I want to be ready. I'm not rolling the dice with her safety. I'll ask Nate for help. He and his men will guard Holly better than any team the Feds can pull together."

Rey broke into a cough that went on for seconds. Holly didn't like the sound.

"Chief?" she asked.

"I'm here."

"You checked yourself out of the hospital, didn't you?"

"I have responsibilities."

"None more important than your health. You need to go back to the doctor."

"I will. I'm sorry about your friend Suzanne." Rey's change of subject didn't hide the fact he sounded weak.

"Thank you. You'll stay in touch even while you're working those other homicides?"

"You bet I will." Rey ended the call.

She leaned across the table toward Jake. "Rey worries me. His cough doesn't sound like he's well enough to work. His voice sounded as if his energy is low. It takes a long time to come back from a bullet wound."

Jake pushed her glass of tea in front of her. "This is a convoluted mess. I'm convinced calling Nate for professional help is the right thing to do."

Jake picked up the phone and was able to key in a few digits before Holly placed her hand over his.

"Their business has grown, Jake. After the new office complex was complete, things picked up. Nate's taken on a lot of contracts, so many that he's hired a staff of former military men."

"Do you really think he won't clear the deck and pitch in?"

"What about Kay? She needs him."

"He'll tell us what he can or can't do. If we're lucky, Marcus and Diablo are available." Jake pulled free of her and finished entering the number.

"Wolfe," Nate said. Holly assumed he was being cautious because his caller ID read unknown.

"This is Jake."

She tugged the phone away, put it between them on the table, and clicked on speaker. "And Holly."

"I take it you spoke with Chief Santos."

"We did."

"Holly, how are you? I'm sorry about your friend."

"She's pretty broken up," Jake answered before she could.

"I know you, and you're blaming yourself. Check those emotions, because there's nothing you could have done to prevent her death."

"You're right there. She's trying to carry this entire thing on her shoulders."

"Stop it." She frowned at Jake. "I can speak for myself."

Nate's laughter rumbled through the phone. "Yeah. I can testify to that. I'm glad you called. Kaycie picked up on your anxiety when you two talked. She's been threatening to find your aunt's ranch and just show up."

"Tell her Holly is in good hands." Jake again took the lead. "Nothing is going to happen to her."

"You two stop talking around me." Holly would not be ignored. "I can speak for myself."

"You can for sure do that," Jake said. He'd snapped her out of the dark hole she'd been wallowing in, which had been his plan, judging by the grin on his face.

"Well, of course she can," Nate said. He laughed, easing the tension.

"You two think you're pretty smart." Holly leaned back in the chair.

"Damn right, we are," Nate said.

"Back to Kay. She shouldn't be worrying about anything."

"The doctor says it could happen any day. Mother and baby are fine."

"Do you know the baby's sex?" Holly asked. "Are you keeping it a secret?"

"No secret. It's a boy. We're going to name him after her brother, Kevin."

Jake's eyebrows lifted. "Kevin?"

Holly realized Jake didn't remember. She started to explain but Nate started talking.

"Kaycie had a twin brother named Kevin." Nate spoke as if Jake not remembering was unimportant. "He had a car accident the night they graduated from high school, and Kaycie took the blame so as to not affect her brother's football college scholarship. He died a few days later, but their dad never forgave her. She finally told him the truth years later, but even then he refused to believe her."

"Thanks for explaining. I'm sorry I don't remember." Jake ran his hand through his hair.

"It's not a problem, but you two didn't call me twice in one day just to chat. Tell me how I can help."

"Rey is turning the investigation over to the Feds," Jake's tone had returned to all business.

"I heard. They have the manpower and equipment he doesn't."

"How booked up are you?"

"Dumb question. If you need something, you've got it."

"I want to hire you. Kay will need you when the baby comes, so you have to stay put. If Marcus isn't on assignment, he'd be a big help. The quicker this crazy bastard is locked up, the sooner Holly can come home."

"Did you think we'd stay out of this? As soon as we heard, Marcus contacted Dalton. And don't insult me by offering money. Whatever you need, and I don't mean just a safe house. We're in this."

Nate's insistence meant a lot to Holly. Judging by the tension disappearing from Jake's face, it meant a great deal to him too. He hadn't forgiven himself, so it was natural for him to believe that none of their old friends had either. She longed to help him see that none of his old friends harbored hard feelings toward him. They'd bent over backward to help him get well and ensure he was a free man. Jake had already lived up to their faith in him.

He pulled his hand from hers. The tension in his face had returned. She'd been rubbing her thumb across his knuckles.

"I appreciate that, but I want you and Kay to stay out of it."

"We'll be fine." Nate's tone was firm. "You haven't been home in a long time. This place is like Fort Knox."

"So I've heard." The nerve in Jake's jaw had always jumped around whenever he made up his mind about something. It was doing a dance right now. "Look, right now we're running blind, and I need a contingency plan in case we have to move Holly. If you can find a place, one that could be available on a second's notice, that would be great."

"You'll bring Holly here. I have a place where you can sleep too. If we reach that point, your ranch will be compromised, and your aunt will need a safe place."

"That's not going to be easy. There are cows and horses that need taking care of."

"Then I'll send a couple of men who know how to do that."

"She might go for that. Listen, this sounds paranoid, but I'm destroying this cell when we hang up."

"Good idea. There's no such thing as being too safe."

"But we don't know the killer will continue to search for me." Holly leaned forward, rubbing her forehead with her fingertips.

"We don't know that he won't," Nate answered. "Is your license to carry valid?"

"Yes. You know it is."

"I figured as much."

She laughed a soft agreement. "You should."

"Nate, once again I owe you," Jake said as he stood.

"Bullshit."

Jake chuckled and picked up the phone. "He hung up."

Alice's footsteps on the back porch drew their attention. Holly stood and walked to the screen door. She pushed it open. Alice opened her arms to Holly and she gratefully accepted the hug.

Chapter 17

Ivan ordered from the room service menu, positioned the soft-cushioned chair next to the window, and then opened the journal. He'd chosen this hotel because it sat directly across from the hospital where Holly and Suzanne had worked.

Before he could start reading, his cell phone rang. For the second time in as many days, he turned down a job from an arms dealer who was pissed and needed a competitor removed. This client wasn't willing to wait, so Ivan reluctantly referred him to a competitor.

That Holly bitch was not only responsible for Angel's death, she was costing him money.

Room service delivered his food, placing it on a small table next to his chair. He grunted, begrudging the man a small tip. Then he settled in, and tried to read while he ate. Unable to concentrate, he pushed away the half-eaten sandwich and fries. He put his feet on the ottoman and went back to the journal.

On the front page, he read Suzanne's return address and wrote it on a notepad. He read all her quips, antidotes, complaints, and comments. She'd hooked up with a couple of men who had turned out to be losers. He scanned that drivel, completely uninterested in who she'd fucked.

Things got interesting about halfway through. She'd met a newly hired nurse named Holly. Suzanne's comments indicated she'd hit it off immediately with the novice. She'd even made notes about where they had lunch and which mall they liked to shop. As he read, he paused and jotted down the things that seemed helpful. After he wrote his last note, he placed the book on his bedside table.

Nothing Suzanne had written made Ivan care that he'd cut her throat. He dealt with collateral damage all the time. That she hadn't mentioned Holly's last name pissed him off.

He put in a call to a hacker friend and put him to work digging into Suzanne's online usage. He could worm his way into any database, and Ivan wanted all the information he could gather on Suzanne Richards.

He took a quick shower, and then dressed in faded jeans, an oversized golf shirt, and a ball cap, an unlikely outfit he'd picked up at a roadside flea market during his drive from Connersville. Normally, he wouldn't be caught dead looking like this, but today it served his purpose. His pistol—with the attached silencer —was cumbersome, so he purchased the loose clothing to hide it.

He popped a pill to help keep him sharp, grabbed his car keys, and left the hotel. He punched Suzanne's address into the GPS and drove away. Grieving people often said things without thinking. Somebody knew Holly's last name and how to reach her. He just had to get them to talking.

Ivan stopped at a red light and rubbed his eyes. The pill hadn't kicked in and his senses were dull. He hadn't been sleeping well. His dreams about Angel lying in a cold morgue alone and unclaimed were relentless. He'd finally figured out what his brother was trying to say. Ivan had made promises. Promises to always be there. Promises he should have kept. And he broke them all. Angel deserved to live, deserved to be protected. But having failed his little brother in life, now all Ivan could do was ensure a proper funeral. How could Angel rest in peace without one?

It was a short drive to the apartment complex that Suzanne had written about in her journal. He parked in front of the office and walked inside. Five minutes later, he emerged with the apartment number written on the back of a business card and the information that a couple of Suzanne's family members had arrived this morning.

Ivan left his car in the visitor's area and walked to 1304. Up the stairs he went, full of determination. Before he could knock, the door opened. A short middle-aged woman with swollen eyes looked up at him.

"You must be Mr. Montgomery." She offered a forced smile. "The manager's office called to let us know you were on the way up."

"Call me Carl, please." He took her outstretched hand and held it tightly. "I had to come when I heard the horrible news." Ivan pulled the woman in for a hug. "I'm so sorry for your loss. For our loss."

"Mother, let the man come inside," a female voice said.

"Of course, come in."

The voice belonged to a younger version of Suzanne. Judging from the firm set of her jaw, she was the one to win over. "You must be Elizabeth."

"And you were a friend?" Her skepticism was showing.

"Yes." He released the older woman and extended his hand. "Lizzie, you and Suzanne looked a lot alike." Her eyes blinked. He knew immediately that she'd taken the hook. "I'm sorry. That was her pet name for you. I had no right to be so informal."

"No. Lizzie is fine." Her bottom lip trembled.

Ivan didn't hesitate. He walked to her and hugged her too. "I won't keep you. I just had to offer my sympathies."

"Nonsense." The older woman took charge, but her voice was weak and raspy. "Stay. Tell us how you knew Suzanne."

"For a minute," he said, taking the spot on the couch she was patting. "I met her through a mutual friend. If I remember correctly, it was right after she went to work at the hospital." He had intentionally not mentioned Holly's name, hoping one of the women would fill in the blanks.

"Holly Hoffman?" the younger woman said.

"Yes." He delivered his most sincere smile. "You've met her?"

"A few times. We've been expecting to hear from her," Lizzie said.

"I'm getting a little worried. She called to tell me about this horrible tragedy, but I haven't heard a word since. I have no idea what's going on."

"We're in the dark too. We can't get answers from anyone. Mother received the phone call that told us what that monster did. We've heard nothing since. I pray the bastard gets the death penalty."

So there it was. Other than having Holly's last name, he was no better off than yesterday. If these people didn't know where Holly was, they were of no use to him. Maybe searching the apartment would be more fruitful.

"Well," Ivan said with a heavy sigh. "I called our mutual contacts and no one has heard from Holly. Is there anyone you can think of that I missed?"

Both women shook their heads.

"I really have to go. When I hear from Holly, I will be sure she calls."

"Thank you for stopping by," the older woman said.

"Sure thing." He walked toward the door. He removed his gun from under his jacket, turned, and then put a bullet in each of their chests. Just to ensure they weren't alive, he put one in each of their brains.

He pushed open the bedroom door to find a small child of maybe six years old asleep on the bed. She didn't stir as he conducted his search, stopping to pick up a stack of journals. He tucked them under his arm. He aimed at the curly brown hair, his finger on the silenced gun's trigger, and then he remembered his brother at that age. Ivan pulled the door closed behind him, leaving the sleeping child alive. For Angel.

Ivan's contact called with Holly's address just as he drove out of the complex. He got directions and made his way to the freeway. This was turning into a productive outing.

****

The sun had barely peeked over the horizon when Jake and Daisy stepped out of the house onto the back porch and walked to the barn. Once inside the barn's office, tucked into the back corner of the wooden building, he prepared the small coffeepot he kept on top of his filing cabinet. Daisy padded over to the bed of old saddle pads he'd made for her and plopped down.

He propped his feet on the corner desk just like his uncle had done for years and enjoyed the peace and solitude of morning while the aroma of the brewing coffee filled the small room.

He checked his email, filled his mug, and started his daily walk. So attuned to his routine, the horses had already moved to the front of their stalls for their daily ear scratch. He set his mug on a bale of hay and began his first chore of the day. He fed the horses their grain, always starting with Duchess first.

He hung the empty bucket on a large hook in the feed room, then headed back toward the office. He bent to pick up his mug, and a headache hit out of nowhere. He sat on a bale of hay stacked next to Duchess's stall, dropped his head into his hands, covering his eyes. Pictures flashed as if he were watching a slideshow. They were just snippets. The helicopter crash in Afghanistan played in his mind in slow motion. A deafening explosion roared through his head. Jake didn't relish the pain, but he didn't want the memories to stop. These were pieces of his past; random snapshots of his history flowed nonstop.

"Jake?" Small hands grasped his shoulders. Holly knelt in front of him, so close her scent wrapped around him.

"I'm good." He pulled his hands from his eyes, lifted his head, and then looked into concerned blue eyes.

"What happened?" Worry lines creased her forehead, tempting him to rub them away.

"A few memories confirmed some of the things I've been told. The explosion of my helo was more vivid than was described to me after the operation." A flash of understanding crossed her face. "Of course, you've heard all this before."

"But not from you." A slight smile lifted the corners of her mouth. "Don't you think it's good to remember?"

"I never want to forget that I let them down." His heart squeezed. "Sixteen men died in my care. They trusted me."

"You had no control over what happened. It was a dangerous mission. Everyone on board knew the helicopter could be shot down at any minute."

"I've got work to do." She was telling the truth, but he didn't want to listen.

"Are you sure?" Cool fingers found the vein in his throat. "Jake, your heart rate is elevated. Let's take a break." He opened his mouth to tell her to drop the subject, but she leaned closer. Her hair was loose this morning, and it fell in waves over her shoulders, stopping just at the tip of her breasts. His body reacted instantly to her nearness.

"Yeah." He started to stand, but thought better of it. The wrong move and his erection would be right in her face.

"Are you dizzy?"

"No." Jake shrugged away from her and willed his erection away.

"Then why did you sit back down?"

"Leave it alone." Jake stood and pushed past her. He took long strides trying to get to the office. Putting a desk between them was the only way to keep his hands off her. Her rapid footsteps behind him meant she hadn't taken the hint. He had barely made it inside when she slammed the door behind her. The click of the lock turned him to face her. "Please, Holly."

"You're going to stop running from me today."

Then she was in front of him, lifting up and kissing him. Her mouth covered his with an enthusiasm that almost buckled his knees. Her hands dug into his hair, dragging him closer.

All the previous talks he'd had with himself, all the warnings that somebody's heart would be crushed, left his thoughts faster than the tornado had moved through. He wrapped his arms around her, pressing her breasts against his. The passion that had been building since the day she'd touched his arm outside the makeshift clinic finally spilled over the dam.

Holly moaned, pushing the last shred of his resistance from his mind. Her hands slid under his shirt. She stroked his skin, digging in with her fingers while holding him closer.

Jake reluctantly broke contact with her mouth. "Be sure you know what you're doing. The last thing I want is to hurt you again."

"No more fighting," she whispered into his lips. "This may not be forever, but it's what I want for now."

Wrapping a handful of her hair around his hand, he tilted her head back and kissed her neck, working his way with his tongue to her neck and the corner of her mouth. He leaned back and studied her beautiful face for a minute.

"You're sure?"

"Yes." Her voice was soft but steady as she dug her fingers into his back. "Don't think for a minute that I can't handle my emotions. I want you to make love to me. Right now. Right here." She nodded toward the desk.

"I have a better idea." Pushing her backward, he unlocked the door, scooped her up, and walked to the last stall on the aisle. Empty and clean, with its high walls and a fresh bed of straw on the floor, it offered all the privacy they needed. He put her down, grabbed a clean horse blanket, and tossed it on the hay.

"Have you done this before?" She looked around the stall.

"Never. You up for it?" he challenged.

"Of course, I am." Her gaze dropped to his bulging erection. "Looks like you are too."

She laughed, pushed the gate closed, snapped the lock, and then turned into his arms. He pushed her far enough away from him to pull her shirt over her head. With one hand, he unhooked her bra.

"My God, you are beautiful." Her breasts fit perfectly in his hands. Dark rose nipples were beaded in anticipation. He dipped his head and pulled her into his mouth.

Jake moved from one breast to the other, tasting her and enjoying her soft moans. She tugged his shirt from his jeans. He reached to help, but she caught his hands and moved them to his sides.

"Wait," she whispered. "Let me and don't move."

"I have one thing to say." He leaned down and captured her mouth.

"What's that?"

"Hurry."

Her eyes sparkled as she slowly started the process of undoing his buttons one at a time. "I don't think so. I waited a long time for this."

Leaving his hands at his sides where she'd placed them was going to be a true test of his will. She kissed the hollow in his neck, driving him wild as her lips trailed down his chest behind each opened button.

"Ever heard of payback?" He lost his words when she unhooked his belt and unsnapped his jeans.

"Damn boots."

"Does that mean I can move?"

"Yes." She rolled her eyes. "I think you'd better."

Her eyes never left his body while he toed off his boots. Before she could stop him, his jeans and underwear were on the floor.

She licked her lips and trailed her fingers down his chest to his abs, leaving a trail of fire behind her. "You are perfect."

"I wouldn't go that far." He pulled her closer and wasted no time adding her clothes to the pile on the ground.

Jake lifted her breasts in the palms of his hands and leaned over, pulling one nipple into his mouth. He switched to the other side, marveling at her response.

Her breathing became labored, "Jake," she moaned.

He knelt on the hay and helped Holly lie down on the blanket. She reached for him but he caught her hand. No taking chances, because he had only just started pleasuring her.

"I'm in no hurry." He kissed her lips, her cheeks, and slowly worked his way down her neck.

His lips journeyed, his tongue tasting her skin with small flicks. Nobody knew what would happen tomorrow, but today he would memorize every soft, curvy line of her body. Softly, gently, he kissed his way to her breasts.

God, he loved how responsive she was to his touch. One more moan and he'd be in serious trouble. He stopped his trip downward at her belly button, where he circled it and drew patterns.

Her hips lifted. Accepting the invitation, he slid between her legs. His thumbs spread her so every delicate inch was exposed. He tasted her with a long draw of his tongue, lavishing her with attention, driving her higher.

"Please." The word rolled off her tongue, needy and pleading. He'd treasure the sound for the rest of his life.

The softness of her plea engulfed him, filling an empty place with a warm feeling. One he'd never dealt with before. He reluctantly released her and grabbed a condom from his wallet.

"Let me. You'll take too long," she said.

"No. If you touch me, everything may be over too soon."

He covered himself under her watchful eye. He leaned over and kissed her, using his tongue to delve into the soft heat of her mouth, wanting her to remember their time together with love. Jake nudged her thighs farther apart and cupped her breasts, rubbing the hard nipples with his thumbs. "I'm going to enjoy watching you come."

Reaching under her hips, he elevated her slightly and inserted just the tip of his erection. Her gaze never left his as he entered her with a quick plunge.

"Oh, yes." Her eyes flashed wide. In that instant, Jake knew he'd found home.

He penetrated deep into her heat, moving in and out, repeating the process until she grabbed his shoulders and pulled him down to her as she murmured.

"Now...with me..."

He slid his hand between them and pressed circles on her most sensitive of places. Her eyes locked on his and she met him thrust for thrust. The honesty of her passion pushed him over. They reached the pinnacle together, her calling out his name while he emptied himself to the rhythm of her spasms.

An era later, or so it seemed, Jake rolled to his side, bringing her with him to lie on his shoulder. Neither spoke. He'd never regret making love with her. She'd given all of herself with complete trust and honesty. Neither of them knew what the future might hold, but for this perfect moment they were together as one.

Holly broke the silence by laughing. It was infectious and Jake joined her.

"That was amazing." She walked her fingers across his chest.

"Yes, it was."

"I have a question."

"Ask away." He rolled to his side and propped up on his elbow.

Color rushed up her cheeks. "Never mind."

"Don't go bashful on me now. Not after what just happened."

She opened her mouth but closed it.

"Don't hold back. We're lying naked on a blanket in a horse stall. There's no reason to feel awkward," Jake said, rolling her nipple between his fingers.

"I'm glad we made love. So many times, I've wondered how it would be. Have you ever wondered what having sex with me would be like?"

Jake weighed his answer carefully. She'd used the words having sex instead of making love. "I'd have to be blind and crazy not to fantasize about you."

"That's not exactly an answer. I've thought about it many times."

"Well, you aren't wondering any longer." No way was he confessing that watching the passion in her eyes was the most erotic thing he'd ever seen. Or that being inside her felt as if that's where he belonged. Or that those feelings scared the hell out of him.

Should they talk about how dangerous their actions could be? What would happen when the killer was caught and this was over? One or both would suffer damage when they parted ways, and that was one thing he was sure would happen. She had a life and a rewarding profession in the city. Sure, he had the ranch, but how much joy would it bring him without her?

She leaned over him and kissed the tip of his nose. "You seem to bring out the animal in me."

"Good thing I like animals." Jake reluctantly pulled himself away from Holly and stood. "If Alice sticks to her routine, she'll be here soon, bringing me a cup of coffee."

"I'm up." Holly scrambled to her feet. "Her catching us acting like two teenagers in heat is not something I want to happen."

The two of them dressed quickly. He would have preferred to spend the day right there in the stall but that couldn't happen. Jake dragged his hand through his unruly hair, thinking again that a haircut was in order. He turned Holly around and picked a few pieces of hay from her hair.

"Does it look like a nest of eagles moved in?" She patted her head as if trying to get a feel for the mess they'd created.

"Hmm." He leaned back and inspected her. "More like the eagles moved out." He pulled a few more sprigs out.

"We've gone completely nuts." Her laughter echoed off the walls. She pulled on her blouse. "Out of our freaking minds."

Jake closed the gap between them. He pulled her into his arms. "The possibility of getting caught excites you, doesn't it?"

"You know better." She pretended to be offended but didn't pull away from him. "Look, you confuse me. Sometimes, I think you hate that I'm here. Other times, I think you might actually like me. Can we start again?"

He kissed her, and she joined him. It was truth time. "I don't hate you. And since we're being honest, this may not have been the smartest thing we've done in a while. When this is over, putting it in the past may be difficult."

She studied him as if searching for something. "I don't believe in holding on to the past. Let's deal with that when it happens. Okay?"

"I better get busy. Alice comes down and I haven't hauled hay to the cattle, she'll want to know what's kept me." He could accept her deal. This thing between them would end and probably not well.

Jake grabbed the horse blanket, threw it across the stall gate, and walked to the four-wheeler. He backed it up, hooked on the utility trailer, and then started loading bales of hay.

"Better you tell her than let her guess." Holly stepped up and sat in the passenger seat. "I'm a guest and don't want her to think I'm hiding something."

He tossed the last bale onto the trailer and turned to Holly. "Tell her what?"

She blanched like he'd slapped her. He wanted to reach for her but didn't. He wanted to tell her that nothing made him happier than being buried inside her, but he couldn't.

He called Daisy to get on, then he slid behind the steering wheel. Holly scooted over to make room for the dog.

"I said I'd pull my weight, so I'll help."

Jake drove out of the barn and met Alice on the walk. He slowed the four-wheeler. "Good morning. I'm taking my helper with me to spread the hay."

"It looks like you've already put her to work." She pointed at Holly. "You've got hay in your hair." Alice passed him a mug of coffee. "Sorry, I should've brought two cups. Jake, you share with Holly."

"Yes, ma'am." He drove toward the back pasture as fast as he could without dumping the hay.

Chapter 18

Ivan waited until midnight to search Holly's apartment. His flashlight exposed an odd picture of her existence. The women he knew had flowers and girly shit all over the place, but every room at Holly's was barren. The drawers had underwear in them, but they were all plain beige or white, nothing to tempt a man into her bed. The clothes in her closet consisted of a few casual outfits, and an assortment of ordinary jeans and blouses. The bulk of her apparel consisted of nurse's uniforms and work shoes. If she had a life outside that hospital, he saw no signs of it. He picked up a few paperback romance novels and thumbed through the pages but found no notes or telephone numbers. Odd that she kept few keepsakes.

He left her apartment no smarter than when he'd arrived. Once inside his car, he removed his rubber gloves and drove back to his hotel.

He sat in the easy chair, wondering if he'd missed something in Suzanne's stack of journals. The biggest point of interest he'd found was that Holly Hoffman had survived being kidnapped and almost killed. A background check on her had provided him with a number of media articles. She had friends who had rescued her. Maybe that's why she lived as if she were in the witness protection program. Had the Lost and Found people helped her disappear?

If she'd burrowed underground hoping he would go away, she was wrong.

Decisions had to be made. Calling in outside help was risky, but clearly, it had become necessary. The journals had produced names, names that needed to be checked out.

His cell buzzed. Ivan answered on the first ring. "You have news?"

"You're brother's body has been recovered. He's on his way to Soto Funeral Home as you directed."

"Thank you. No troubles?"

"Things got a little messy, but we cleaned it up."

"How messy?"

"It's nothing to worry about."

"How fucking messy?"

"Your brother wasn't at the morgue in Connersville. It was overloaded with bodies of people killed by the tornadoes. The night attendant looked up the address, and the boys drove over to Monroe County and picked him up."

"But you left no witnesses?"

"None breathing."

"Good. I'll send you enough money to cover expenses."

"Do I sound worried? A cash exchange is fine if you prefer to wait. One of the boys wanted you to know it was done with respect."

"Tell him I appreciate it." Ivan made a snap decision. "I need a couple of men."

"How many do you need?"

"Start with two. Make one of them the dude who treated my brother the way I asked. Set them up in a motel close to the Lost and Found, Inc. agency."

"What the fuck is that?"

"A company of private investigators. They could be trouble."

"You want the best, right? Might cost a little extra."

"Fine. Just get them here. If I need more, you'll know."

Ivan ended the call. His frustration grew daily.

Something he'd read in that stack of journals troubled him. He vaguely remembered hearing about the guy who'd kidnapped Holly just a couple of years ago. Why did the name ring a bell?

****

The glaring hot sun didn't seem to bother Jake, but the heat was cooking Holly's brain from the inside out. Still, she was determined that nothing, including heatstroke, would stop her from helping spread the hay out in a long line so even the young ones would get their share.

Standing in the pasture, she could see for miles. An occasional tree dotted the landscape but not enough to block the view. She couldn't imagine a more beautiful place on earth. It reminded her of a comment she'd read somewhere. "In Texas, the sky comes all the way to the ground."

"Sorry. What did you say?" Jake tossed the last section of hay to the ground.

"It was nothing. Just rambling about how breathtaking it is here."

A gust of wind caught Jake's hair and rearranged the already messy style. The sun had lightened it, giving him gorgeous highlights, like the ones she'd paid dearly for over the years.

She worked to keep her mind busy, but the memory of Jake's hands on her body kept creeping into her thoughts. She had instigated the episode on the horse blanket. Had she been wrong to force his hand? Maybe they didn't have a future. Right or wrong, she intended to seize the time they had together and enjoy every second—if he cooperated.

Jake whistled and, like children when the recess bell rang, the cattle came running. Holly grabbed an armful of hay and helped feed the cows. One particularly pushy one came right up to her and ate from her hand.

Daisy ran over and stood in front of her protectively. Holly bent down and scratched her head. "It's okay, girl, I think they like us."

Jake chuckled. "It's Alice. She loves being out here with them. They gather around her and vie for attention."

His cell buzzed. He pulled it from his hip pocket. "Donovan."

Holly rubbed her face with her hands and uttered a silent prayer that this nightmare was over.

"What's up, Rey?"

Her hopes vanished as she watched Jake's gaze harden as he listened. The nerves in his jaw twitched.

"Yeah." His eyes blazed like blue ice. "Thanks for calling."

Holly had to know. "What's happened?"

Jake's expression shifted from anger to sorrow as he stuffed the cell back into his pocket and walked to her. He put his hands on her shoulders. "Suzanne Richards's mother and sister have been murdered. They were found at Suzanne's apartment in Dallas yesterday."

"No." Holly sank into Jake's arms. "No more." The weight on Holly's shoulders was unbearable. Tears flowed as if they had a mind of their own. Anger and despair mingled in her heart, pumping rage into her veins. "They didn't know anything to tell that madman. And how did he know about them?"

"He must have learned something from Suzanne before he killed her."

"No way. She would have never told him about her family." A memory flashed. "Her sister had a little girl. Please tell me she's okay."

"Let's get back to the house. We'll get in touch with Nate or Dalton and find out." He pulled her against his chest. "Holly, this is not your fault."

"So you keep telling me." This was too much. Her body felt numb as she let him guide her onto the four-wheeler's seat. Daisy jumped up and sat extra close as if she sensed something was wrong.

Jake joined her and began the drive back to the house. He was quiet and deep in thought. She didn't press him. Instead, she allowed him time to process whatever was on his mind. When he stopped at the gate, his hand caught hers, preventing her from hopping off to open it. Then it hit her—he hadn't told her everything.

"What else did Rey tell you?"

"Somebody broke into the coroner's office and took Angel's body."

"Who would want the body?" Holly's stomach turned over. "The killer and the dead man must be related. Maybe they're father and son? Brothers? The bastard couldn't come forward to claim the body, so he had someone steal it. What for?"

"The cameras caught three men dressed in black, but their faces were covered. They killed the night attendant and drove off in a stolen ambulance."

Holly stepped off the four-wheeler, walked to the gate, and opened it. "You go ahead. I'll walk the rest of the way."

A frown creased Jake's forehead. "You sure?"

"Yeah." She closed the gate after he drove away.

Holly started the short walk back to the house. How had the killer known where Suzanne lived? Her laughing face, big heart, and plans for the future played through Holly's memory. She pictured Suzanne, feet up after a long day at work, making notes in her..."Oh, my God."

Holly broke into a run. She was bursting with the news. She pulled open the screen and stepped inside to find Jake on the phone. "Jake, I have to talk to you."

"Hang on, Dalton. Holly just came in. I'm putting you on speaker." Jake placed the cell on the table.

"You okay?" Dalton's voice was tinged with worry.

"Yes. Listen, Suzanne kept a journal and usually had one in her purse. She had a stack of them in her bookcase. She'd make notes during lunch if something memorable had happened. She was planning on writing a book about being a nurse."

"Nobody has mentioned a journal. I'll talk to Rey and get back to you." Dalton disconnected without saying another word.

"Jake, you know what this means if the killer has the journal. I don't know how much Suzanne wrote about me, but I confided a lot in her."

"Did you discuss our chance meeting in Connersville?"

"Sure, over coffee and donuts the next morning." Holly had confided in only a few people about her kidnapping, and Suzanne had been one of them. "If this man was in Suzanne's apartment and took her journals, he knows about you." Holly rubbed her temples. "Kay's name is probably in one of the recent journals. She occasionally joined me and Suzanne for lunch or shopping."

Jake didn't respond. Instead, he opened the refrigerator, removed two bottles of water, and returned. His hand covered hers as she accepted the bottle, and heat exploded up her arm into her heart. The thought of him or Alice being killed for protecting her was more than she could bear. She would not be responsible for anything happening to him.

"I have to go. Get as far away from you and anyone else I know."

"That's not the solution."

"Then what is?"

"We'll figure it out together." Jake leaned toward her. "If the killer knows about Kay and Nate, they have to prepare for his possible visit."

"Then let's alert them. At the same time, I can tell them I want to leave here. This bastard apparently has resources. If he digs into the names in those journals, he'll find out about you. Sooner or later he'll show up here, and I can't let that happen to you or Alice." Holly's nerves were screaming through her system. She paced back and forth. "I have no money. What if he has the ability to track my credit card? Okay, I'm being silly. He doesn't know where I bank, but paying with cash would make it harder for him to find me."

"Stop talking like that." Jake snapped out the words, harsh and cold. "You're not going anywhere alone. Let's call Nate. Together we'll work out a plan." He picked up the cell.

"I hate being part of a continuous phone call. That's all we do, talk."

"I do too. We're frustrated and on edge, and that's a helpless feeling." Jake put down the phone. He crossed the room to her, lifting her chin with his finger. "But you're not alone."

The panic she'd been riding like a rolling wave dissolved as he leaned down and covered her lips with his. Strong arms wrapped around her, holding her tightly.

"Oops." Alice's voice had Holly jumping backward. "Don't mind me. I'm just passing through. Claude is taking me to supper. I'll be in my bedroom for a while. "

"Wait." Jake held out his hand. "We have news and a phone call to make. All of it involves you." He waved her and Holly to chairs at the kitchen table.

"What's going on, Jake?" Alice slowly sank to a chair.

"More people have died." Holly watched the fear in the older woman's eyes blossom.

Jake turned a chair around and sat. His strong jaw looked to be set in cement. His shoulders were straight, and his face was the definition of composure. Something had happened in the past few seconds. He looked even stronger and more confident.

"Holly, you were right. So far we've existed between a series of phone calls. The recent events have changed that. Today we stop just existing and start planning. We have to be ready for what we thought was impossible."

He punched in a number on the cell.

"Nate, we have a problem. You know about the two murders and the missing body?"

"Yeah. It's all over the news."

The call lasted a long time. Everyone argued against Holly taking off on her own. Leaving Alice alone was out of the question, even though she thought it a long shot that the killer would find her.

"I think you two should go. I don't want to know where," Alice said. "There's nobody going to bother me out here."

"Miss Alice." Nate's tone was soft and reassuring. "What if I send a couple of men who know how to care for livestock to manage the ranch?" Nate asked. "Both of these men are coming off an assignment and will jump at the chance to spend time in the country."

"They'll be here to protect me?" Alice asked, shifting in her chair.

"No," Nate answered quickly. "They will be there to take care of the place. Is there somewhere you can go? Somewhere safe?"

Jake's hand reached over and covered his aunt's. "Claude would keep you safe. Think he'd take you to his fishing cabin for a week or so? He doesn't have to tell anybody where he's going. He's a smart man. He'll come up with something."

Alice pulled her hand away. "I don't know...all this cloak-and-dagger stuff sounds like something out of the movies."

"Will you at least ask him?" Jake glanced at Holly, and she read the concern in his eyes.

The room was quiet as they waited for her answer. "Are you sure this is necessary?"

"No."

"Then why—"

"Let me finish." Jake leaned closer to Alice. "The killer we're dealing with is much stronger and has more information than we knew. He probably already knows about me. If he decides to locate me, he won't hesitate to kill you."

"Which means we prepare for the worst," Nate spoke up.

Alice suddenly looked much older. Her normally straight shoulders slumped in submission. Holly couldn't hold her tongue.

"I am so sorry that I brought this trouble into your house. I shouldn't have come."

Alice shook her head. "You cannot blame yourself for other people's sins. This man is a murderer, and you're not responsible for his actions." She leaned back in her chair. "I'll have to clear it with Claude, but I'm sure he'll do what's necessary."

"Then it's settled. Jake and Holly will come here." Nate's tone didn't leave room for discussion. "It doesn't get dark until close to nine, so I can safely say Tank and Paul will be there today. Marcus will pick you up. Bring clothes and toiletries, nothing else."

Holly studied Jake's face, wondering if he agreed. Or would he stay behind? Over the past hour, he'd changed right in front of her. His face had hardened. His back was straighter. And he was furious. The man she'd made love with was gone. Had the murders brought back some of Johnny Darling's personality? Was that even possible?

Nate spoke to someone, but Holly couldn't identify the voice in the background. "Tank says they can be ready in twenty minutes, so look for them in, say, four hours."

"We'll be ready." Holly tried her best to sound positive. In her heart, she feared all they were doing was putting more people in danger. "Nate, Suzanne had a niece. Can you find out if she's okay?"

"A child protective worker stayed with her until her father came. I'm sorry. I should have mentioned her."

"I couldn't have taken it if he'd killed the child."

"Holly, I hear the fear in your voice." Nate had always been the perceptive one. "You're one of the bravest women I know. You'll be safe here. This son of a bitch better bring the SEALs with him if he wants to breach our security."

Again, Daisy had sat close to Holly as if sensing she was troubled. One paw rested on Holly's foot. "Do you have room for one more dog?"

Nate laughed. "Sure. Diablo is here a lot. We have plenty of room for them both."

A shiver rolled up her back as the call ended. Nate was right. She couldn't let fear paralyze her. Not with so many lives at stake.

"Alice, I am licensed to carry a weapon. If you have an extra pistol, I'd like to borrow it."

"I don't own a handgun, but you're welcome to take one of the hunting rifles from the gun safe in my bedroom." Alice stood and left the room, returning with her purse and keys. "I'm going to talk to Claude. Nate, it was a pleasure."

"We'll meet under better circumstances soon."

"Hang on, Nate." Jake walked Alice to the door. "The ranch will be in good hands. I trust Nate."

"And I trust you to keep this place safe."

Holly went to Alice. "Thank you. You welcomed me with open arms and I can never repay you." Holly pulled the woman close.

Alice kissed Holly's cheek and then opened her arms to Jake. He hugged her tightly for a long minute.

"Take your time in town. Tell Claude I appreciate his help."

"You still with us?" Jake asked as he and Holly went back to the conversation.

"Nice lady "

"She certainly is," Jake said. "Holly tells me your business has really grown."

"I've hired seven new investigators over the past two years. All former military and well trained before they got here."

Holly seized a pause. "Now that Alice is gone, I want to revisit her situation. This ranch is sacred to her. The two men can take care of the livestock?"

"I would lie. Tank and Paul are country boys raised right here in Texas. They will stay until this is over. Let me get them started your way."

Jake nodded at her. "Good. As soon as they get here, I'll show them around and explain the schedules."

"You're sure the stress won't be too much for Kay?" Holly couldn't bear the idea of her problems upsetting her friend.

"I think she'll be calmer with you here."

"Then we'll see you later tonight." Jake ended the call.

"I keep hoping I'll wake up and this will have been a dream." She almost retracted that to explain that didn't include her time in his arms. But she sensed he wouldn't have heard her.

Jake stood and walked to the back door. Daisy jumped to attention and joined him. He pushed the screen open, and then looked over his shoulder. "Life won't be just a series of phone calls any longer. I'm going to start a schedule for Tank and Paul. Why don't you pack?"

Holly watched as Jake walked to the barn. She went to her room, started pulling clothes out of drawers, and then remembered she had nothing to put them in. She returned to the kitchen and rummaged under the counter until she found Alice's stash of plastic bags. The memory of her mother saving every bag she brought home popped into her mind. An ache in her heart reminded her how much she regretted that after her dad's death, she and her mother had drifted apart. She hadn't even been invited to the wedding.

Holly quickly folded her few hanging clothes, removed everything from the dresser drawer, and stuffed it all into the bags. Her makeup and hair care products went into a bag by themselves.

So this was it? Her life reduced to four grocery bags? Not that she had a lot of possessions—she'd never been one to care for material things—but now she couldn't even go back to her own apartment. Tears filled her eyes as she looked at the bags on the bed. She angrily blinked them back. Digging deep, she mentally prepared herself for the days ahead and prayed the FBI would figure out who the killer was and put him away. She carried her bags to the kitchen and put them by the back door.

Jake was walking back to the house, carrying a clipboard. The way he moved, the confidence in his step, and the grim, hard line of his mouth scared the hell out of her.

The peaceful young man she'd run into in Connersville was gone.

Chapter 19

Jake opened the door for Daisy, then followed her inside. She trotted to Holly, who was leaning on the counter, and dropped down at her feet. He saw tears brimming in Holly's eyes. Had the dog picked up on her emotional state? He realized the situation was getting to her, yet he was at a loss for words.

"I'm sorry." He waved his hand in the direction of four plastic sacks on the floor. "I should have remembered you'd need a suitcase or two for your clothes."

"The bags worked just fine."

Jake caught the heartbreak in her eyes. Holly was grieving over the recent murders. He wanted nothing more than to comfort her, to promise he'd make things right. But bold statements wouldn't help. She'd have to sort through the heartache in her own time.

But Jake couldn't give in to such sentiments or emotion. His job was to keep her safe, to remain alert and on guard at all times. And there would be no giving in to his desire to hold her.

"I called Alice and reminded her to take the battery out of her phone and ditch it." He made a few notes, then dropped the clipboard on the table. "I'm trying to write out every detail of all the jobs that have to be done."

She cleared her throat. "That's a good idea."

He thought for a moment. "I'll have to call the feed store and give approval for Tank and Paul to charge to our account." He picked up the home phone and dialed. While giving instructions to the owner, Jake walked to his bedroom, returning to the kitchen with a couple of suitcases. He ended the call and offered them to Holly.

"I don't need those." Holly opened a cabinet door under the sink. "Since I'm ready, I'll clean my bedroom and wipe out all traces I was ever here." She pulled out a plastic tote and some cleaning utensils.

Jake covered her hand with his. "Just removing your personal items is enough."

She tugged it back. "I need something to do."

Jake released his grip and stepped back. He understood how keeping your mind busy gave it a chance to calm and heal, so he gave her space and returned to his own bedroom to pack. He gathered enough clothing to fill a small duffel bag, rolling up each item and tucking it in neatly. His bathroom items and a pair of tennis shoes went in a backpack. He carried them to the kitchen and dropped them next to Holly's bags. Then he walked down the hall and found her sitting on the edge of the bed, staring at the floor.

"Hey," he said, giving her warning that he was coming in. "You can't dwell on what-ifs. They'll eat you alive."

"You would know." She lifted her head and met his gaze. "I'm sorry. I shouldn't have said that."

"Don't apologize. You're right, I speak from experience." She hadn't offended him, so he sank down next to her. His hand hovered over her knee, but touching her would only make him want more. "What were you thinking?"

"I was visualizing myself at Nate's gun range."

He chuckled. "That's an out-of-the-blue thought, isn't it?"

"Not at all."

"When did they add the gun range?"

"Last year. I've practiced out there a couple of times."

"Let's hope you never have to test your skill on a human being." The idea of Holly wielding a gun against a killer sent his stomach into freefall. "Are you finished in here?"

She held up a rag and furniture polish. "I wanted to dust before I left."

"If you have an extra one of those, I'll help finish up."

Together they dusted and put clean sheets on both beds. Holly opened the drawers and then closed them. "Just double checking."

"You're becoming more withdrawn by the minute." He could feel her looking at him from time to time. "Do you want to talk about it? You can cut the tension in this room with a knife."

"I was thinking how much things had changed within the span of a few hours. This morning we were lovers, and now you're a completely different person. Stiff and distant. These last killings and leaving the ranch has changed you, and not for the good."

"I don't know what you mean." Of course he understood completely, but now wasn't the time for him to tell her. Surely, she knew that going to the Lost and Found compound would change everything.

Daisy wandered into the room.

"You need to go?" He stood and patted his leg. Daisy followed him onto the front porch, where he sat on the steps while she took off trying to catch a grasshopper.

He felt Holly standing behind him just inside the screen door. He wouldn't invite her to join him. The urge to wrap her in his arms and never let go was too strong. He absolutely had to rein in his foolish emotions.

"When will our ride be here?"

"Probably at the same time as the two men who will stay."

"What about Alice?"

"Claude may not let her come back. Either way, I'll call before we leave." A bitter laugh bubbled up from inside his sour stomach. "Very soon, they'll be using burner phones, and we'll do the same. Staying in touch just got harder."

"As long as Dalton is working with Rey and the FBI, they will find a way to communicate with us."

"Right." Clouds of dust rolled up in the distance. Two vehicles were coming in fast. Just to be safe, Jake went inside to the gun cabinet, pulled out a couple of rifles, and then loaded them. Holly was on the porch waiting. He handed her one of the weapons. "It's old but it shoots true."

"You think we'll need these?"

"Probably not, but wait inside until we're sure that it's Tank and Paul."

She didn't speak a word. She simply turned on her heel and did as he'd instructed.

Jake stepped off the porch and walked a few yards away from the house. He waited patiently as the vehicles drew closer. The cattle guard rattled when their tires rolled across it and onto Donovan property. A pickup and an SUV stopped in front of the house. The SUV driver's side door opened and Marcus Ricci stepped out.

The screen door slammed and Holly bolted past Jake and across the porch at a run. "Marcus."

Laughter rolled across the yard as the big man braced himself. Marcus's and Holly's faces lit up with smiles. It was good to see her happy.

Jake hung the rifle over his shoulder by the leather strap and walked to meet the two men getting out of the pickup. It was a safe bet that they were friendly. Both stepped out holding their hands where they could be seen.

"You Jake Donovan?"

"That's right." The one doing the talking had to be Tank. The name fit him perfectly. The man had to be six foot five. Filling out that height was a thick and wide body. If Jake was right, running into Tank would be like hitting the proverbial brick wall.

"Tank Jorgenson." He extended his hand. "I hear you got problems."

"That's true and I appreciate your help." Jake immediately liked the man's strong grasp. It was a weird feeling considering his hands were on the large side. "It's good that you're here. You made good time."

Tank introduced Paul Torbin, who'd been scanning the property, seemingly taking in every inch.

"Nice place. We'll take good care of it." Paul was smaller than Tank and closer to Jake's six-two height, but he was built to handle himself in a fight.

"Please do," Holly said with her typical smile and welcome. "This ranch is very important to friends who've put themselves in jeopardy because of me."

The three of them went inside the house. Before Jake could follow, a hand clamped down on his shoulder. He turned to look into the eyes of his old friend Marcus Ricci.

Normally soft-spoken and easygoing, Marcus turned deadly when one of his friends or family was threatened. Twenty years ago he'd crawled into a shell and hidden after his wife died in an automobile accident. Not that Jake remembered any of it. Marcus had helped Nate and Kay nurse Jake back to health, filling in a few of the holes in his memory along the way.

"Good to see you." Marcus pulled Jake in for a hug and pounded him on the back.

"Same here." Jake stepped back and looked at his old friend. "You're looking good. I can tell Chris is feeding you well." He'd met Marcus's wife a couple of times before leaving for the ranch. "Where's Diablo?"

"I heard you had a dog. I figured we'd wait until we got home to let them get acquainted." He glanced around. "Where is she?"

Jake whistled and within seconds, Daisy came running from the barn. "This is Daisy. She needed help one night, and afterward, she just stayed with me."

"Dogs know who they can trust." Marcus walked a few steps away, motioning Jake to follow. "I've been briefed on your situation." He pulled a cell phone from his pocket. "Your aunt is on her way to a safe place. There's a message here for you, along with a list of items she needs. We'll make a drop on the way back to Dallas."

"We should push off soon," Marcus said.

Jake went to his aunt's bedroom and packed her things as requested. He could hear Holly in the kitchen, covering his list with Tank and Paul. The warmth in her voice while she discussed the ranch pleased Jake. He carried the suitcases into the kitchen, and she stopped speaking the second she realized he was standing behind her.

"Tank and Paul are waiting for you to do a walkthrough." Holly backed away.

"I'm ready." Jake set Alice's cases down.

"Let me have them," Marcus said. "I'll put them in the back of the SUV."

The worry lines around Holly's eyes that Jake had noticed earlier seemed to have relaxed. Tank and Paul towered over her and were all but drooling. Jake pushed a zing of jealousy aside. She deserved to be happy. Tank, with his Jethro Gibbs haircut, would probably be a good match for her.

"Jake?" Holly's voice snapped him out of his thoughts. She'd turned her attention to him and he saw that the worry on her face had returned. He got it. He represented everything bad in her life.

"We need to go soon." He saw no need to sugarcoat the situation. She knew. "Tank, I'll take you and Paul through the feeding process, then we'll stop by the office. I'll show you all the important telephone numbers and files."

Jake walked through the kitchen and out the door. Leaving meant trusting that these two men were as reliable as Nate believed.

****

Ivan stood and stretched his arms overhead. He fixed himself a coffee, ordered breakfast, and then dressed. This waiting for a break was making him crazy. Holly Hoffman would suffer before she died. She'd pay for every second of his trouble. And the longer he waited, the more determined he became to exact a painful justice.

After he'd put a couple of good men on the payroll to watch the Lost and Found compound, he'd left Dallas for two days to do a job. In his line of work, he couldn't have word getting out that he was turning down jobs. Being away for a few days had not diminished his need for revenge.

Researching the Lost and Found agency had been easy. They'd experienced a large growth spurt after building a facility outside of town, prompting the newspaper to do a story on Wolfe and his team. The article included the backgrounds of the partners. If Holly had gone to them for protection, his job had gotten tougher. Not impossible, just more of a challenge.

Ivan slipped his Rolex on his wrist, glanced at the time, and automatically reached for his cell, which rang right on time.

"Go." Patience wasn't his long suit, and he'd received the same bland report for the past few days. So much so that he could almost recite it verbatim.

"There's been an increase of activity at the compound. People coming in and out."

"Anyone of interest?"

"Two men we'd never seen before. Both of them stopped at the gate, got out, and shook hands with the guard."

"They were probably operatives coming off a job. Any women?"

"No."

"You're positive?"

"As much as I can be from this distance."

"Go on."

"The two men came in separate pickups but later they left together followed by an SUV. They hadn't returned when I left."

"Interesting." Ivan wondered where the little caravan was headed.

"Today was a lot busier than yesterday." The line was quiet for a long moment. "Look, I can't be here twenty-four seven."

Ivan couldn't argue that point. "I'll have somebody at your motel tomorrow morning at seven. Take him with you for a day or two. Then you follow Kay Wolfe every time she leaves the compound. I want to know where she goes and who she sees."

"I'll cover her."

"Good."

Ivan ended the call and immediately placed another. Hiring a third man to help watch the compound wasn't a problem, but he had other ideas. So he asked for two.

He reread one of the last entries Suzanne had written in her journal. The man who'd previously kidnapped Holly had just happened to be in Connersville at the same time. Ivan was intrigued that somebody else could be stalking Holly. There hadn't been a lot to read, except how surprised Holly was to have run into Jake Donovan.

Ivan logged on to his computer and started a new search.

Donovan had been a helicopter pilot who'd been shot down in Afghanistan. Everyone on board had died except him. After his return to the states, he'd had gotten involved in some nasty shit while working for a group who kidnapped and sold young women.

A newspaper article indicated a tumor had caused the change in Donovan's personality. How interesting that after the tumor had been removed, he'd managed to dodge jail time altogether. How the fuck had he pulled that off?

Locating Holly was becoming more difficult. Had the crazy-ass pilot taken her again or was she hiding out somewhere? It was time to locate this Donovan and rule out one option. While it was a long shot, nothing would be left to chance.

If the son of a bitch had taken her again, Ivan would kill him for it.

Ivan finished dressing and drove his rental to a local branch of his bank. His men worked on a cash-only basis, which Ivan happily obliged.

Donovan's whereabouts nagged at Ivan. The Internet had provided no information on what had happened to him after the case was settled, so he'd called someone who could dig up that information. His patience had stretched its limit when his cell rang. He made notes as some of the blank spaces on Donovan's disappearance were filled in. The call ended and Ivan already had a plan.

Chapter 20

Holly walked through the barn one last time. As she headed down the aisle toward Duchess and her colt, the lump in her throat grew with each step. She opened the stall gate and slipped inside. The mare lifted her head as if looking over Holly's shoulders. Then she stepped closer and lowered her head. Holly rubbed between the horse's eyes, closing her own as a longing she couldn't explain swamped her.

She'd been on the ranch just a short time, yet she felt as if her roots were being ripped from the ground she stood on. Life here was so normal, so routine and peaceful. She'd let her guard down just enough to see a side of life where she could have been happy.

"You were looking for Alice, weren't you? She had to leave because of me." Duchess shifted her weight and leaned closer. "I promise, she'll be back."

A warm nose drew her attention. The foal had decided to get his share of petting. Holly turned and wrapped an arm around the colt's neck, scratching the underside of his jaw for what was probably the last time. She completely understood why Jake had found happiness here on the ranch. Leaving the sanctity of this place scared her more than she wanted to admit.

Tears flowed like tiny rivers down her cheeks. Her heart ached at the thought that the colt would leave here someday just like she would in a few minutes. Neither would ever return.

She leaned down and rested her head on the colt's warm back. "Alice will find a really good family for you."

"Holly?" Jake's voice roared through the barn aisles.

Holly flinched at his tone. Duchess reacted and began to paw the floor with her hoof. A spooked horse was dangerous, so she smoothed her hand down Duchess's strong neck. "Easy," she whispered. "It's okay."

"Holly?" Jake yelled again.

She did her best to wipe off any signs of crying, exited the stall, and then answered. "Stop shouting. I'm right here."

She'd barely had time to call out when Jake appeared at the other end of the aisle. In ground-covering long strides, he closed the space between them.

"Damn it. What the hell are you thinking?" His jaw looked to be set so tightly it might crack any minute. "You can't just vanish without letting me know."

"I wanted a minute alone." Holly instantly went on the defensive. "What's wrong with that?"

Jake blew out a long breath. "You scared the crap out of four men. Not one of us knew where you'd gone." He turned and started out of the barn. "We need to leave."

She'd frightened him. He did care for her. Her heart leaped with joy and crushed her with guilt at the same time. Damn tears brimmed again. "Wait. I'm sorry. I just needed time to say good-bye." He kept walking. "Jake. Don't shut me out."

Jake stopped, standing with his back to her. "It won't work. You and me. It was never in the cards."

"Why? What cards?"

He returned and stopped a few feet away from her. "You know that old saying 'that's water under the bridge'? Our bridge washed out a long time ago. You belong in the city, nursing the sick back to health. My home is here, caring for livestock. They don't give a damn about my past."

"I don't—"

"Stop." He cut her off. "It's time we faced facts."

"Jake." But the tone in Dalton's voice ended any hope she had of convincing Jake he was wrong.

"Down the first aisle." Jake stepped to the side for Holly to pass.

Marcus rounded the corner, stopping at the first stall. "You found her."

"Yeah. We're ready."

Stunned, Holly gathered the shattered pieces of her heart and pride, straightened her shoulders, and pushed past Jake. "Yes, we are."

Holly hurried to the house, grabbed her grocery bags of clothes, and then started walking to the SUV.

Tank intercepted her, reaching for the sacks. One long tattoo of barbed-wire snaked around his right arm, vanishing under his shirt sleeve. He moved too quickly for her get a good look. "I'll carry those."

"Thank you, but I've got them."

"My mama would tan my hide with a switch if she knew I didn't help." His face softened. Dark hair, cut military short, matched the deep brown of his eyes. He smiled, showing off deep dimples on both cheeks. She'd been too caught up in the drama of the situation to notice that Tank was not only built like a linebacker, he was utterly gorgeous.

Suzanne would have loved him. Holly's anger subsided, replaced by sadness. She relinquished the bags, but the pain of loss didn't cut her a break. "Thank you. I wouldn't want both of us to be in trouble."

"Cut him some slack." He referred to Jake with a nod of his head. "Men, in general, overreact when someone they love scares them. He's worried about keeping you safe."

Holly laughed. Unfortunately, the sound was extremely bitter. He put her belongings in the back of the SUV and turned to her.

Tank shrugged one shoulder. "I'm just saying."

"Thank you. You've been very kind. This ranch is very important to Jake and his aunt. I have a feeling you'll take care of the place."

"Paul and I are both country boys. We'll treat this place as if it belonged to us. If anybody asks, we've been hired on to help expand the ranch."

"Thank you. When did you go to work for Nate?"

"A few months ago. It was time to get out of the military and settle down."

"You call working for Lost and Found settled?"

"In comparison? Yes, ma'am. I guess I could have gone back to bulldogging, but this made more sense." Tank took out a business card and a pen. He jotted a number on the back. "You put this somewhere nobody will look. Shit hit the fan, and you can't find help? Call that number."

The big man shook her hand, then placed the card in her palm.

"I will."

"I'll load Jake's things next to yours."

Holly opened the back door to the SUV and got inside. While Jake and Marcus were still walking back from the barn, she calmed herself.

"You loaded and ready to go?" Marcus reached in and captured her hand with his.

"As I'll ever be. I wish there was another way."

He squeezed her hand. "Want to ride up front with me?"

"No, thanks. I'm good right here."

Marcus closed the door and started the engine. The cold blast from the air conditioner was welcome. Jake said good-bye to Tank and Paul, loaded Daisy in the back with Holly, and then hopped in the passenger-side seat. In less than five minutes, they were driving through the gate and toward the highway.

She wanted to reach forward, to grasp his shoulder and say she was sorry that he'd gotten involved. But she couldn't for fear he would shrug her hand off. Deep in her soul, she ached that their time together was over. For a minute in time, she'd shared her heart with him. Maybe she'd given him a glimpse of true love.

Together they'd created a memory that would have to last her a lifetime.

****

Marcus stopped the SUV at the Lost and Found guard shack. "Gary, this is Jake Donovan."

Jake leaned across Marcus and shook Gary's hand. "Pleased to meet you."

"Likewise." Gary leaned down and looked through the driver's side window.

"Welcome home." He winked at Holly. "I had coffee with Kay and Nate this morning. She couldn't stop talking about you. She's excited for sure."

"Thank you," Holly said. "I can't wait to see her."

Jake leaned back and tried to relax. The ride back had been long and tedious, leaving Jake time to second-guess his decision. If something happened to the ranch, he'd never forgive himself, but deep in his soul, he knew protecting Holly was worth any cost.

Jake was familiar with the architectural plans for the Lost and Found compound, but the drive back to the compound showed him that major changes had taken place. The hot and dry Texas summer weather hadn't managed to kill off enough heavy shrubs and trees to expose the layout of the business at first. The tree-covered road opened and Jake whistled. "The place is larger than the blueprints I remember."

"Wait until you get a look around," Marcus said. "We've grown a lot since we moved out here, adding additional buildings within the first year.

Nate's established the company as the go-to place for solutions not only for individuals but the government."

"I'm guessing Dalton coming on board helped with Uncle Sam."

"No doubt, Dalton added to our credibility."

The road wound through the trees a few minutes before opening up at the mouth of a clearing. The plans Jake remembered called for an office building, a house, and a gym/training facility. A long, narrow shotgun-type building had been added to the back of the property.

"That's the gun range and a bunkhouse of sorts. It helps when there's a big case and we're in and out." Marcus laughed to himself. "My wife doesn't like it when I crash here, but sometimes, all I have is a couple of hours."

Jake understood why Nate had been so adamant that Holly would be safer here than just about anywhere. "The compound appears to be secure, but it's never been really tested. Has it?"

"Have we protected someone from an outside attack?" Marcus's gaze slid to the rearview mirror. "No. But we can."

Holly leaned forward. "An attack?" Her surprise was evident in her tone. "It sounds as if you expect a small army."

"We always plan for the worst," Marcus responded.

Daisy stood and stuck her muzzle over the back of Jake's seat. He leaned his head toward her. She rewarded him with a sloppy lick across his cheek. "You about ready to stretch your legs?"

Marcus scratched her behind the ear. "She's a good dog. I almost forgot she was with us." He drove into the office parking lot and stopped. "There's a huge fenced-in area behind the bunkhouse. Diablo loves it out there."

"How is he around other dogs?"

"I have no idea. But if we handle it right, they'll be fine."

Jake hoped so.

The door to the office opened and Kay burst out onto the walk. About the same time, Holly exploded from the backseat. Within seconds, both women were in each other's arms, laughing and crying at the same time. They turned and went inside as if there was nobody else in the world.

Jake felt a giant boulder drop on his chest. Bringing Holly here had been the right thing to do all along. He'd been wrong to fight so hard against the idea. She had no family and these people were her friends. They loved her and would ensure her safety much better than he could. He watched as the two women linked arms and walked inside.

He'd been so sure that nobody could protect her like he would. Had it been vanity or fear of losing touch with her completely? Had he allowed his desire to have her near him put her in jeopardy?

"Jake, I don't give advice readily, so tell me to shut up if you don't want to hear what I think."

Jake would listen to anything that took his mind off Holly. "No way. You have thoughts. Let me have them."

"You're a fool if you let Holly get away. She hasn't been the same since you left...what is it, two years now?"

"That wasn't the kind of advice I expected." Shit. Jake's memories of his college days were fairly clear. He and Marcus had been good friends. Those were the good old days, now long gone. "Now if you have ideas how we're going to stop this crazy motherfucker from killing her, I'm all ears."

Marcus held up his hands in surrender. "I'm just saying." He nodded toward the office. "Looks like somebody is waiting for us."

Nate had stepped out onto the walkway. His dark, piercing gaze could cut a person in half, but today, even his eyes were smiling. He held out his arms as if frustrated. "Are y'all coming inside today?"

"Be right there," Jake said, walking to Kay and wrapping his arms around her. Her belly was big so he was extra careful.

Jake and Daisy walked to Nate for a hug.

"Damn, it's good to see you." Nate tugged at Jake's hair. "Damn shame there aren't any barbers in Murdock." Nate looked down at the dog watching every move. "So this is Daisy?"

"She's a good dog," Marcus said. "She needed a friend. Jake made that happen."

"You two attract animals." Nate waved in the direction of the front door. "I have news."

Jake followed the two men through the expansive office area. Nothing resembled the small office in the strip center where Nate had first set up his business. Offices lined two walls and a huge conference room filled the back wall.

"Jake Donovan." Kay's tone stopped him in his tracks. "I could use another hug."

He turned and swept his friend into his arms, lifting her off the floor. "You," he said kissing the top of her head, "I missed." He glanced at Nate and Marcus. "I can't say the same for these ugly bastards."

"Liar," she said with a laugh.

"True." He carefully put her down. "Are you feeling up to all of this?"

"I'm better now that all my chicks are in the coop. All we need is for Ty to be here."

"I haven't seen him since my surgery. How is he?" Jake felt Holly's presence without turning. She was standing to the side, watching.

"He's great. We've accepted the fact he'll never move back to Texas."

Jake told Daisy to sit. "Where's Diablo?"

"In the conference room. Let's put..." Kay leaned over and patted Daisy. "Let's put her in the yard. She can stretch her legs for a while before we put the two dogs together."

Jake followed Kay to a large, fenced grassy area. He led Daisy outside and removed the leash. She immediately put her nose to the ground and started exploring.

"She'll be fine." Kay looped her arm in Jake's and escorted him to the conference room.

He paused at the door. These people were his closest friends, but he didn't feel comfortable here. He remembered a great deal of the past and understood how they'd been inseparable in college, but he didn't fit in anymore. Too many years had passed.

Diablo sauntered over when Jake sat next to Kay. He sniffed Jake's jeans and shoes, checking out Daisy's scent, before returning to plop down on Marcus's foot.

Holly reached down and patted the dog. She hadn't made eye contact with Jake in hours. She'd had a long time to think during the drive. Had she accepted that the city was her home, not some ranch in the country?

"Sorry we're late," Kay said. "We decided to keep the dogs separate for a little while."

"You did the right thing." Nate beamed at his wife. Jake felt a stab in his chest. Surely, love like Nate and Kay's only happened every few hundred years.

Nate said, "We heard from Sheriff Santos and Dalton today. The FBI ran the DNA on two unidentified men who were murdered outside of Connersville instead of waiting for the state. At first blush, they initially thought the murder of the older couple and these men weren't related to Holly's killer. Now they are not so sure."

"My killer?" Holly's tone made it clear that she wasn't going for that nickname. "You need to call him something else."

"Sure thing. I'll let you come up with something." Nate was abrupt, but he patted Holly's back, indicating he meant no offense. "Santos sent a deputy out on a wellness check for an older couple whose daughter hadn't been able to reach them. Three men and two women's bodies were found."

"He told us that he was working a murder case." Jake's interest jumped. Had they found a lead? "He thinks that case might be connected to ours?"

"The autopsy results provided a lot of information. The older male and female had been dead approximately a week prior to the two unknown men. The men's fingerprints easily identified them as small-time hoods from Houston. The older couple's daughter has never heard of either Lavon Kelly or RG Rogers. The thing that ties this together is the second female. She was identified as a reporter who'd been at the school the day that Holly was almost kidnapped. Add that to the stolen drugs found stashed in a horse trailer and the missing guns from the old man's cabinet and the identity of both men became very interesting."

"They were some of the looters Santos was worried about," Jake said. "Killed the older couple for a place to hide."

"But the reporter?" Kay said, shifting in her chair. "They thought she knew something?"

"You are probably right," Nate said, smiling at his wife. "Sheriff Santos has a friend who is a Houston police detective. He's recovering from a gunshot wound and is on medical leave. I'm going to contact him. If he's interested in some off-duty work, I'll hire him to investigate both Lavon Kelly and RG Rogers. We need to know a lot more about them."

"Somebody in Houston knows why they were in Connersville," Marcus added. "I can fly to Houston today and work with this detective."

"You might be needed here." Nate looked at Marcus. "Dalton has done about as much as he can from Connersville. He can go to Houston."

Nate's cell chirped, stopping the discussion. "This is the front gate." He put the call on speaker. "What's up?"

"We have company. Monk spotted him during the routine perimeter check. The sun bounced off the guy's binoculars and caught his attention."

"Can Monk get to him?"

"He can try to circle back. He pretended not to notice and kept walking."

"Have our peeping Tom escorted to my office."

"Copy that."

Nate placed his hand on his wife's arm. "You and Holly go to the safe room."

Chapter 21

A chill raced up Holly's back, creeping around her rib cage to her lungs. "This is the safe room-tornado shelter you told me about?"

"Wait until you see it. There's even a small TV." Kay stood, leaned over, and kissed her husband. One of his hands cupped her cheek while the other rested on the swell of her stomach. Holly realized that she'd been so preoccupied, she'd failed to question Kay about her pregnancy.

Jake got up and walked around behind Holly's chair, his nearness engulfing her heart. His hands gripped her shoulders. "Nobody's going to get hurt." His voice sent tears to her eyes. "This is just a precaution."

"I'm going." Holly stood as he pulled her chair back for her. When she turned, his gaze held hers for a long time. Was he trying to tell her something?

"Be safe." Kay took Holly's hand and led her out of the conference room, past the offices, and into the break room. She opened the pantry, pushed something on the back of a shelf, and waited as the panel slid out of sight. Kay keyed in a code on a metal door, pushed the lever down and opened the entry.

"Cloak-and-dagger stuff." Holly walked inside and looked around. "Wow, I could live in here."

"I wanted somewhere we'd be safe if a tornado struck." Kay stepped in and closed the door behind her. The thick door swung shut with a thud. "The keyword is football."

"Football?"

"Nate and Marcus designed this room. Sometimes, they act like they're still in college."

The room had a small couch, an easy chair, an apartment-size refrigerator, and the television Kay had mentioned. Holly opened a door and found a small half bath.

"All the comforts of home." Kay sat in the chair.

Holly perched on the arm of the couch. "Now that we're alone, put your feet up and tell me how you're feeling. I want to know everything."

"I'm fine. Better than fine. We're both healthy. The doctor says the baby is in position. He may come any day now." Kay pulled the lever on the side of the chair and it lifted her feet, showing swollen ankles to Holly.

"How long have your feet been swelling?"

"A few weeks. It happens when I am up and about for long periods of time. It's nothing to worry about." Kay kicked off her sandals. "Come here."

Holly got up and stood next to Kay.

"Put your hand right here."

Gently, Holly placed her hand on Kay's belly. The baby pressed against his mother. Holly smiled, rubbing her palm in a circle. "Another football player."

"Kevin Nathanial Wolfe."

"Your brother would like that." Holly hesitated before asking the question on her mind. "Are your parents excited?"

"Mom is over the moon. I never know about Dad. Even though I wasn't driving, he still blames me for Kevin's death."

Holly regretted bringing up Kay's father. "I'll bet Papa is pleased about the baby."

Kay chuckled. "Pleased doesn't begin to describe it. Now that he's fully retired, he can't wait to spoil his first great-grandson."

Holly moved back to the couch. "I hope they catch that guy who's watching us. Jake might just beat some answers out of him."

"I'm sorry you're going through this. You've dealt with enough trauma and danger to last a couple of lifetimes." Kay groaned softly as she shifted in the chair. "But it brought you and Jake together. That's a good thing. Right?"

"It's proved once and for all that we're not meant to be together."

"How so?"

"His guilt is as strong as ever. He can't or won't accept that he wasn't in control of his actions."

"So you talked about your relationship?" Kay's eyes widened.

Holly's cheeks heated as the memory of their lovemaking flashed through her mind. "He opened up once but then slammed the door closed."

A sly grin spread across Kay's face. "You two had sex."

Holly bit her lip.

"You did." Kay's laughter filled the room. "Didn't you?"

"Once." Tears filled her eyes.

"Details. I need details." Kay's excitement was contagious, and Holly's mood lightened. "What happened?"

"I kissed him."

Kay laughed. "You just walked up and laid one on him?"

"I did. Somebody had to open that door." Holly was still shocked by her actions. "It was wonderful."

"I'm so proud of you."

"Don't be. Before we left Murdock, he told me that a relationship between us wouldn't work. If you think about it, he's right."

"Bull." Kay shook her head. Her wavy chocolate-brown hair swirled around her shoulders.

"You look beautiful. Pregnancy agrees with you. Even your hair seems fuller."

"Don't try to change the subject. You love him and he loves you. He's either too guilt-ridden or too stubborn to admit it. You can't give in to him."

"I'm not sure I can change his mind."

Kay leaned closer. "Has he remembered more of his past?"

"Yeah. Sometimes the memories come with a headache. But he's at the point of not knowing whether it's a real memory or something he's been told."

"He did some terrible things as Johnny Darling. Even if he wasn't responsible, he's not the kind of man who will use the tumor as an excuse."

"You should have seen him in Connersville. He worked tirelessly and saved lives. It's almost as if he feels the need to redeem himself."

"And nobody can help him decide when he's accomplished that."

The door lock clicked, then opened, and Nate stepped into the room. "The conquering heroes have returned. You ladies can come out."

He extended both hands, helping Kay from her chair. "In other words, you didn't find anything."

"Right." He smiled down at his wife, and Holly's heart clenched. "We were being watched, for sure, but whoever it was is long gone."

****

Ivan rose from the stiff-back chair, preferring to stand rather than sit on the uncomfortable piece of wood. He shifted the scabbard riding on the back of his hip and struggled to maintain a look of interest in his current conversation.

He'd come upon this place quite by accident. A chance meeting with a grizzled old man at the gas station a few days earlier had been a stroke of luck. The man had just kept talking to Ivan while they filled their respective fuel tanks. His interest had been piqued when he learned the old bastard lived alone in an isolated area and seldom left the property.

Figuring it had worked for Lavon and RG, he'd followed the old man to his farmhouse outside of Dallas and killed him. Ivan was staying at a luxury hotel and wasn't going to discuss business there, but this dump had the privacy he needed.

The weather-beaten mobile home had seen better days. However, the place sat in the middle of a patch of scrub oaks and bushes, shielding the place from prying eyes.

Ivan returned his attention to his spotter as he tried to explain why he'd abandoned his post. Preferring to not know the men personally, he'd learned first names only, and Benito was currently bemoaning the heat. Not once had he apologized for being seen or almost getting caught.

"That guard didn't fool me. I knew the minute he spotted me. His back straightened and his pace slowed. Bastard tried to look casual as he glanced around, but I had already backed out of sight."

"Tell me more about the guards." Ivan would glean what information he could before sending Benito to meet his ancestors.

"They run in shifts, patrolling throughout the day. There's always a few on duty."

"Did you see any women?"

"Not while I was there today." Benito's hand shook as he handed Ivan a flash drive. "Here are the pictures I took before the guard spotted me."

Ivan said nothing. The entire compound knew they had been under surveillance and would be on high alert. This incompetent bastard had fucked up and didn't have the sense to know it.

Benito stood. He rubbed his hands on his jeans and shifted his weight to his heels. "So you want me to find a new place to watch tomorrow?"

"No. They will be extra careful from now on." Ivan stood and walked to the door. The air conditioning barely kept the mobile home from becoming an oven. Benito's nerves seemed to be sucking every ounce of cool from the air. "Our business has concluded."

"I'm sorry it turned out this way."

Ivan bit back a smile when Benito backed to his car with both hands at his sides, fingers spread. "Relax. I'm not going to shoot you."

Benito smiled. "Sorry about that. Just being cautious."

Ivan laughed and walked the man to his car. "Drive safely."

"Will do." Benito turned his back to open the door.

Ivan quickly drew his knife. The sharp blade pierced Benito's flesh, sliding up through the kidney, into the liver, then punctured the diaphragm. He was helpless, unable to breathe, and would bleed out fast. Ivan shoved his body inside the car and slammed the door closed. He went inside the trailer and ripped the place apart.

He would not quit until Holly was pleading for mercy. It was the only way to end the nightmares he'd started having. Again and again, he dreamed about Angel's death. The only way to make it right was for her to suffer the same fate.

Ivan returned to his hotel, showered, and then opened the flash drive Benito had given him. The drivers of the two pickups he'd mentioned appeared to be all male, but the angle was so shitty Ivan could only guess.

Calmly and with purpose, he moved to the next step. He'd located Jake Donovan's only living relative, an aunt who lived on a ranch in a barren area of Texas. Ivan had to be sure the lunatic hadn't discovered Holly in Connersville and kidnapped her again. He drove to a men's clothing store, made his purchase, and returned to his hotel. He quickly changed, grabbed his fake ID, got in his rental, and started the four-hour drive from Dallas to Murdock.

****

Ivan eased off the gas pedal of the black sedan. He'd swapped his rental for a car more likely to be driven by a federal agent. Dust rolled up from the tires as he turned down the long driveway, coating its shiny paint job and making it look more authentic.

The house was a good couple of miles off the main road and appeared to only have the one way in and out, which made him a little nervous.

So this was Donovan's new home. Ivan knew nothing about ranching, but the sheer size of the spread impressed him. Why anyone wanted to live this far from town was beyond him. Of course, after the shit Donovan had pulled and gotten off with a slap on the wrist, he should be keeping a low profile.

Before he'd reached the house, two men were standing on the front porch waiting. Ivan had pulled off the disguise at the sheriff's office, but she'd been as dumb as a fucking brick. He'd have to be careful here.

He adjusted his tie, which reminded him of a hangman's noose every time he put one on. It wasn't something he'd normally wear, but he'd dressed for the occasion. The black suit, white shirt, and polished black loafers he wore screamed FBI.

He parked, got out, and nodded as he approached the house. "The young lady at the sheriff's office called ahead, right?"

"You're Ben...?"

"Salter." Ivan flashed a black wallet with a fake ID and badge inside. He stopped and waited while trying to size up the two men.

The smaller of the two men stepped off the porch. He was maybe in his mid-thirties, but the T-shirt he wore said he was in great shape. "She said you were looking for Jake. How can I help you?"

The man hadn't exactly identified himself as Jake Donovan, leaving Ivan at a disadvantage. Whoever the guy was, he was older and had brown hair, which was different than the pictures Ivan had studied carefully. And the gorilla on the porch was probably born larger than Donovan.

"I understand he was in Connersville after the storm. I'm looking into a couple of drugstores that were ransacked during that time. I'm talking to anybody who might have heard something."

"Paul Torbin." The man extended his hand and met Ivan halfway. Their handshake was swift and strong.

"Pleased to meet you," Ivan said.

Torbin tilted his head toward the porch. "That's Tank Jorgenson. Jake's not around and neither of us can help you."

"Neither of you were with Mr. Donovan in Connersville?"

"No. Somebody had to stay to work the ranch with Mrs. Donovan." The one named Paul motioned to a chair on the porch.

"Is she around? Maybe he said something to her." Ivan sat, wondering why he hadn't been invited inside. The temperature was hovering at ninety-five, and his suit was getting hot. What was in there they didn't want him to see?

"She's not here either."

Did he fucking look stupid? The man named Paul was lying through his teeth. Was Donovan hiding inside? Hiding behind his aunt? Or maybe they were trying to keep Holly out of sight.

"Mind if I wait for Mr. Donovan?"

"You can, but it won't do you any good." The big guy could actually talk. Without making eye contact with Ivan, he walked to the other end of the porch. "He and his aunt are on vacation."

"Really? They just left you two here alone?"

"Yeah," Paul said. "We're in charge while they are away."

Ivan wasn't going to be blown off. He needed information. He stood. "Look, I don't know what your problem is, but if you interfere with my investigation—"

"We don't know anything that would help you," Paul snapped. "Tank doesn't take kindly to threats. You might better move on."

These two assholes were either born suspicious or they knew a lot more than they were saying. He had to get inside that house. Had to know if she was there.

"I'm just trying to close a case. When Donovan comes home, tell him I'll be back."

"What did you say your name was again?"

Ivan stood without answering. They both reeked of either the military or law enforcement. He walked to the car. Opening the door, he positioned it between him and the two men. They reached at the same time he did, but he knew it was coming and that gave him the edge. He shot them both before they had a chance to fire their weapons.

Ivan jerked off the hot jacket and tie, throwing them in the backseat. He strode across the yard into the house and conducted a thorough search. Ivan found women's clothes in one closet but nothing more than boots, jeans, and a couple of dresses. They had been shoved to the back and replaced with men's clothes. A couple of the shirts he pulled from the closet had to be the big guy's.

Which brought up lots of questions, like why were the hired help living in the main house? Where were Donovan and his aunt?

He searched the house and barn but learned nothing, his temper now hovering on the edge of sheer explosion. He was fucking tired of hunting Holly. She had to be at that compound in Dallas. He went into the barn's small office and dug through the desk drawers and file cabinet but found no helpful information there either.

A small box of matches sitting on the desk caught his attention. He picked them up. On his way out, he lit a match and dropped it on a bale of hay sitting in the aisle. The sudden whoosh of flames startled him. Time to go. He jogged to his car and in minutes, the ranch and burning barn were far behind him.

"Fuck." He slammed his foot on the gas pedal. He had a four hour drive in front of him. Between here and Dallas he would work on a plan to get inside that compound.

Chapter 22

Jake and Marcus stood close watching Daisy and Diablo get acquainted. They took turns walking around each other, sniffing each other's butts. Daisy's tail relaxed, lifting and swinging back and forth like a rope. She'd accepted the submissive role.

Jake scratched her behind the ear. "Let's try them off leash."

Marcus nodded, leaned down, and released Diablo. Jake unhooked Daisy. Both immediately took off running, leaping at each other, and, in general, celebrating a new friendship.

Nate joined them. "Marcus, are you up to an interview with a reporter?"

Marcus raised an eyebrow. "You know the answer to that."

"Marcus is camera shy." Nate laughed and pounded Marcus on the back. "We had a couple of reporters and cameramen out when we first opened. The community was curious even though we're a good five miles away from the city limits. I decided to at least try to ease their concern."

"Diablo and I had business to take care of that day."

"Chris just happened to need them at the shelter all day."

"Who wants to come out?" Marcus asked.

"A WKGA reporter."

"Where is that?" Jake couldn't remember the last time he'd watched television, except for sporting events.

"Amarillo, I think. Kaycie will vet him thoroughly before he sets foot out here."

"I thought everyone called her Kay." Jake remembered her going by Kaycie back when they all were in college together, but years later, it had been shortened to Kay.

"Everybody but Nate." Marcus winked at Jake. "It's a lover's thing."

"Fuck you." Nate grinned. "That's her name."

Jake picked up a tennis ball off the ground and called the dogs to come. From the way Diablo twisted, he knew exactly what was coming. Daisy just stared at him. Jake tossed the ball toward the back fence. "Go get it."

Both dogs took off at a run. Diablo got there first, snagged the prize, and returned it to Jake. He scratched Daisy's ears. "You'll figure it out."

"You should have been with us in Colombia when we first saw that dog. Marcus changed his life. Frankly, I didn't believe Diablo could be rehabbed. Not after I saw the damage he could do."

"You'd never know it now." Jake threw the ball again.

"Just don't speak Spanish around him." Marcus whistled and Diablo brought the ball to him. "Even though it's been a few years since he's heard any of those commands, I don't know what he'd do."

"And I don't want to find out." Nate's cell buzzed. "It's Kaycie. Let's go see what she learned about this reporter."

Jake watched as the two dogs drank from the water bowl. He relaxed and followed Nate and Marcus inside. Gone were the cubicles that had done nothing to muffle private conversations. Everyone had their own office, complete with ergonomic chairs and glass-top desks. The whole setup was too uptown and elegant for his taste, but image and presentation were part of the package. He preferred the weather-beaten metal desk and file cabinet in his office at home.

"Conference room." Kay's face was ashen. "I have a Murdock deputy sheriff on the line."

Jake got there and found Holly waiting for them. She was even paler than Kay had been. Tears streamed down her face. She mouthed the words, "I'm sorry."

Nobody sat. Nate punched the speaker button. "This is Nate Wolfe. I have Jake Donovan with me."

"What's wrong, Mac?" Jake braced himself for the worst.

"The two men working out at the ranch were shot earlier today. Jake, there's been an incident at the ranch." Silence filled the room for a long heartbeat. "Somebody set fire to the barn."

"Son of a bitch. Are Paul and Tank okay?" Jake's throat closed.

"Paul Torbin died on the front porch. Tank Jorgenson is in critical condition. He'd lost a lot of blood and is suffering from all the smoke he inhaled. He was transported to Connersville. They are better equipped to care for him."

"The livestock?" Jake couldn't utter the words mare or colt, hoping they were in the pasture.

"Looks like Jorgenson rallied and realized the barn was burning. He opened the stalls and got the livestock outside. The mailman spotted the smoke and called the fire department. Mr. Jorgenson had collapsed just inside."

"What's the prognosis?" Jake asked.

"He'll pull through. The bullet passed through the side right under the rib cage. The biggest concern is smoke damage to his lungs."

"I'll get one of my men on his way to the hospital," Nate said. "And I'll notify his sister."

"Thanks. I contacted Sheriff Welborne. Miss Alice wanted to come home but I assured her the animals were fine. I'm supposed to tell Jake they're not coming home yet."

"Thank you," Jake said.

Kay leaned closer to the phone. "We'd appreciate it if you'd alert the hospital that someone from our agency will be there to take care of all Tank's expenses. He's to get the best of everything."

"I'll do that right away."

"Do you have anything else for us?" Nate asked.

"No. I'll call if we learn anything." The deputy ended the call.

Nate turned to Kay. "It was a good idea to send someone to be with Tank. Will you contact Jeff? Pull him off rounds and get him headed to Tank."

"Right away." Kay stopped on her way out of the room and squeezed Jake's shoulder. "I'll reach out to Paul's parents. See what we can do to help."

Nate nodded. "Tell them we'll take care of all the expenses. I'll call them later."

Jake couldn't sit any longer. He stood, walked back and forth. He was ready to explode. "The son of a bitch doesn't care who he kills."

"I agree," Nate answered. "But it's a good thing you moved Holly when you did.

He must have thought she was in Murdock with you."

"Smart bastard took the trip to Murdock as a process of elimination." Marcus had been quiet until now. "Now he'll concentrate his efforts here."

"It was Suzanne's journals." Holly turned to Jake. "It never occurred to me that I should ask Suzanne not to write anything down."

"That wouldn't have occurred to any of us." Kay rejoined them at the conference table.

"Regardless of how he knows"—Nate dragged his hands through his hair—"he knows more about us than we do him."

"That's an understatement." A pain pierced Jake's temple. Flashes of the past flooded his brain.

"Jake?" Kay's voice sounded far away. Hands massaged his shoulders. "What can we do?"

"I'm fine." The pain subsided as quickly as it had hit. He glanced around the table at the worried expressions.

"You remembered something." Marcus's voice was calm and reassuring.

"Nothing whole, just bits and pieces, fragments of the things I did as Johnny Darling."

"That's in the past," Marcus said.

Jake caught Nate's gaze. He nodded his agreement. "Marcus is right."

"I appreciate it." Jake stood. "I have to go home. You'll double your guard on Holly?"

"She's in good hands. Take the SUV parked at the front door. The gas tank is full." Nate took keys from his pocket and tossed them to Jake.

"You'll follow up with the detective in Houston?" Jake asked.

"Go. I'll handle things from this end." Nate smiled.

Jake had tried to avoid looking at Holly. No doubt her fear was like the raging fire that had taken the barn. He took a breath. "I don't know when I'll be back."

"You take care of your ranch," Kay said, lifting up and kissing Jake's check. "We'll take good care of Holly."

Jake turned on his heel to leave. A small hand caught his. He didn't stop. Didn't look at her. Instead, he twisted his fingers through hers and led her from the room. Once at the exit, he turned to face her. His heart ripped open at the sight of tears streaming down her face.

"I'm sorry you were dragged into my mess."

"I'm not." He pulled her into his arms and held her tightly. He understood. He identified with her emotions. Many times he'd been pushed to the brink of breaking down.

"How can you say that? Because of me, people are dead. Your aunt is in hiding. Your barn burned."

"All circumstances out of your control. You'll have to come to grips with that to ever move on." He thumbed the tears from her cheeks.

Holly stepped back and suddenly his arms ached to hold her. "I guess we both have things we need to deal with before we move on."

He didn't respond. How could he when she'd hit the bulls-eye with that statement?

"Stay out of sight." He reached over and tucked a stray lock of hair behind her ear. "I'm leaving Daisy with you."

"I'll take care of her." Holly turned away and returned to the safety of her friends.

Jake ran to the SUV and headed home.

****

Jake ignored the speed limit signs on the four-hour drive down I-45. Forty-five minutes north of Houston he turned west off the Interstate, expertly swerving onto the farm road leading to the ranch. He finally slowed down before crossing the cattle guard at the entrance. The smell of charred wood filled the inside of the SUV even before he reached the barn. He drove past the house and parked.

Jake walked to the back gate and whistled. If the firemen had put the animals in the pasture, they'd come running. He waited a minute and whistled again, then breathed a sigh of relief when Duchess and her foal came trotting over the rise. Jake opened the gate and went to meet them.

She nickered and stopped in front of him.

He murmured words to calm her while he ran his hands over her body and did the same to the colt, glad to find that neither had a scratch on them. "Nothing's going to happen to you or Hollywood." He rubbed the colt's nose. "Hollywood," Jake repeated.

Holly would like having the colt named after her. He immediately put her out of his mind and checked the rest of the livestock. Once he was satisfied all the animals were okay, he walked to the barn.

Tank Jorgenson had risked his life to save the horses, and Jake owed him a huge debt of gratitude.

He circled the barn and discovered that most of it had gone up in flames. He struggled to check his temper as he stepped into the blackened remains. The four-wheeler sat in the corner, twisted and melted into an almost unrecognizable pile.

The feed and tack room was on the west end of the building. Previously filled with grain, saddles, bridles and blankets, it was now a pile of charred lumber. Silver conchos, which had previously adorned a leather headstall and saddle, lay in the rubble. Jake wanted to start cleaning up right away but had to wait for the insurance agent. After years of showing horses, all Alice had left were a few trophies, ribbons, and pictures. In the meantime, he'd empty the equipment barn and convert it into a makeshift storage and shelter.

Jake stepped out of the barn and took a deep breath. He wanted the scent of burned wood and leather burned into his memory. His hands ached to be wrapped around the throat of the bastard who'd done this. Hate grew with each step.

He stopped in his tracks. Wet and resting on top of a soggy pile of charred wood was part of a red winter horse blanket. Was this the one he'd spread on the hay when he and Holly made love? What had he been thinking?

"I'll bet that day left a bad taste in her mouth. That was real classy." He glanced down, expecting Daisy to be looking up at him as if she understood every word. He'd gotten used to talking to her as if she were human. He missed that she wasn't at his side today.

He'd alerted the sheriff's office that he would be on the property, so he didn't hesitate to duck under the crime scene tape and enter the house. A few phone calls later, Jake had arranged for hay and grain to be delivered along with a few supplies.

The next few hours went by in a blur. He moved the horse trailer, tractor, front-end loader, and brush mower out of the equipment barn. The trailer he relocated to the far end of the building to serve as a makeshift storage for the feed and hay. Only sick or injured livestock were kept inside, so he left minimum space for them. Duchess and Hollywood could stay in the pasture.

The late afternoon heat was relentless. Inside the metal building, the temperature had risen to roast-your-brain hot, leaving Jake's clothes and hair soaking wet. He refused to stop until satisfied he could store the food that would be here soon and could shelter livestock if needed. He stepped out into the evening air, appreciative of the slight cooling effect of a breeze.

He'd avoided going in the house, dreading what he'd find, but the time had come to go inside. He walked to the back porch, turned the water on, and then hosed himself down. He pushed the door open and stepped inside. It was nice and cool. Nothing in the kitchen seemed unusual. The air conditioner hummed as if it were a normal summer day. The irony struck Jake hard, as he felt there was nothing normal in his life.

Closet doors stood ajar; drawers were wide open; several items of clothing had been tossed carelessly on the floor. Jake realized the bastard had searched the house, and his gut curled and tied into knots from the sense of invasion. Tank and Paul had been shot simply for being at the ranch. One had given his life for people he didn't even know. Did he have a family? A wife and child?

He had to find the man responsible, but was torn between hurrying back to Holly and staying here to fulfill his responsibility at home.

He grabbed a bucket, broom, and bottle of bleach, hauling the lot to the porch. After a few minutes, he pulled off his shirt and put his back into the job of removing the bloodstains. After soaking and scrubbing, rinsing and repeating a dozen times, he quit trying. He'd build a new porch.

The sound of an engine alerted Jake that a vehicle was approaching. It turned out to be two. The insurance agent and the owner of the feed store drove up in separate vehicles and stopped. Jake slipped his shirt back on and led the agent through the barn, pointing out everything that needed to be replaced. He left the guy to make notes and went to help unload the feed.

He missed Holly and Daisy as he ate a bologna sandwich. Tired to the bone, he took a badly needed shower and then landed facedown on his bed.

Just as he hit the edge of sleep, his cell buzzed incessantly. "What's up?"

"I just wanted to be sure you're okay." At the sound of Holly's voice, Jake was wide-awake.

He rolled over and pushed a couple of pillows behind his head. She sounded sad, vulnerable, and too damn far away.

"Jake?"

"Sorry. I was almost asleep." His heart rate fluttered. She'd actually called to check on him. "How are things there?"

"Quiet. I was worried about the animals."

"Sorry, I should have called. It's no excuse, but I got caught up in everything that needed to be done."

"Duchess?"

"There were no injuries to any of the livestock. The cattle guard kept them from wandering off until one of the firemen put them in the back pasture."

"The barn?" Her voice was so soft he had to listen closely.

"I'm going to push the whole thing down. I'll bury the pieces in the back pasture."

"The back forty as Alice calls it." The tension in Holly's voice seemed to have eased now that they were talking about the ranch.

"Right. Alice has insurance, so everything will be rebuilt." He pushed an image of her lying beside him from his mind.

"Have you heard from her?"

"No. Claude's deputy contacted them, but I didn't follow up. I was afraid I would only upset her."

"I understand. You'll let us know how things go?"

Jake hated to end the conversation. "Has Nate heard from Dalton or the detective in Houston?"

"Nothing yet."

A lull hit the conversation. He couldn't allow Holly to continue to be his pseudo-caseworker or caretaker. "I'd better get some shut-eye. Big day tomorrow. Tell Nate I'll check in soon."

"I will. Take care."

"You too." Jake ended the call. He wasn't tired anymore, so he got up and roamed around the house. Nothing interested him. Holly had sounded far away. In reality, she was where she belonged.

Shit. Had he had fallen in love with her? And why did that question fill his heart with fear?

Chapter 23

Jake was up before dawn the next morning. He fed the livestock and then salvaged what he could from the barn, storing it in the equipment barn. That finished, he drove the front-end loader to the charred remains. With the push of a lever, the bucket raised high, and he began knocking down the burned walls.

The day wore on and the sun grew brighter and hotter. Jake, totally absorbed in his work, paused only for an occasional drink of cold water. Once he bent over the hose and ran water over his head. His mind was so occupied by the job at hand that for the first time in days, he was at peace with himself.

He methodically scooped up the pieces and hauled each load to the pasture, where he'd earlier dug out a large chunk of earth. His anger grew with each lift and lowering of the bucket. After he pushed the last charred load into the hole, he pounded the pile with the backhoe bucket, and then covered them with dirt. At last, nothing remained of the ruins but small pieces of rubble and the dark scorched earth where the barn had stood.

This piece of heavy equipment had served him and Alice well, but as it lumbered along in an attempt to return to its station in the equipment barn, the engine developed a miss. He reversed the backhoe into its new parking spot, hopped off, and began to hunt for the reason.

The metal clang of the cattle guard drew his attention. Claude's pickup came into view. Jake wiped his greasy hands on a rag and went to meet him.

The pickup didn't stop at the house. It sped down the drive, stopping next to Nate's SUV. Alice was out and running toward the empty spot where the barn had stood before Claude killed the engine.

"Alice," Jake called out, running to intercept her.

She stopped and turned to face him. The worry and pain on her face tore at his heart. "Duchess?"

"They're all fine. One of the men guarding the place managed to let the animals out before the fire engulfed the barn."

"We heard, but I need to see for myself."

"Then come with me." He took her hand and led her to the back gate. "She and Hollywood are fine. All of the livestock are fine."

"Hollywood?" Alice tugged a tissue from her pocket and dried her eyes. She looked up at Jake. A frown tugged her brows together briefly. "Oh. I get it."

"I'd like to keep the colt."

"It's a great idea. She'll love—"

"No. She won't know."

"What makes you think she won't be back?"

"I know."

"What are you going to do about it?"

"I'm going to find the S.O.B. who did this. Then I'm coming home to help you."

"I meant about Holly."

Claude joined them on the walk back to the house thankfully ending the conversation. Alice tucked her hand under his arm and together they walked back.

"I wish you two had stayed gone a few more days." Jake considered the ranch to be safe, but he'd hoped to have construction on the barn started before she came home.

Alice caught Claude's hand. Color flooded her face. Something was up, and Jake was pretty sure it was good news.

"Claude and I wanted to talk to you about something."

Jake forced back a smile. "What's up?"

Her cheeks flushed red. "We..."

"Finally. You stepped up and told her how you feel about her?"

"I did." Claude stepped back. "You tell him."

"He proposed."

"And she accepted." A smile burst across Claude's face.

Jake slipped his hands under her arms, spun her around, and then set her down next to Claude. "Congratulations," Jake said. "You two have wasted enough time."

"I hoped you'd approve." She let out an audible breath.

"Approve? I'm thrilled. While I'm getting the barn construction going, I'll find an apartment in Murdock."

"No," she answered quickly and firmly. "We don't want that. Not at all."

"You two need your privacy. We both knew my living here was temporary."

"Will you shut up long enough for me to tell you something?" She laughed at her words. "We are going to live in Claude's cabin. It's beautiful and peaceful. Has a covered fishing dock and space for me to plant a flower garden. Claude's going to retire and sell his house in town."

"This is your home. You love this place."

"You're right. Over the past few days, I realized there was something missing in my life. This ranch doesn't hold me when I'm frightened. It doesn't bring me coffee in bed every morning." Her eyes misted as she reached for Claude's hand. "It doesn't look at me like I'm still a beautiful young woman."

"Well said," Claude crooned like a schoolboy.

"Jake." Alice pinned him with a look. "Your uncle always worried that someday this ranch would fall into the hands of someone who didn't love it like he did. He would want me to give the ranch to you."

Jake had gotten so caught up in her emotional words that it took a second for her last statement to hit home. "No. You're not giving me anything. I owe you...remember?"

"Bull. Your hard work turned this place around and made it something to be proud of." She pointed her index finger at him. "Don't argue."

Jake studied Alice's face. Her eyes definitely had a new twinkle. Damned if she didn't look younger. "You've made up your mind?"

"Yes. Claude and I love each other. We're going to enjoy every moment we have left in this world together."

"Then I'll buy the ranch. The salary you've been paying me has been sitting there waiting for me to spend it. I'll make payments just like any buyer would." Alice opened her mouth as if to speak, but Jake held out his hand.

Alice was shaking her head. "You'll need that profit sharing money for operating expenses."

"It's the only way I'll take it."

Alice shook his hand. "Deal. But you'll pay the price I set or the deal is off."

Jake opened his mouth to argue but changed his mind. Arguing over money would throw a wet blanket on the celebration. The sting of the barn was enough. He wouldn't spoil her day.

Claude released Alice long enough to offer his hand. "You're okay with this?"

"More than okay. It took you long enough," Jake said with a laugh. "Glad to have you in the family."

"I'm honored to have her." Claude's face flushed just like Alice's had.

"Something good has come from this disaster." Alice leaned her head on Claude's shoulder. "Now show us what we can do. We're here to help put things right."

Jake clapped Claude on the shoulder. "I should probably warn you. The woman's a task master."

The three of them walked through the barn, discussing plans. The insurance had promised quick results, and Claude knew a reputable contractor. The more they planned, the more Jake thought about returning to Dallas. Alice and Claude would take care of the ranch.

They moved to the kitchen and Alice immediately began asking questions. "The two men who were staying here, did the one who was killed have a family?"

"Tank Jorgenson has a sister. I don't know about Paul Torbin." Jake's anger rolled through his blood. "We didn't share personal information."

"I hope Holly is well protected," Claude said. "This killer, he has no conscience at all."

"She is." Jake truly believed she was safe. "She's with friends who will do whatever it takes."

"You need to go make sure," Alice said, reading Jake's thoughts. "We'll ride roughshod over the construction."

"I can't dump this on you."

"You've done the hard work. All we have to do is supervise the construction."

Jake walked away. How could he not return to Dallas? He needed to make sure Holly was protected. If anything happened to her... He returned to Alice.

"Are you sure?"

"Positive. So shoo."

"Then I'll shower and head back." Jake turned to Claude. "You're staying here?"

"Yep. I'm resigning today. I'll be right by Alice's side until she runs me off." He laughed, taking a quick peek at Alice.

"And that's never going to happen," she said, joining Claude in a chuckle.

"Good enough." Jake walked to his room for a change of clothes. His shaving gear was at Nate's, but that was the least of his worries. Clean was good enough, so he showered, dressed in clean jeans and a shirt, and went to say good-bye.

Alice stood at the stove with her back to him. He wasn't surprised to find her cooking. It was her way of showing affection.

"Something smells good."

She turned, drying her hands on her apron. "I'm putting on a pot of chili. Claude says the weather doesn't get too hot for him to want a big bowl. It won't be ready until long after you're gone."

"You'll spoil him," Jake teased. "Where is Claude?"

Alice met him halfway. "Down at the barn. The sheriff in him wants to be sure no clue was overlooked."

"You'll tell him I said good-bye?" Jake asked.

"I will." She grasped his arms. "We will take care of things here until you get back. In the meantime, I'll be planning a wedding."

"You're glowing."

"I am not."

Jake tipped her chin up with his finger. "Yes you are, and I'm glad."

"Holly loved this ranch. You should bring her back with you."

"That's my cue to go." He kissed Alice's forehead. "You two keep your eyes open. I don't think the bastard will come back, but don't take any chances."

One last hug and soon Jake was driving Nate's SUV across the cattle guard. Jake called Nate when he hit the highway to explain the situation.

"I'm glad you're coming back."

"Why? What happened?" Jake's heart rate jumped.

"We heard from Dalton. I'll fill you in when you get here."

"How's Daisy?"

"Great. She's asleep at Kaycie's feet. Diablo is on one side and Daisy is on the other."

"I hope she's not too much trouble."

"None at all. Kaycie loves them and they love her. She thinks Marcus and I don't know about the treats she sneaks them when she thinks nobody is looking."

"Tell her I said thanks. See you soon."

Jake ended the call and concentrated on the highway in front of him. Daisy had managed to accomplish something Jake had failed to do in two years. She fit in with Wolfe's Pack.

The traffic on Interstate 45 was hell most of the way back to Dallas, but then it always was horrible. Jake was ready to stretch his legs by the time he pulled up to the gate and stopped.

The guard stepped out to meet him. His stoic expression morphed into a smile. "They're expecting you."

"Thanks," Jake said. "Gary, isn't it?"

"Yep. I'll let Nate know you're coming in."

Jake started to ask Gary if he worked twenty-four seven because he was always at the gate. Instead, he drove on, ready to get out of that SUV for a while. The thought of seeing Holly had crept into his thoughts a number of times since leaving Murdock.

He vowed not to spend so much time inside his own head.

Chapter 24

Ivan slammed his empty glass down on the table and barely throttled back his temper in time to speak courteously.

"Sir, is there a problem?"

"Bring me my check."

Ivan paid the bill and left the restaurant. He'd waited two days for that bitch at Lost and Found to call him back. Of course, she'd vetted his credentials. Let her check all she wanted, because his background would check out as legit. No way had she uncovered anything that might have tipped her off. So why hadn't she called?

He drove back to his hotel. The waiting was driving him crazy, but he wasn't giving up. Ivan would kill the bitch who'd cost him his brother. Maybe he should have done more for Angel. Found better caretakers to watch him while he was out of town on a job. But over the past few years, Angel had gotten harder to control. They'd lost more than a few handlers because he'd become so aggressive.

"Enough," Ivan grumbled. Holly Hoffman needed to die. Soon.

He left the car with the valet and returned to his room. Once inside, he dialed the number of the Lost and Found office.

"Lost and Found. How may we help you?" The voice was female but not the same woman he'd devoted twenty minutes of his time to smooth talking. None of the men who'd watched the compound had mentioned a new female on site.

"Mrs. Wolfe?" A chill sizzled up his spine. Had he finally caught the break he needed? Could this be the elusive Holly? He'd play this carefully.

"She's not available at the moment. Is there someone else who can help?"

"Is this her assistant?"

"No. Just a friend. May I tell her who's calling?"

Ivan was so excited to have his target pinpointed, he almost couldn't speak. "My name is Mateo Medina with WKGA TV Six. I spoke with Mrs. Wolfe about writing an article on her husband and his company."

"She mentioned you. Let me see if I can get you an answer. Please hold."

Damn right, he'd hold. His heart pounded like a schoolboy about to get his first blow job. Holly was inside the compound, but was she staying there all the time? He had to get this interview. He'd read the earlier newspaper article. The fucking compound was huge. That wouldn't stop him from sneaking inside and killing every person there.

"Mr. Medina?" Here was the voice he'd originally spoken with.

"Yes. Mrs. Wolfe?"

"We're terribly busy—"

"I'm leaving for Dallas shortly to do another interview. I'll only be there one day. If there's any way you can squeeze me in..." He paused for effect. "These two stories could get me face time on the news." He didn't have to pretend to have panicked. Time was running out and he needed to get this done. He'd turned down another job, putting his reputation in jeopardy.

"Would nine in the morning work for you? Things should be quiet around that time."

"I'll be there." Ivan took a deep breath. "You have no idea how important this is to me."

"You'll have to provide identification at the gate. I'll put your name on the list, but the guard will still check."

"Not a problem. Thank you."

Ivan disconnected the call, dropped his cell onto the bed, and jumped out of his chair in one motion. Finally. If Holly wasn't there, he'd find out where she was hiding. Tomorrow, he'd settle the score.

Only then would he pick up Angel's ashes. Only then would he be rid of the burden. Only then would the nightmares stop.

****

Nate announced that Jake was back, sending Holly's pulse pounding. She stood and stretched, doing her best impersonation of an uninterested woman.

"You're not going to bed this early?" Kay asked.

"No. I just need to move around."

Holly wandered from the room, then walked up the stairs to the guest bedroom. She slept in the main house, which had been built directly above the massive office area. It was tastefully done in beige and creamy off-white colors, offset by dark mahogany furniture. The décor was quite a contrast to downstairs, which consisted of mostly glass and shiny steel desks.

She went to the window and pulled back the corner of the curtain. She stayed unmoving, peering into the dark, until the SUV drove into its parking spot. The door swung open and two western boots hit the pavement as Jake unfolded his long frame from the confines of the front seat. He rolled his shoulders while dragging a hand through his tousled hair. Unshaven, with his blond locks approaching his shoulders, he couldn't have been more appealing. The urge to rush out to meet him almost overwhelmed her. She turned away, walked to the bed, and sat.

Was Kay right? Would taking matters into her own hands work? She's done that once, but later, Jake had rebuffed her.

"He's only been gone two days," Kay said from behind her, "but it feels like forever, doesn't it?" She crossed to Holly and eased herself down. "It's that way for me every time Nate leaves for a few days. I'm sure Chris and Ana feel the same way. We just don't say it out loud. At least not to our husbands."

"Yeah. Well, he's not my husband."

"That will happen. Trust me."

Holly couldn't allow herself to believe she and Jake had a future. She'd share what time she had left with him and then let him walk away in peace.

She couldn't talk about possibilities, so she changed the subject to Marcus's wife.

"Have you seen his wife lately?"

"Not for the past few weeks, but we talk on the phone. Since opening the animal rescue center, she stays so busy. Lately, she's been in Austin lobbying for stiffer penalties for animal abuse."

"She's taken a big legal engine on, but I hope she gets a law passed." Holly kept the conversation going. "Have Ty and Ana said anything about coming home? I miss him."

"We all miss him. But they have no plans to come stateside." Kay's hand landed on Holly's knee. "You can keep dodging the subject all you want. Sooner or later, you'll have to decide how hard you're willing to fight for Jake."

"I know." Holly patted Kay's hand.

"Then let's go downstairs for an update on the ranch."

The sound of Jake's voice grew louder as they descended the stairs and walked to the conference room. Holly recognized the anger and frustration in Jake's words. He was facing away from her when she and Kay sat down.

"Alice and Claude came home? Is she okay?"

Jake turned her direction. The fire in his eyes softened, and the corners of his mouth lifted slightly. "She's a trooper. I had most of the mess buried before they arrived. I didn't want her to see the barn. She'd have carried that picture in her mind forever."

His lips tightened and his blue eyes darkened. "I owe Tank a lot. Thanks to him, the only losses were things. Some had sentimental value but the rest can be replaced."

"I was so afraid Alice would be upset."

"She's taking it better than I expected. I'm sure Claude has a lot to do with that. They're going to get married." Holly noticed his focus was on her as if no one else was in the room.

"That's wonderful news. I'm so happy for her."

"They've been playing this game for a while. I guess a few days in his cabin on the lake was all it took for them both to admit to their feelings. They are going to stay at the ranch until we catch the killer."

"What do you mean? Until?" Holly asked.

"After the wedding, they're moving to the lake permanently."

"Does this mean you're moving back here?" Nate leaned forward. "I need a good man for investigations and to help train new hires."

"Thanks, but we all know I can't work here."

"Bull. You can't register for a private detective's license, but you can do a hell of a lot without one. Besides, you're part of this family."

"I appreciate that, but I belong in Murdock. Alice is selling me the ranch."

Holly's chest tightened. Her heart pounded against her rib cage. She understood the pull the ranch had on Jake. He loved the land and the animals. But for him to be so cavalier about it without so much as a glance her direction cut at her like a knife.

"What have you heard from Dalton?" Obviously, Jake didn't want her opinion and wasn't interested in her reaction.

"According to the interviews Dalton and Ash Hunter conducted, this RG and Lavon had been hired as caretakers for Angel Garza. I'm sure we'll get a medical definition later, but evidently Angel was hard to control and couldn't grasp what was right from what was wrong."

"So where was the brother and why wasn't he taking care of Angel?" Jake asked.

"That's where it gets interesting," Nate said. "Word on the street is Ivan Garza was very protective of Angel, but he'd run out of reliable caregivers for Angel."

"This is about revenge." Jake shook his head. "And guilt for not taking care of his brother."

"I think you're one hundred percent right. The rumor is that Angel's brother is a hit man. It wouldn't look good if word got out that he hadn't retaliated."

"We're finally getting somewhere."

"Marcus said that Ash Hunter knew where to go and who to talk with. The information came together quickly."

"Sounds like a possible recruit?" Kay asked at the end of a yawn.

"I understand he's happy where he is," Nate said. "Why don't you get some rest?"

"I think I will." Kay stood and kissed her husband. "See you in the morning," she said to Holly.

Nate watched Kay leave the room and then turned back to Jake. "Hunter is going to dig up a picture of Ivan. When he does, he'll fax it to Chief Santos and us."

"Good." Jake dragged his hand through his hair. "I'll be so glad when this is over."

Holly stood and did her best to look casual as she walked from the room. Jake and Nate were so engrossed in their conversation, neither acknowledged her as she left. She eased open the back door and escaped outside.

Daisy was alone, so Holly walked out to check on her. She found her under the overhang on the dog bed Marcus had brought her. She stood and trotted to the gate.

"Hey, girl," Holly said as she went inside. Daisy leaned her weight against her almost directing Holly to the lounge chair next to the enclosure. She sat and the dog climbed up, stretched out, and rested her head on Holly's lap. "You're too big for me to hold, but this works."

She rested, scratching behind the dog's ears for a long time. Her thoughts kept coming back to Kay's advice to force Jake's hand. She couldn't do it. Jake had to decide what was right for him. She closed her eyes, remembering his mouth on hers, his fingers stroking her body.

Chapter 25

A voice penetrated Holly's sleep. She thought she heard Jake whispering her name. His fingers were stroking her face. His long tongue licked her cheeks. "No, Daisy. No licking."

Holly opened her eyes with a start. Was Jake really standing over her? She touched her hand to her cheek. Daisy had left a damp trail, which meant she was awake. Dog slobber meant that Jake was really there.

Holly pushed herself upright and patted Daisy. "She's a good dog."

"That she is." He squatted next to Holly's chair and rubbed Daisy's back. "What are you doing out here? We thought you'd gone to bed."

"I came out to check on Daisy."

"Me too, but I grabbed a quick shower and shave first."

The outside light highlighted his wet hair that was slicked back off his face. A breeze gifted Holly with his clean scent. She breathed in deeply, hoping to call up his scent in the future. Instead, she remembered his earlier statement. He couldn't wait to get back to the ranch and away from her.

"Well, I won't keep you two apart." Holly stood and started to the gate. His hand wrapped around her wrist.

"Holly," he whispered.

Anger sizzled up her spine. Anger that he didn't love her. Anger that she cared. She turned. "What? Why did you bother to come back?"

Jake frowned and opened his mouth.

"Don't." Holly threw up her hand to stop him from speaking. "Don't you dare feel sorry for me. I was fine before I ran into you in Connersville, and I will be again."

"I don't. I feel sorry for me."

Confusion flooded her. "What the hell does that mean?"

He pulled her against his chest. His kiss was hard. Rough. Demanding. He ravaged her mouth with his tongue and sent fire licking through her veins. His hands buried in her hair, molded to the back of her head, and held her in place.

Holly surrendered to the sensations coursing through her body and melted into him. She ran her hands up his neck and cupped his cheeks.

When he stepped back, her knees were weak and her head was spinning. It was nothing compared to the ache between her thighs.

"You have no idea how much I want you." His hands slipped under her arms and lifted her off her feet.

This kiss was warm and tender. His tongue swept inside her mouth. The blood in her veins hummed as need blocked out everything but him. She pulled her legs up and locked them around his waist, giving back every ounce of desire she'd been holding inside.

Without losing contact, they made it to the gate, laughing out loud as they fumbled with the latch. In a few long strides, Jake carried her into the bunkhouse and to his room, pausing to kick the door closed.

As if understanding her unasked question, Jake said, "Nobody is staying here except me."

Holly unlocked her legs, and he slid her body down his. Without hesitation, she stepped back, unbuttoned her blouse, and pushed it off her shoulders to the floor. Jake's gaze lowered to watch her every move. She reached around, unhooked her bra, and then dropped it also.

A low moan came from Jake as he lowered his head and kissed her nipple. His hands cupped her breast. Taking it in his mouth, he rolled his tongue in circles. She bowed her back, offering herself to him. A cry escaped her throat.

Holly surrendered to her need and the desire to make love with him. There was no denying how she felt about him. She'd take this time and show him how good they could have been together.

He caressed her breasts, whispering how beautiful she was. She leaned into him, held his head tight against her. In his arms, the outside world faded away.

He pulled away, smiling at the way her nipples seemed to stand at attention and beg for more. He jerked his T-shirt over his head and tossed it on the growing pile of clothes. Holly reached for the snap on her jeans but his hand stopped her.

"Let me."

His chest rose and fell rapidly as he knelt and slowly slid her jeans down over her hips. He hooked his thumbs in the sides of her thong and pulled it down. Holly lifted a foot to step out of it, and Jake leaned in and kissed her between her legs.

Her knees buckled. He chuckled, scooped her into his arms and placed her gently on the bed. Jake toed off his boots and socks before crawling over her.

"No way." She reached for the snap on his jeans. "I'm naked. You need to get that way."

"You tend to be a bit bossy." His blue eyes sparkled, and his lips curled into a smile.

"But you already knew that."

"I did." He jumped off the bed. Without taking his gaze from hers, he unsnapped and slowly slid down the zipper.

Holly's eyes tracked every move he made. In one motion, his jeans were at his ankles and he was stepping out of them. His broad, muscular chest and defined abs were clearly works of art, made more beautiful because Jake's incredible body came from hard work, which made him even sexier. Her gaze dropped to his erection. It was huge and all hers.

"You are beautiful," she whispered in awe.

"I'll bet you say that to all the guys," he joked as he climbed between her thighs, nudging them farther apart.

"I do not." Her breath caught as his mouth descended on hers.

His tongue traced the outline of her mouth. His teeth nipped at her bottom lip. The torture continued until she reached for his face and pulled him to her.

"Kiss me."

He cupped her cheek, slanted her head, and studied her face. Slowly, his head lowered until his lips covered hers, softly and tenderly. This wasn't a wild, passionate, I'm-going-to-ravage-your-body kiss. His tongue explored the inside of her mouth as if he needed to experience every part of her.

He increased the strength and passion of his kiss, and Holly ached for him, needing more. She buried her hands in his damp hair and challenged his tongue for dominance. She uttered a protest when he pulled away, and he silenced her by working his way down her neck.

With their hands and lips, they tasted, experienced, mapped each other's bodies, learning and searching out new, exciting spots to explore.

He lowered his head, pulling a nipple into his mouth. She bent further backward, pressing herself deeper into his mouth. Need turned into a craving. She craved his mouth on her breasts. Craved his lips on her body. Craved a release that only Jake could give her.

Jake sat back on his heels, leaving her grasping for him. "Open your eyes."

She did as he asked. "I didn't realize they were closed."

"Leave them open." He smiled and any bashfulness she might have felt vanished.

"I will."

"Good. You should see your body through my eyes. You are the most beautiful woman I've ever seen." His head dropped to her belly as his body slid farther down the bed.

His lips explored, licked his way down her body while his fingers searched out her most sensitive parts. Holly held her breath as he settled between her legs.

His fingers parted her. His tongue stroked her tender flesh. Relentless, he pushed her to the point of begging. Her hips moved, faster and faster, until she exploded in a body-racking orgasm. She soared out across the atmosphere for a long time, pulsing stronger and longer than she'd believed possible.

"My God, you are wonderful," she whispered as he kissed his way back up to her lips.

Her hand slid across and down his body, but he stopped her, pulled it to his mouth, kissing each finger one by one.

"Not yet. We just got started." His lips crushed hers.

Jake's hand slipped into her warm, moist heat, and her body instantly responded to his touch. She'd never had back-to-back orgasms, but she was on her way.

He nipped at the corners of her mouth and then skimmed it with his tongue. He kissed her breasts, pulled at her nipples with his teeth, and rimmed them with his tongue while his fingers worked their magic, driving her back to the edge. His thumb found her most sensitive part, and her body bucked into his hand. She was lost. He'd take her heart to the ranch, leaving a shell behind.

Jake withdrew his hand, and Holly almost cried out in protest. That was until she realized he was getting protection from his wallet. Fascinated, she watched as he deftly ripped open the package and rolled the condom over his erection.

"I like that smile," he said, climbing over her again.

"What can I say?" Heat rushed up her cheeks. "I already said you are beautiful."

"Your taste in men is questionable." His lips covered hers before she could challenge that statement.

Jake nestled between her legs, positioning himself at her entrance. He entered her slowly, allowing her to adjust to his size while his lips captured hers. Sensations flooded her body and love filled her soul.

He made slow, teasing movements until he slid one hand under her and lifted her hips to the perfect angle. Holly locked her legs around him and met him thrust for thrust.

He brought her to the edge. Just when she teetered on the edge of another orgasm, he stopped moving, lavishing her breasts with kisses. He repeated the process until Holly was sure she'd explode.

"Jake," she said. "Please."

Her heart beat wildly as he drove into her body. Harder and harder, he pounded into her core until suddenly release hit her. He continued until she was riding the wave again. Her passion was fierce. Primal. She writhed, bucked, and ground into him. Jake pulled her to the edge and nudged her over.

He gave her no time to rest as his fingers found her sensitive spot. Her breathing quickened and her hips moved with his rhythm. He kissed her neck, tracing circles with his tongue until she caught his head in her hands and guided his lips to hers. He lifted her hips higher as he slammed into her, thrusting harder and deeper with each stroke, pounding, as they both approached the edge.

"Come with me." He groaned as she felt him pulse inside her.

Holly whispered his name as she climaxed. And again when he throbbed, pulsed, and emptied himself into her.

****

Jake wrapped a long curl around his finger. Holly's head rested on his shoulder. They were enjoying each other's company, relaxed, and content in the afterglow of unbelievable sex. They had spent the past hour talking about everything but their relationship. He was grateful for that because he had no answers to give.

His gaze trailed over her body. Her long hair was pulled over one shoulder, caressing the tip of one breast. Damn, she was incredibly luscious and almost asleep. Sure, he could stir her passion if he tried, but he decided to let her rest.

She made love as she lived life, with every fiber of her being. It was too bad they didn't have a chance in hell at a life together. Jake pushed the thought of going home without her from his mind and closed his eyes.

Chapter 26

Jake opened his eyes. He took a minute to bask in the warmth of Holly's body spooned against his. He lifted his head and checked the time. The news wasn't good. In another hour, Nate and Kay would be up and moving around.

He glanced down at the sleeping beauty next to him. Studied the soft curves of her body. He hardened as he took this visual tour. No way could he not touch her.

Jake's fingers slowly roamed across her back, sliding around to softly caress her breasts. He lifted her hair and kissed the back of her neck. His tongue flicked at her shoulders.

She moaned and pressed her breast deeper into his hand while he tweaked her nipple making it hard and erect. He drifted on the sensations, letting each touch, each stroke, awaken her desire. His hand drifted downward and found her warm and wet.

"Make love to me," she whispered. "Now."

He moved inside her slowly, reveling in the sound of passion in her sighs. The need to push her higher, to give her pleasure, consumed him. She took his hand and slid it down her body, stopping when his fingers found her clit. He stroked her, pushed her to the edge as he deepened his penetration, moving faster and faster. She gasped out loud.

"More," she whispered.

Her one word sent his brain to overload. He was starving for her. His body, his mind needed to feed his passion. He turned her over and used his hands, his mouth, and his tongue until she screamed his name and released herself to him.

Jake rolled to his side, facing her. He pushed a lock of her hair off her face. "Good morning."

"Great morning," she said with a smile. "That was way better than coffee. I like your alarm clock."

He laughed. He'd wondered if she'd feel awkward or uncomfortable, but he should have known better. Holly was content with who she was. She would stand behind her decisions. Warmth gripped his heart.

Without speaking, she sat up and straddled him, impaling herself on his erection. She rested her hands on his chest and shifted her hips back and forth.

Jake realized he hadn't used a condom. "Holly. I didn't use protection."

"I know. It's okay. I won't get pregnant."

"Still, it was careless of me."

"I trust you." She cupped his cheek, staring into his eyes. "Shh."

Maybe she did love him. But she deserved so much more than he could give her.

"Stop analyzing what's happened between us." Holly read his mind.

He grasped her hips, and for a few minutes, nothing existed but the two of them. Holly tightened around him, squeezing as she rushed to another orgasm. She came hard and took him with her. She collapsed on his chest, where she stayed for a long time. It killed him to end their time together.

"Nate and Kay are up by now."

Holly laughed but she grabbed her clothes and started to the bathroom. "Do not join me unless you want to explain what we've been doing to Kay, because you can bet she will ask."

That warmth from his heart spread across his chest. He shook it off. When the time came for him to go home, she'd return to work at the hospital. She'd understand that her life was here in the city.

****

Ivan stopped the rental in front of the Lost and Found, Inc. guard shack. By the time the guy reached his window, his identification was in his hand.

"Good morning." Ivan handed his identification to the man. "Mateo Medina. I have a nine o'clock appointment."

The guard studied the fake license and then the business card. "Wait here."

What the fuck for? His name had to be on the clipboard in the man's hand. Ivan slid the pistol he'd hidden between the seat and console forward so the grip was at his fingertips and the silencer faced the floor. A minute passed before the man walked back to Ivan and handed him his paperwork.

"Go straight to the fork in the road and stay to the right. Mrs. Wolfe is expecting you." His expression hadn't changed until he delivered the instructions and then he smiled.

"Thanks." Ivan put a bullet in the man's forehead.

He jumped out, grabbed the dead man, and dragged him to the guard shack. When he shoved the body inside, he noticed a sign, which he placed in the middle of the road.

How fortunate, he thought. The sign read...*Closed.*

Ivan mopped the sweat from his forehead with his handkerchief and then straightened his shirt and tie. He removed the silencer, stuffed it in the glove compartment, and then secured the gun behind his back so it was hidden by his suit coat. The drive through the compound took a few minutes. This was a large property and the buildings were a good distance from the entrance.

As he approached the main building, a man walked out the door and stopped on the sidewalk. He recognized Nate Wolfe. The articles Ivan had found during his research hadn't done the man justice. He was much larger than he'd expected. Not that his size worried Ivan. It simply meant that a kill shot for Wolfe would have to be on target.

Ivan's gut reaction when he'd heard the new woman's voice on the phone convinced him that his target was here at the compound. If he had to kill every person at the compound to find her, he would.

Ivan had never been comfortable going with his instinct. He'd made a name for himself by planning every hit down to the last detail, and this scenario was a little unnerving. He liked to know everything about his target before eliminating the person. He always carefully, meticulously located the optimum spot to kill, but today he was winging it. Even last night he'd tried to plan today's events, but finally had to admit to himself that he'd be flying blind—and he hated that.

He parked, grabbed the newly purchased notebook, and got out of the car.

Wolfe walked forward. "Mr. Medina."

"Call me Mateo, please." Ivan shook the man's hand. His grip was strong and quick. "I can't tell you how much I appreciate you seeing me. I had another interview here in Dallas and this will save me a trip back."

"No problem. Let's go inside."

Ivan followed the man through the door and past the reception area. The area was empty. The desk chair had been pushed flush with the desk. Disappointment hit him. He'd hoped to find Holly immediately.

"Something wrong?" Wolfe asked. His deep voice grabbed Ivan's attention.

Shit. Ivan realized he'd stopped walking and was still at the front desk. "No, not at all. Your wife has been so kind I was hoping to thank her in person."

"I'm sure she'll check in with us. She's moving a little slower these days."

Ivan followed Wolfe into a large office. Stainless steel and glass furniture filled the room. The only solid wall was covered with pictures of the compound in various stages of construction. Ivan walked to the first picture, then looking back at Nate he asked, "May I?"

"Of course. I'll talk you through the expansion."

Ivan listened closely as Wolfe talked through the growth of his business by explaining each picture. He committed the layout to memory. This knowledge was a bonus that might come in handy.

"Good morning," a female voice said from behind them.

"Good morning." Wolfe's smile as he turned dashed Ivan's hopes. This woman wasn't Holly. "Mr. Medina, my wife, Kaycie."

"Pleased to meet you," she said, extending her hand as she came to greet him.

"My pleasure. I'm glad I have the chance to thank you personally for squeezing me in this morning."

"No problem. If you two will excuse me, I'll let you get back to the interview." She stopped at the door. "May I bring you two a cup of coffee?"

Ivan shook his head. "None for me. But thank you."

"I'm good," Wolfe said.

Ivan had never killed a pregnant woman but would if necessary. He had to stall until he figured out where Holly Hoffman was today. He set his notepad down and removed a recorder from his pocket, noting how Wolfe tensed when Ivan slid his hand inside his coat.

"If you prefer I not record, I'll take notes."

"You're fine. What would you like to know about the organization?"

"Start at the beginning. How did you get started?"

****

Jake entered through the office front door. He'd intentionally stalled, staying behind and giving Holly time to get inside the house before making his appearance. The lights were on at the front desk, and the computer screen was bright, but Kay was nowhere around.

He walked through the office area toward the sound of male voices. Nate's interview was today, so Jake bypassed them and went to the break room for a cup of coffee.

Holly and Kay were leaning against the counter when he walked in. Holly's cheeks turned pink so he tried to keep Kay's attention on him.

He took a deep breath. "Something smells good."

"Thank you." Kay followed her comment with a laugh. "Oh, you meant the coffee."

"I admit it. The idea of a caffeine drip sounds wonderful. Good morning," he said to Holly. "Sleep well?"

She choked, coughed, and said, "Like a baby."

Kay's eyes narrowed but she didn't comment. Her hand rubbed her lower back. "I think it's time for me to sit for a while. You two kids don't need me hanging around." She slipped out the break room door, wearing a knowing smile on her face.

Holly poured him a cup and passed it to him. "You might as well have hung a sign around our necks. Kay will be on me all day."

Jake crowded Holly, backing her against the counter. "You're not ashamed of last night, are you?"

"Not one bit. I just know she's going to want details."

"So you women do swap sex stories. Do you rate us too?"

"No. If you're fishing for a compliment, forget it."

He couldn't help himself. Her lips were just too tempting. So he kissed her. It was a sweet relief when she returned his kiss.

Suddenly Kay burst back into the room holding a sweater to her chest. She closed and locked the door. Her color had faded to gray. She was pale and her hands trembled.

"Is it the baby?" Jake pulled one of the chairs over for her.

"No." Kay handed him a fax. "I just received this from Dalton and Ash Hunter."

"Finally. We have this bastard's face to go with the name," Jake said.

Kay tapped the picture with a trembling finger. "That man is sitting in Nate's office. Oh, God. I bought his lie and invited him here."

"Did he see you run back here with this?" Jake glanced around the office for some kind of weapon.

"No. His back was to me." Kay's face was damp with sweat. One hand rested on her round stomach.

"You need to take a few deep breaths. This stress isn't good for the baby." Holly wet a paper towel and handed it to Kay. "Jake and Nate will handle this, it'll be okay."

Jake jumped in quickly. "She's right. First let's get you two in the safe room." Holly's trust and belief in him made him feel ten foot tall.

"I'm okay." Kay stood. "Don't worry about us."

"How do I get to the guns?" Jake asked.

Kay dropped the sweater she clutched against her chest and handed Jake a pistol. "I keep a small .380 in my pocket, but I figured you'd prefer the Berretta 9mm with the fifteen-round clip."

"Smart woman. Now go quietly. After the door is secure, call Gary. Tell him to get here fast."

"I called the gate," Kay said. "He didn't answer. We're alone until Marcus gets here. Everyone else is on assignment or with Tank at the hospital."

"Did you call the cops?"

"No," Kay whispered. "Sorry."

Holly steered Kay to the pantry door. "We'll call as soon as we're in the safe room."

Jake moved to stand with his back to them. He kept his gaze and the gun trained on the hallway.

"Do not open that door until Nate or I tell you it's all clear."

Holly's hand slid up his arm. "Please be careful."

He glanced back at her. The fear in her eyes fueled his anger. "This nightmare ends today."

The second he heard the lock set, he closed the fake pantry door and carefully entered the hall. He flattened himself against the wall and silently moved toward Nate's office.

A gunshot cracked through the silence. Jake squashed the urge to bolt into the open and run to Nate's office. If Garza had fired the shot, he was on full alert too.

Jake paused at the end of the hallway before cautiously stepping into the open. The office area was empty. He paused, listening for the sound of footsteps. A soft moan from behind Nate's desk drew his attention. Jake stepped to the corner of the desk and found Nate pushing himself upright.

Blood trickled down Nate's face just in front of his ear. Jake knew better than to hover.

"Good to see you. The girls are in the safe room." Jake kept the Berretta facing the open area of the offices while extending his free hand. "Need help getting up?"

"Fuck no." Nate pulled himself up using the corner of his desk. He blinked rapidly.

He picked his gun up off the floor, pulled up his shirt, and wiped his cheek. "I should have made that motherfucker as a phony sooner. The second I did, he nailed me."

"Ready?" Jake asked.

"Yeah." Nate moved next to Jake.

Step by step, they made their way out of Nate's office. Jake snagged a roll of paper towels from a tote full of cleaning utensils and ripped off a handful. He handed them to Nate. "Two inches over and that wouldn't be a flesh wound."

"Yeah. Dazed me for a minute. Fucking room keeps spinning."

"Kay called the gate. Gary may be dead. She's calling the cops once the safe room door is locked."

"Shit. Gary was a good man." Nate looked out the window to the parking lot. "The shooter is still here."

"Yeah. He came to kill. He's not running." Jake handed over the fax.

"That's him." Nate wiped the blood from his face, smearing it but not stemming the flow. He dropped the towels. "This son of a bitch dies today."

Nate stumbled and Jake grabbed his arm. "You sure you can do this?"

"I am." Nate's growl would have been funny under different circumstances.

"Then let's split up," Jake said.

"Okay. I'll go upstairs and you take the bunkhouse. Be careful. It will take a while for the cops to get here."

Chapter 27

Holly called 911 and tried to explain the situation succinctly. She gave the operator the address and the information that a killer was on site. But she didn't remain on the line as instructed.

Kay was pacing back and forth in the small space. Adrenaline was probably pumping through her veins at record speed and Holly was worried about her.

"What kind of maniac actually comes to the compound like ours to kill somebody? He's insane."

Holly struggled to appear calm. "Your blood pressure is probably too high. Try a couple of deep breaths."

Kay was staring at the thick door. "I heard the gunshot. So don't pretend you didn't."

"Of course I heard it. But freaking out won't help. There's nothing we can do but wait." Holly's heart was racing and her nerve endings were screaming, but she concentrated on her friend. "Come sit in the lounger. Let's get you off your feet."

"I have to pee. This baby is sitting on my bladder."

"Go. Where is Marcus? Why isn't he here?"

"Chris needed his help at the shelter this morning." Kay closed the door to the bathroom. "Call him."

Holly dialed Marcus's number and waited.

"Good morning, what's up?"

"The killer is in the building."

"I'm on my way." Marcus had never cared for small talk.

"Kay and I are in the safe room. I called the police."

"And?"

"Jake went to find Nate, and we heard a shot just as we closed the door."

"You two stay put."

Holly disconnected. She was the one pacing now as she waited for Kay. She'd been in the bathroom a while. Holly knocked on the door. "You okay?"

The door opened and Kay stood there wearing her blouse and a towel wrapped around her waist. Tears rimmed her eyes. "My water broke."

Holly wrapped her arm around her friend's waist. "C'mon, let's get you to the couch."

Once Kay was resting, Holly ran to the closet, threw open the door, and grabbed a blanket, pillow, and a small stack of clean towels. Kay groaned again.

"You just relax and breathe deeply. Everything will be fine. This is just the beginning of your labor." Holly helped Kay clean up and then eased her back down. She elevated Kay's feet with the blanket and pillow.

"I can't do this. I want Nate with me when the baby is born."

"I know, sweetie." Holly wet a washrag and wiped Kay's face. "Stressing doesn't help."

Kay moaned. Her head lifted with a contraction, and Holly suddenly feared this baby wasn't going to wait.

"The police and Marcus are coming. So let's concentrate on your breathing."

"But the pains are coming too fast." Kay moaned, pulling her knees to her chest.

"I'm calling the paramedics."

"Don't call anybody. If the killer is still here, a lot of innocent people will die. Besides, I read first babies take their sweet time." A contraction hit, doubling her over again. "But maybe not mine."

"Babies can't read a calendar and don't know if the time's convenient or not." Holly dialed 911 again. "I have a pregnant woman in labor and need an ambulance stat."

Holly explained an active shooter was on site, and that the police had already been called.

"I'm sorry, but the police will hold the ambulance off site until it's safe for the paramedics to enter."

No way was Holly telling that to Kay. "We're in the safe room."

"I need you to stay on the line," the dispatcher said.

But judging from her contractions, Holly needed to devote her attention to Kay, so she disconnected the call.

"Breathe through the contraction. That's it." Holly wiped Kay's forehead again.

"What if Nate was shot? What if he is injured and needs me?" Kay's eyes were filled with a mixture of fear, pain, and grief.

"Jake will take care of Nate. You have to trust in him. Besides, I can feel it in my bones. Nate is just fine." Holly tried hard not to show her concern, but it ate at her insides.

"Help is on the way. I know this is hard but please try to relax."

"I wish Nate was here."

"The police can take over the search with Marcus and Jake. Nate can go to the hospital."

Kay spoke through gritted teeth. "This baby isn't going to wait. I have to push."

"Don't push. Do your breathing exercises."

"You are going to deliver this baby." Kay gave a weak smile.

"No. I'm a nurse. You need a doctor."

Kay screamed. The sound ripped through Holly. Help had to get here soon. "The baby's coming, I can feel it. I have to push." Kay drew her knees to her chest, her face contorted with agony. "I have to," she cried.

A sense of calm came over Holly. It was time to take command. She shoved the coffee table out of the way and crawled on the couch between Kay's knees. Holly started talking, keeping her voice even and relaxed.

"That's it, breathe. We're not going to panic." She prayed the cops and paramedics would hurry. "Look at me. No, don't close your eyes, look at me. Do not push, do you hear me? Do not push."

Holly ran her training through her mind over and over. She'd been timing the intervals between contractions. They were coming hard and getting closer.

"The baby's coming," Kay gasped. Another pain hit and her face turned blood red.

"Then we'll do this together." If she had to deliver this baby, well...so be it.

"Oh, God." Kay's voice reached a higher pitch with each contraction. Her head went back, and her knees came up tighter to her chest.

"I'm right here. I'm not going anywhere." The baby had crowned and Holly knew it was time to take action. "Looks like we're having a baby."

****

Jake slowly opened the door to the bunkhouse and crept inside. Knowing Holly was safe, he moved with purpose. No man would harm her. Not while he was alive.

He turned left and walked quietly down the hall. He entered each room and ensured it was empty before moving to the next.

The room he'd been assigned was next. The bed remained a tangled mess of white cotton. The top sheet reminded him of when he'd tossed it carelessly to the floor. Holly's face filled with passion flitted through his mind. He picked up the sheet and tossed it on the bed.

From the corner of his eye, he caught movement from his right. Shit. He'd allowed himself to be distracted.

"I knew you'd brought her here."

Jake started to turn.

"Don't move. Toss the pistol on the bed."

"You only have a few minutes before the cops arrive."

"Toss it now! It takes less than a second to pull the trigger." He moved closer, shoving the nose of the gun into Jake's back.

Reluctantly, Jake complied. His mind raced. The opportunity would come, and he'd take that gun away from this bastard.

"We're going to the office area, and you're going to take me to Holly."

"Fuck you." Jake protested because it was expected. He'd let the bastard think he was going back inside only under protest. Nate would end this before anyone else was hurt.

"I'm perfectly willing to kill you."

The gun was shoved harder into Jake's back. He grunted as if in pain.

"Walk ahead of me. Slowly." The pistol pressed against the base of Jake's skull.

"Fine. But I have no idea where she is. I told her to hide when we heard the gunshot." Jake followed instructions. This time, he didn't try to hide his footsteps.

"I'm not stupid. Stop trying to attract attention."

"What you are is a sorry excuse for a human being. A bastard who kills for no reason has no right to live."

"My brother deserved to live."

"Then you should have taken better care of him."

"Shut the fuck up."

"That's what this is about. Your guilt. You let your brother down. His death is your fault." The back of Jake's head exploded with pain. He stumbled but stayed on his feet.

"Move."

They entered the office area through the side door. Jake turned right, leading the bastard away from the safe room. He listened for sirens but heard none. Making the bastard mad was dangerous, but it was a chance Jake had to take. Nate would hear them arguing and kill the bastard where he stood.

"I didn't tell you to go this direction. Go upstairs."

"There's nothing but living quarters." Jake was happy Garza wanted to climb the stairs. He'd find Nate waiting at the top.

Halfway up, Jake saw Nate facedown. Hate boiled through Jake like hot lava as they stepped over the body. Was his friend dead? They searched every room and found no one just as Jake had known they wouldn't. Nate hadn't moved when they walked downstairs.

He turned left, away from the safe room. He had to stall until help came or he could distract Garza for just a second.

"I didn't tell you to go left. Turn around. Let's see what you didn't want me to find."

Jake led the way down the hall to the coffee machine. "Would you like a cup? It makes all kinds. Just select a pod and I'll drop it in."

"Cute. What's behind that door?"

"The pantry."

"Open it."

"It's empty."

"An empty pantry? I think not."

"Open it yourself."

A second blow to his head sent him to his knees. Darkness engulfed his brain, but Jake fought to stay conscious. A losing battle.

He was aware of the pantry door opening. A loud knock sent shards of pain through his head. He could not give into the darkness and let the bastard get to the women.

"Open the door. I have one dead and another with seconds to live. Come out or I'll kill him."

Jake tried to stand. Holly would never put Kay at risk, but he couldn't take a chance.

"Open the door now." Garza's crazed behavior got worse by the second. His voice had escalated to a scream. Nate was dead. There was no one left to help.

The safe room lock clicked. Holly stepped out and slammed the door behind. Jake blinked rapidly, willing his body to respond.

"Don't kill anyone else because of me."

"Then walk calmly to my car. I have plans for you."

Jake had to act now while Garza's focus was on Holly. Jake rolled to his belly and pushed up onto his hands and knees. He reached up to grasp the edge of the counter, but instead, he pulled open a drawer. Extending his arm, he dragged himself to his feet.

As he stood, his eye caught the handle of a knife. Memories shot through his mind at record speed as he picked it up by the tip. He turned, the knife left his hand, and the blade found its target. Only the handle protruded from Garza's left rib cage.

"Nice hit."

Jake whirled to see Nate propped against the door facing with his gun pointed at Garza's head. Together they watched the bastard fall to the floor. His eyes went vacant and blank.

The entire mess was over. Jake slid to the floor. "I didn't know I could do that."

Holly was shaking all over. She pointed to the safe room. "Nate. Hurry."

He stumbled into the wall, shook his head, and said, "I've got this."

Nate dragged the body aside, keyed the lock on the door, and opened it to the sound of a baby crying. In the distance, dueling sirens harmonized with the newborn.

Jake took a deep breath and extended his arm to Holly.

"Your pupils are dilated." She looked at the back of his head. "You'll need an MRI and a few staples." She tucked his arm over her shoulder.

"I'm fine."

"Let me be the judge of that."

"Garza had a thing for heads. He nicked Nate's and clipped mine a couple of times with the butt of his gun."

She took a stack of napkins from the counter and pressed them against his head. "This is one bloody mat of hair."

"Alice will be happy if they cut it all off."

"I've never been so scared." Tears broke and trickled down her cheeks. She turned into his arms.

Sirens screamed loudly. Help had arrived.

"We need to get out front and talk to the police."

"You sit. I'll go," she insisted. "You're injured."

"I'm fine. It will take more than a couple of taps on the head to kill me."

"Police," someone yelled.

"Back here," Holly called out. "We'll go together."

"We can do that. The baby?"

"Mother and baby are fine."

Chapter 28

Holly appreciated Marcus taking the lead when the Dallas Police demanded answers. He'd contacted Dalton, who'd given names and telephone numbers of the FBI and the Connersville Police Department for corroboration of their story.

Holly broke all the local speed limits getting to the hospital only to learn that Jake had been whisked away, under police escort, into one of the examination rooms. Then he'd had been taken for an X-ray.

One of the duty nurses in the emergency room confided that Nate had sustained head trauma and lost a lot of blood. Holly had no doubt he would recover quickly. His love for Kay and Kevin would drive his need to get on his feet. He and Kay would be allowed to share a room.

Holly hoped she hadn't overstepped her boundaries by calling Dallas Police Department Detective Tomas Mendez. Tomas had been a friend long before the agency had been formed. His affection for Kay was acknowledged by everyone but him. As a group, they'd been through a lot together, and she knew he'd come without asking questions.

She turned to see Tomas walking down the hall to the waiting room. He smiled as he crossed the room. Holly met him, giving him a grateful hug. "I hope you don't mind me dragging you into this. I really just needed a friend."

"You'd have been in trouble if you hadn't called." He slipped an arm around her waist and walked her to a couch by the window. "Nate kept me in the loop just in case he needed backup. Everything will be fine after all the loose ends are tied off."

He held her hand while they talked, allowing her to bring him up to speed without interruption. She began with her first encounter with Angel Garza.

"Guilt does funny things to people. From what I understand, he'd promised his brother that he'd take care of him." Tomas studied her for a moment. "Nate says you and Donovan have reached détente. Are you sure that's wise?"

"I don't know where this is going. Our relationship has been like a seesaw, up and down, all over the place. I know how I feel, and the rest is up to him now."

"I understand the crime scene unit cleared your apartment."

"I haven't been inside my apartment since Ivan Garza ransacked it."

"Want me to go with you?"

"For the time being, I'll stay with Kay. I promised I'd help with the baby."

"How is she?"

"Great. The baby is beautiful."

Tomas looked away for a second. "How about I go nose around. See what I can learn."

"I'd appreciate that."

Holly reread the same paragraph in a magazine a couple of times before putting it back on the rack.

"Ms. Hoffman?" The nurse behind her spoke softly.

Holly turned and braced for news about Jake. "Yes."

"Mr. Donovan wanted you to know that he's fine. There's no concussion, but he has a nice row of staples. He'll have a headache for a few days."

"May I see him?"

"A detective is with him, but he said to tell you he'd be out in a minute." She smiled and backed away.

Holly leaned back in the chair. Relief was just now settling her nerves. If she could see Jake, look him in the eyes, would she be able to tell how he felt about her? They had made love, taken comfort in each other, but that didn't guarantee that he loved her. Her heart hurt at the thought of losing him.

Marcus surprised her with a cup of coffee. He sat next to her, taking a sip from his cup. "I'm sorry that I didn't get there in time to help. I'm just glad it's over."

"Is it really?"

"Just about. The police will need more statements, but Chief Santos has been on the phone providing information." Marcus studied her. "What about you? What's next?"

"There are so many things to decide. I have to see if I can get out of my lease. Living in my apartment isn't an option."

"A fresh start sometimes helps."

"All those people died and we're expected to just go on?"

"Yes. We have to because they died. Survivor guilt is always hard."

"I just don't understand the why of it all."

"Some things aren't explainable." Marcus set his cup on the side table. "I have some good news."

"Tell me."

"Tank expects to be released from the hospital next week. Dalton will drive him and his sister to the family ranch outside of Weatherford. But he'll be back to work as soon as possible."

"You guys never quit coming."

"We can't." Marcus stood.

Tomas returned. He crossed the room in long strides and shook hands with Marcus.

"Marcus. You're looking good."

"Good to see you too."

Tomas turned to her. A frown pulled his eyebrows together. "I believe somebody is looking for you." He nodded his head in the direction of the doorway.

Her heart skipped a beat. Jake stood just outside the waiting room. A bandage circled his head, and he wore a hospital gown over his jeans. His gaze was locked on hers.

"I convinced the nurse to let him keep that stylish top." Marcus leaned down close to her ear. "Tell him how you feel or he'll walk away. There are times that you women have to hit us with the truth before we see it." He handed her a set of keys. "I'm on the second level in slot B83. Chris will pick me up."

"Check in with Kay for me?"

"Right away."

Holly did her best not to run to Jake. Keeping her cool wasn't easy. She wouldn't do as Marcus suggested. Jake had to take that first step. Until then, she'd distance herself, protect her heart.

In the middle of the corridor, Jake pulled her against his chest. Holly had been functioning on adrenaline, and now that the excitement was over, her hands shook and her knees wanted to fold under her.

"How does it feel to have delivered a baby?" His words caressed the top of her head.

"I really didn't do anything." She heard her own voice quiver. "Kay's water broke and the contractions came really fast."

"You were there for her when she needed you. Your patients are lucky to have you."

Holly leaned back and looked at him. Aside from the white bandage around his head, he looked good. The disheveled look made his angular features, square jaw, and sultry eyes even more intense. God had been in a good mood when he'd given Jake his looks. She thought the same thing every single time she looked at him.

"How's the head?"

"Hurts a little. Nothing to worry about." He grinned and his eyes sparkled. "I have a bald spot, right here." He pointed to the side of his head and winced.

"Marcus gave me his keys. I'll drive you back to Nate's."

"Are you sure you don't want to see Kay first?" he asked before they exited the hospital.

"It's an intimate time for her and Nate. They need this time together." She shouldn't be jealous, but the love Nate and Kay shared had always made Holly envious. That's what she wanted, a love that would stand the test of time.

Jake was quiet as they walked to the car. He reached around her to open her door. "You've been through hell. How are you doing?"

"I'm wonderful."

"Liar." His blue eyes seemed to pierce through her outer layers and see what she was truly feeling.

Before she could say another word, he'd pulled her into his arms again. His hands rubbed up and down her back, and she forgot she'd been trying to distance herself from him.

"I'll bet you were cool and calm."

"Not at all. I was terrified something would happen to you or Nate." Inside the circle of his arms, she relaxed, her tension vanished. "You saved our lives. How you remained conscious during what was going on is a miracle."

"My stubbornness finally came in handy."

"Don't try to be humble with me. I knew you would keep me safe. That was the second time you threw a knife and saved my life."

"I remember."

"You do?" Holly's heart soared for him. "Everything?"

"I think so." Jake's eyebrows pulled together.

"Get in. You need to get off your feet." Maybe a parking garage wasn't the ideal location to have this conversation, but if he wanted to talk...well, she'd sit here all night.

He nodded and closed her door. Her heart ached for him. His eyes had lost their usual brightness and were shadowed with pain, but talking about the kidnapping was the only way forward. Jake paused and rested his hand on the hood. Holly reached for the door handle but stopped. This mental trip had to be Jake's decision, one only he could make. To accept his tumor had driven his actions was the path to self-forgiveness.

He straightened his shoulders, walked around to the passenger's side, then got into the SUV. Holly turned in the seat to face him. Maybe today he'd put his demons to rest. She extended her hands and his icy cold fingers intertwined with hers. Jake's gaze dropped and he seemed to study their joining.

Holly wasn't a psychological counselor—maybe she had no business doing such a thing, but she refused to second-guess her ability. Jake deserved happiness, and she'd do whatever it took to help him.

"You can tell me." She squeezed his hands gently and spoke softly. "You're safe with me."

His head shifted up and down in a small nod. "You're the only one I can tell." He lifted his gaze to meet hers and took a deep breath.

Holly smiled and waited, because now wasn't the time for her to speak.

"I remember most of that last tour in Afghanistan when my helicopter was shot down. But not the rescue or the trip home. The next time I was cognizant of my surroundings, I'd been flown home to America and was in a hospital in Dallas. I heard male voices outside my room discussing performing surgery on my brain."

"You had been unconscious during the few weeks prior to coming home."

Jake closed his eyes for a long second. "My memory was a blank. I had no name. No past. I heard the doctors say that I could die on the operating table. I didn't know about the tumor then, so nothing made sense; in my mind, they were going to kill me. I waited until I got a chance and ran. Ran into the early dawn, barefoot with my ass exposed. But I was running for my life."

He paused, scanned the parking garage, and then pointed to the grassy area outside. "See those homeless people? Did you know some of them hang around hospitals? Lucky for me, a couple of homeless vets who'd come home as fucked up as me took me into their group. They clothed me, shared what little food they had, and I lived under the Baker overpass with them until one day, Mr. A stopped. He picked me out of the crowd and asked if I wanted to make a buck."

"That was Anthony Walsh?"

"Yeah. He didn't seem to care that I didn't know my name. He liked my looks and called me Johnny Darling. All I had to do was follow orders. And I could do that. Next thing I knew, I had a new name, I had new clothes, and a fat paycheck. I became a hunter. A hunter of women. Women he and his sick-fuck of a son, Hank, auctioned off to the highest bidder."

Jake's grip on her fingers tightened. She inhaled sharply and he relaxed his hands.

"I'm sorry. Did I hurt you?"

Holly pulled a hand free, reached across, and cupped his check. "You have never hurt me. Scared the hell out of me but you never caused me pain."

He made a sound of disgust, blowing air from his lungs and shaking his head. "Business was booming, until Hank started snorting cocaine and deciding to "sample the wares" as he called it. He raped and beat up a teenager, then left the door unlocked, assuming she was dead. But she managed to escape with his signet ring, a fancy ring his dad had designed and crafted by a jeweler who could identify its owner. I searched everywhere for that ring. I finally learned that Kay Wolfe was the last person to see her alive at the hospital." Jake's chest rose and fell hard. He closed his eyes and rubbed them vigorously as if trying to see into the past. "How could I have been a part of that? I should have remembered Kay. We'd been part of Wolfe's Pack in college. Close friends. But the tumor...well, she was nothing more than a problem to be eliminated. Somehow I found her and...."

Jake pulled his hand away and wiped a bead of sweat from his forehead. Was he shutting down? As painful as this had to be, Holly couldn't let him stop. "But Kay had protection. Nate had called Ty Castillo and Marcus Ricci to come help solve the mystery. So you kidnapped her best friend."

"Oh God." Jake dropped his head into his hands. "Yeah. I took you right out of your bed."

"Not to kill me, to trade for the ring." Tears brimmed in her eyes at the pain she was forcing on him. Still she pushed. "I never believed you'd kill me."

"Don't you get it? There was never going to be a swap. The minute Hank's ring was in my possession, I was to kill you and Kay."

"But you didn't."

"Somehow, someway, you reached a part of me the tumor didn't control. The part that was still human. Still Jake Donovan. Nobody was going to hurt one hair on your head."

Jake reached over and picked up a stray curl that had escaped her ponytail earlier. His eyes reflected pain and exhaustion. Even his smile seemed weary. Emotionally drained, he needed a break. Her heart twisted in her chest as tears slid unchecked from her eyes.

"Jake, I'm so happy for you. Maybe now you'll stop punishing yourself."

"I had heard it all before, back when I had to get square with the law. But fragments of what happened came and went." He brushed the tears from her cheeks. "I have to admit that actually remembering what happened is a lot better than hearing."

"Let's get you back to the bunkhouse. You can rest while I clean up the safe room."

"I'll rest later. Maybe I'll help you."

"I think you'll find that bending over isn't an option for you. The numbness and medication will wear off soon. You will go to bed as soon as we get to the bunkhouse."

Holly fought back the urge to confess her feelings. He needed to heal, to accept, to go forward. She'd always love the man she'd gotten to know in the country. The man who cared for his livestock with a love for all living things. The man who'd made love to her in the barn. He'd won her heart and she wanted to spend the rest of her life with him. But she tucked her emotions away and started the SUV.

****

Within the week, Jake was almost back to normal, successfully making daily runs around the indoor track without a headache. Nate was home, bossing everyone around and back to his old self. Holly kept busy helping Kay with the baby, doing the grocery shopping, and cooking for the four of them. Today she and Kay had gone apartment hunting.

Regardless of how Jake felt, he and Holly were from two different worlds. Even if he talked her into living in the country, how long would it take before she resented sweating in the sun while tending to livestock when she could be using her talent to care for the sick? He couldn't bear seeing pain in her eyes.

Watching the nurses in the emergency room, Jake had finally understood Holly's passion for helping people. Her soft, loving nature would flourish in a hospital setting.

The time had come to gather his belongings and go home. The investigation on Ivan Garza's death was closed, and Jake was free to leave town. But he couldn't just disappear on her. Tonight, he'd have the talk with her.

He waited to join her until she made her nightly trip to pet Daisy. Holly had gone inside the pen and was perched on the edge of the lounger. Daisy's head was in her lap. He stopped and took a picture with his mind. This was the way he'd remember her.

"I wondered when you were going to give me the talk," she said, drawing him out of the shadows.

Jake didn't go inside the enclosure for fear he wouldn't be able to keep his hands off her. "It's time for me to go home."

"It doesn't matter that I love you?" She lifted her chin in defiance, firing a spear with her eyes.

"Sure it does. It's something I will cherish until the day I die. But your life is here, and I can't turn my back on the ranch. We both knew we didn't work from the start."

She stood and walked to the fence. "Look me in the eye and tell me that you don't love me."

His heart crumbled in his chest. "I can't. I won't. But part of loving you means I have to let you live your life." His fingers itched to touch her cheek one last time. He didn't. "Claude is picking up me and Daisy in the morning."

Her eyebrows lifted. "So you had this all planned out before our little talk." She held up her hand to stop him from answering. She turned away, walking back to Daisy. "Then you don't mind if I stay out here with her for a while longer."

"Stay as long as you like." Jake swallowed the lump in his throat, turned on his heel, and went into the house. He'd say good-bye to Nate and Kay tonight and leave without fanfare in the morning.

****

Holly watched from the guest room window until Claude's pickup was out of sight. Jake loved her but didn't want her. She sank into the corner chair, pulling her knees up under her chin. Tears ran down her cheeks.

"I can't believe you let him get away with that." Kay entered the room, placing the baby in the middle of the bed.

"He made his choice."

"No. He made your choice without even having a conversation with you. Since when do you let any man make your decisions?"

"What was I supposed to do? Demand he ask me to come with him?"

"He really believes that you'd come to hate him."

"How do you know that? Did you two discuss it?"

Kay pulled the footstool over in front of the chair and sat. "You forget that Jake and I were friends long before I met you. We were the youngest of Wolfe's Pack, so we always had each other's backs. I think Jake filled a void made by my brother's death."

"I wish he'd be as comfortable talking to me."

"Then give him a few days and go to him."

"I sign the lease on my apartment tomorrow."

"Take my advice," Nate said from the door. "Don't sign anything until Jake understands that you want to live in Murdock, Texas. That is if you do." Nate stepped in, lifted the baby and carried him from the room.

"I'll go too. Nobody can decide for you. But I've seen the way Jake looks at you. He loves you. Believe me—Kay glanced toward the hall—I know what true love looks like."

****

Holly picked up the phone for the third time. This time, she dialed the number and waited, hoping Alice answered. She was going to see through Holly's pretext of checking on Jake's injury, but it was the best she could do. "Alice. This is Holly."

"Hello, sweetheart. I'm glad you called."

"I..." Holly's words stuck in her throat. "How's Jake's head?"

"His head is fine. It's his heart that I worry about. He's been growling and snapping at everything that moves. You two must have had a whopper of a fight."

"No fight. I love him, but..." Again words failed her.

"He loves you too. So what's the problem?"

"He thinks I'll hate the ranch, and in turn, I'll eventually hate him."

"Is he right?"

"No. Not even a little bit. I love the ranch."

"Then do something about it. Holly, sometimes you gotta take the bull by the horns. Pardon the pun. But it's especially true with men."

"I keep hearing that same sermon from friends."

"Must be something to it then."

"Must be." Holly's heart was lighter just talking with Alice.

"Claude and I have moved the wedding date up a week. I was just making out your invitation. I'd like for you to come."

"I don't know if Jake will want me there."

"Bull. He hasn't been happy for one second since he got home."

"I'll be there."

Chapter 29

Holly's nerves were tied in knots as she battled back the fear of rejection. What if he didn't want to see her? What if he turned her away? Would he give her a chance to prove she loved the ranch? She pulled her emotions in check. Reminded herself to tell Jake the truth and speak from the heart.

She drove across the cattle guard at the ranch with hands wet from nerves.

Alice stepped onto the porch and waved. Holly scanned the grounds but Jake was nowhere in sight. She parked in front of the house and walked into Alice's embrace.

"Welcome home," Alice said.

"Thank you. Does he know I'm coming?"

"Wasn't my place to tell him. He's in the corral behind the equipment barn. He's riding Duchess and teaching Hollywood to lead."

Holly frowned. "Hollywood?"

"The colt. He's decided to keep him. He was probably planning to geld him for you as your horse."

Tears rushed to the surface. "He named him Hollywood?"

"Yep. Wonder where he got that name?" Alice winked and took Holly's suitcase. "Now go on. He's due a nice surprise."

Holly walked to the corner of the barn, her heart pounding against her rib cage painfully. Daisy spotted her and raced to her. Holly knelt and quieted the dog. Would Jake be as happy to see her?

From where she stood, she watched Jake use his familiar gentle manner on the horse. He spoke softly, leaning down to pat the mare's neck and sharing a treat with the colt.

His sun-streaked hair had been cut short, making him even more beautiful.

She stood at the corner for a long time. Jake was totally unaware he had an audience. The wind whipped around the building so hard her blouse fluttered in the breeze. Silently, she walked to the railing and climbed up.

Her movement must have caught his attention, because he turned Duchess around to face her. She could see the surprise on his face, but no joy.

Tears breached the surface and ran untouched down her cheeks. Her love for him filled her every fiber of her being.

He wrapped the reins around the saddle horn, sat as straight as an arrow on his horse, and studied her, silently. The breeze suddenly died down, and the air stood still as she waited for a sign or a reaction.

Had she misunderstood Alice? Maybe she'd made a fool of herself. If she had, so be it. He would have to be honest with her if he wanted to send her away. She waited, listening to the deafening sound of her heart beating. She forced herself to remain still. Jake had to make the next move.

A low moan came from deep within her heart when he slung his leg over the horse's neck and slid to the ground. His dazzling smile blinded her as he sauntered toward her. She gripped the fence rail with her fingers and counted the seconds as he drew nearer.

He stopped in front of her, pulled her off the post, pinning her between him and the fence. Still silent, he reached for her face, wiping away the tears streaming down her cheeks. His expression told her everything she needed to know. Just as Kay had described, Jake's eyes were full of love.

"What took you so long?" Without waiting for an answer, his lips crushed hers.

Holly slid her arms around his neck and pulled him tight. They were both grinning like school kids when they finally came up for air.

"I got a speeding ticket."

"Of course you did."

"I love you."

"Of course you do," she whispered. "I love you too."

Holding Holly in his arms, he laughed, a sweet calm washed over him as the world finally shifted into place.

Coming Soon
Till the Dead Speak

Samantha Anderson exited the Los Angeles airport shuttle dragging her suitcase behind her. She scanned the rows of rent cars, pausing to slip on sunglasses against the glare of bright California sunlight. Under different circumstances she might have stopped to admire the green trees and many colors of the flowering shrubs, but she hadn't come to enjoy the scenery. This was a get-in-and-get-out-quick trip.

A strong arm wrapped around her waist from behind and jerked her backward just as a black SUV brushed past them so close she felt the breeze on her face. Her heart slammed into her chest, escalating from normal to supersonic. Their feet tangled and both of them tumbled to the pavement. Samantha landed on top of a rock hard chest.

"Oh my God!" Her words whooshed out. Fear crippled her thought process as she fought to extricate herself from the strangers grip.

"Hang on." He rolled her off his chest, stood, and then pulled her to her feet in one motion.

"That…" Her words failed her too. She took two steps back, trying to calm herself.

"I'm sorry I startled you but there wasn't time."

"Thank you." Samantha looked up into Texas-sky-blue-eyes. His voice, deep and rich as warm caramel, didn't do a thing to slow the rapid kathump kathump kathump of her heart.

"Welcome to California." He smiled and his stern expression vanished. "Are you hurt?"

"Scared the crap out of me, but I'm fine. Are you? You took the brunt of the fall."

"That was nothing. You're Samantha Anderson?"

"That's right." Her knees wobbled slightly as fear circled her chest like water down the drain. "How do you would know my name?" Everything about this trip had her spooked, and he wasn't helping matters.

"Easy. I've got you." His hand caught her by the elbow. "Lincoln Hawkins." He extended his free hand. "Your grandfather was my friend."

"That statement isn't exactly endearing." she reluctantly took his hand. "That Charles Pearson was my grandfather isn't something I've wrapped my mind around."

Her left eyelid twitched. Great, she'd never had a twitch of any kind, not before she'd heard the name Charles Pearson.

"It had to have been one-hell-of-a-shock." He nodded his head as if he understood her situation which he couldn't possibly.

"That's an understatement." A chill rushed up her arms. "Why are you here?"

"We can get into that later. Right now, we need to talk about your safety."

"My what?" She pulled her hand from his warm grasp. "I don't normally walk out in front of moving vehicles."

"I don't believe that was a coincidence."

"Why would anyone wants to run me down?" Samantha's heart started to rumba inside her chest at the seriousness on his face.

"Did the driver stop?" The stranger's eyebrows drew together. "Is he standing here apologizing profusely?"

She held back the sizzle of temper rising in her chest. Okay. So the driver didn't stop. That didn't prove it was intentional.

"Run your name by me again."

"Lincoln Hawkins. Most people call me, Linc. I'm convinced your grandfather was murdered. And it looks like you might be next."

The word ludicrous formed on her tongue, but she kept it to herself. No word in Webster's Dictionary could possibly describe the past few days. She smoothed her hands over her hair and straightened her blouse.

"The attorney who contacted me in Fort Worth said Charles Pearson drowned."

A DNA test had proven the lineage, but Samantha couldn't bring herself to refer Charles Pearson as grandfather. Not without betraying the memory of the two men she'd grown up calling Papa and Grampy. She had one grandmother left, and all attempts to reach her had failed. Samantha was beginning to believe the first lengthy message she'd left had sent Nana into hiding.

"I haven't convinced Hank yet, but I will." His gaze swept the rental parking lot, constantly moving. His walk reminded her of a predator ready to pounce.

"Hank?"

"Charlie's lawyer, Henry Davis. You spoke with him on the phone. He goes by Hank." Linc nodded as if she should've known. "Look, can we go somewhere and talk? Somewhere not so..." He waved a hand through the air. "Open."

"Surely you don't expect me to leave my rental here, get in a car with a complete stranger and ride off?" She inched her way a few feet from him.

Linc's blue eyes softened. "I get that you're angry and confused, but you have friends here."

"You're very good at understatements. This morning I packed my bags and left my job and flew to the land of movie stars. I'm beginning to think I've fallen down a rabbit hole and landed in Wonderland."

What Others Are Saying

Jerrie Alexander has truly done it again. If you haven't read any of her books you are missing out. I have read them all and can't for Jake's story next. If you're looking for something thrilling with some romance thrown in then you need to pick up Jerrie Alexander's Lost and Found Inc series. You won't want to put it down.

The Book Maven

I've never been disappointed with any of Jerrie's books and this was no exception. Looking forward to the next book in the series.

SNS Reviews

This series features hunky alpha males who share an unbreakable bond forged back in their college years. The former military heroes put their resources and skills to good use, helping those who have run out of other options. The most thrilling part of any Jerrie Alexander book, for me, is the villain's POV. Out of all of her villains, this one made me squirm the most.

I highly recommend this series.

Ms. Romantic Reads

About the Author
Jerrie Alexander

My husband and I live in Texas with Buddy, the little dog who rescued us. I write alpha males and kick-ass women who weave their way through death and fear to emerge stronger because of, and on occasion in spite of, their love for each other.

If you enjoyed this book, please help me spread the word. Facebook and tweet your approval. A review on Amazon, Barnes & Noble and Goodreads would be greatly appreciated. Send me an email if you post a review, I'd love to thank you personally.

Get up to date information on new releases. Sign up for my newsletter at http://www.JerrieAlexander.com[1] and connect with me on Facebook[2] and Twitter[3].

---

1. http://www.jerriealexander.com/

2. https://www.facebook.com/pages/Jerrie-Alexander%20/
121521571355959?ref=hl

3. http://www.twitter.com/jerriealexander

About the Author

A student of creative writing in my youth, I set aside my passion when life presented me with a John Wayne husband and two wonderful children. A career in logistics offered me the opportunity to travel to many beautiful locations in America, she revisits them in her romantic suspense novels.

I write alpha males and kick-ass women who weave their way through death and fear to emerge stronger because of, and on occasion in spite of, their love for each other. If they're strong enough, they live happily ever after.

I hope you enjoy the story.

My books are standalone so if you read them out of order no worries.

Read more at https://www.jerriealexander.com.